Beginnings

by
Edward Galluzzi

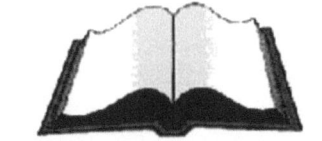

CCB Publishing
British Columbia, Canada

Beginnings

Copyright ©2008 by Edward Galluzzi
ISBN-13   978-1-926585-10-9
Second Edition

Library and Archives Canada Cataloguing in Publication

Galluzzi, Edward, 1951-
Beginnings / written by Edward Galluzzi – 2nd ed.
ISBN 978-1-926585-10-9
I. Title.
PS3607.A423Z46 2008   813'.6   C2008-907169-7

United States Copyright Office Registration # TXu-769-672

Publisher: CCB Publishing
              British Columbia, Canada
              www.ccbpublishing.com

Acknowledgements

I wish to thank Antonette M. Burks (Toni) for her proofing of the manuscript and her suggestions for the final edit. I also wish to thank my mother Roberta, my sister Diane, my brother Rick, and my father William, who passed away on February 23, 2004, for enriching our family history and Italian culture.

Contents

Introduction

Beginnings is based on the lives of Greg and Charly that propels the reader on an emotional roller coaster, as events unfold in their lives, including the more absurd and amusing aspects of life. B*eginnings* traverses the singledom lives of Greg and Charly and bring them together. The global benchmarks that help define them and a people unfold for each decade of their lives. Life is a continuing series of choices and adjustments that we all face. To not make choices or to leave these choices to others surrenders our personal control over life events.

We all encounter collectively many *beginnings* and *beginnings of the end*. We share them for they are part of what we call the human condition. Some *beginnings* are quite important; others we hardly notice in passing. Greg and Charly experience many *beginnings* and *beginnings of the end*—some predictable, some unexpected. *Beginnings* can have tranquil effects, bring humor into our lives, balance absurdities, or end periods of misery and pain. Some *beginnings* are critical moments in our lives as they forever change us for better or worse—they bring us together or tear us apart. They recycle through our existence and impact on us and on those around us with whom our lives intersect. They are intimately tied to human relationships as they strengthen or weaken the stuff that binds us. *Beginnings of the end* do not ask permission to intrude and their meddling can change our lives forever. Instead of anchoring our lives in stability, they create mayhem and conflict, and push us on unplanned paths.

The *beginnings* that impact on Greg and Charly unfold in the pages to come. Yet, these are not necessarily unique experiences and readers can relate to their own *beginnings* and *beginnings of the end.* However, I am getting ahead of myself. I would like to tell you about the circumstances of my world just before my *beginning* and the woman in my life, Charly . . .

Chapter 1

The Sum of the Parts

They say you cannot understand the whole of anything without putting together and understanding its parts—sort of the jigsaw puzzle of life. Although one's memory might fade and specific reminiscences are forgotten with age, each generation owes the richness of their lives and perhaps their life's paths to the beliefs and events of their era; even though at the time of their happening they may have gone unnoticed or unappreciated. The events of our times give testimony that no matter how hard we try or protest we are neither isolated nor living in a vacuum. No people are an island. Indeed, no man, woman, or child is an island.

The decade before my own *beginning* that influenced my parents' lives and choices was the 1940s. Franklin D. Roosevelt was president of the United States. World War II dominated half of this decade and perceptibly defined the decade's entirety. My mother, Roberta, who was born and lived in Carrara in northern Italy at the time, was in her late teens and trying to live to tell the tale of World War II. Italy was part of the Axis powers until they changed alliances to the Allies, as the Allies prepared their Sicily campaign in 1943. Italy also changed alliances shortly after the start of World War I in 1914 from the German-Austria-Hungarian alliance to the Great Britain-France-Russia coalition. Indecisiveness is typically not beneficial for a person or a people, but Italy defied the odds each time.

What is part of my mother's fortitude, willful nature, and tenacity of today likely had much of its roots in her survival during World War II. The aerial bombings of Italy by the

Allies and Axis powers not only reduced Italian cites and towns to rubble, but also reduced the survival rate of the Italian people. The bombings forced mother and her family to run into the local caves, as they were the natural and only bomb shelters of the time. Her family also had to hide her two brothers in their home's attic from time to time, much like Anne Frank and her family, as the Nazis often came to town looking for male *volunteers* to swell the ranks of the German army… or to suffer a much worse fate. What humans can do to each other under the banner of hatred defies the imagination. Mother often related her fears and anger brought about by these world events seemingly never able to escape them.

My father, William, was born in Memphis, Tennessee after his parents immigrated to America from Carrara, Italy—born American, forever Italian. He was a clerk and draftsman at the time of his induction in the U.S. armed services on March 11, 1942 at the age 27. My father served as a corporal in the U.S. army having achieved this noncommissioned rank on May 21, 1942. He served in the 347th Air Base Squadron, 5th Ferrying Group stationed at Love Field in Dallas, Texas. His army specialty was identified as "Artist (296)." My father was discharged honorably on February 22, 1944.

Prior to the world war, the people of America and all humanity had been suffering deeply from the Great Depression of the 1930s. The stock market had crashed on *Black Tuesday*, October 29, 1929. War production of the 1940s helped significantly to lift the Great Depression in the United States. It was during this period that my family experienced for the first time what to all Americans was unparalleled and mandatory life adjustments during the war: rationing. Many products were rationed during World War II: coffee; meat; sugar; shoes; typewriters; fuel oil; gasoline; cars; and rubber. Even certain fabrics like silk and synthetic fibers were not made available to ordinary civilians.

During the war years, my father shared that food rationing was the most difficult experience to balance for his family. Each American was issued a monthly book of ration coupons. Rationed goods were assigned a price and point worth, but not restricted as to how much of each rationed goods one could purchase.   Once families depleted their allotted coupons, however, rationed goods could not be purchased again until the next month at which time new ration coupons were distributed. Family members in the same household were allowed to pool their ration coupons, which indeed helped to stretch a family's budget each month. I guess at the time there was more than just safety in numbers. With rationing, families were also encouraged to plant what were popularly called *Victory Gardens*. These gardens supplied most of the vegetables for each family, including my father's.

Rubber and gas were the most essential products rationed during the war, and restriction of these products affected American driving habits.   Driving for enjoyment was considered nonessential and prohibited in America. Automobile owners were required to display a sticker on their car windshields to enforce the restriction that they were not simply driving for pleasure, but for some strategic grounds supportive of the war effort.

During this decade, the U.S. Allied troops created their own impetus for the War's *beginning of the end* with the D-Day beach landings in Normandy on June 6, 1944. We, as a people, should be thankful that the 24/7 news coverage *and* analysis of today were not in place for project *Overlord*. The plan would never have maintained its secret success of steaming nearly 4000 ships and 133,000 troops to the beaches of Normandy. The landings would have occurred much later if at all while congress argued about whether such a landing had merit—across party lines, of course. Political correctness may signal the *beginning of the end* of life in America, as envisioned by our insightful forefathers.

By mid-decade, President Roosevelt died from a cerebral hemorrhage in April 1945 without experiencing the victory that would soon be celebrated by each and every American. Following Roosevelt's death, Vice President Harry S. Truman was sworn in as our president. It was said that Truman attempted to comfort Mrs. Roosevelt; however, she reportedly returned the favor by replying, "You are the one in trouble now!" How perceptive Mrs. Roosevelt was and how clueless Mr. Truman would be about the complexity of the trouble ahead.

Yet, the world war was brought to its methodical conclusion. V-E Day, Victory over Europe, was celebrated on May 8, 1945. Japan later surrendered on V-J Day, September 2, 1945 after two atomic bombs decimated Hiroshima and Nagasaki in August 1945. With the Allied victory, the United States emerged as a superpower that militarily could only be challenged by the U.S.S.R. With the end of World War II, The North Atlantic Treaty Organization (NATO) was created in 1949 in response to the emerging tensions of the Cold War between Russia and the United States.

Well, now you have a slice of my parents' life as well as many people of the era. The value of the dollar and scrimping were lessons taught to them by the world depression, a lesson they bestowed daily upon us whether through the sharing of a nickel ice cream cone among 3 children or sustaining a weekly food budget of $30.00 for 5 family members. The value of rationing and sacrificing for the common good were taught to them by world war. The violence and death of war was thrust upon my mother, as a matter of the time and place in which she lived. My father, like many other fathers and sons, volunteered

4

for the armed forces to serve his country. My father came home a proud veteran—many others did not. My mother survived in Europe—many others did not. Yet, survival had its price. To this day, mother becomes quite angry with presidents and other government officials who make decisions to wage wars and conflicts that put our young men and women in harms way.

World events aside, my mother and father were introduced to each other by a 'mutual friend of sorts' and married in early 1948. My *beginning* was in 1951—the decade of the 50s, three years after the birth of my sister Diane and four years before the birth of my brother Rick. Yes, I can say it now... I am a middle child. I know some of you are nodding empathetically, but more of you are snickering, "Oh, a middle child!" Anyway, if I count backwards correctly, I became more than a gleam in my parents' eyes in cold February of that year—either by happenstance or by plan—as I was born in October 1951. OK, now you are snickering because I am an old fart!

To continue, when I was born the world population was 2.5 billion people. I was born in the United States where I was one of nearly 155 million people in 1951—a statistic that almost makes you feel dwarfed and insignificant right off the bat—does it not? Life expectancy was 71 years—for women of course. For men, life expectancy was beaten down to a mere 65 years. Are women just stronger than men or does marriage just make men weaker?

Anyway, the world was at war again as it seems that the only way to achieve fleeting peace is through victory—this time, the Korean War—or "police action" depending upon your political reference and point of view. President Truman ordered Naval and Air Force service men to Korea in June of 1951. The 1950-1953 Korean War ended with an armistice, not a peace treaty. In essence, the war never ended, only the fighting among nations involved in the conflict at the time. In Japan, the United States signed a pact that permitted U.S. troops to stay indefinitely in Japan... and the unrelenting warrior of World War II, Winston Churchill, was elected to form a new government across the Atlantic in the United Kingdom.

On the home front, Harry S. Truman was president of the United States and Alben Barkley was vice president. Alben who? Truman submitted the biggest peacetime budget to date in U.S. history to fund American's participation in the Korean War. The 22nd Amendment was ratified, which limited the number of terms a president may serve—good for us when we elect an ineffectual president; bad for us when we elect a productive, influential one. Julius and Ethel Rosenberg were sentenced to death for treason for passing atomic secrets to the Russians, and their execution in 1953 sparked controversy.

The federal debt was $255.3 billion compared to the over $8 trillion dollars of today. For those of you suffering and/or benefiting from obsessive-compulsive disorder (OCD), the debt of at this very moment to the penny is: $8,392,042,389,042.07. For today's U.S. population, your share of this debt comes to $28,071.41.

Minimum wage was 75 cents an hour back in 1951 and the annual average income was $3,515. However, commodities were also much more economical at the time: first-class stamp, 3 cents; loaf of bread, 16 cents; milk, 92 cents a gallon; 72 cents per pound for ground coffee; eggs, 24 cents a dozen causing many chickens to leave the coop due to slave labor; and ground hamburger for 50 cents a pound, which was not enough to cover the cost of cow flatulence! You could own your own home for $9,000, buy a new car for $1,520, and drive your roadster to the hottest hangouts for a mere 19 cents a gallon, or if you preferred, to the movies for 65 cents—a really cheap $1.30 date as long as she did not ask for popcorn and soda!

Super glue was invented in 1951 in case you had the urge to dangle yourself or any part of yourself from a construction beam or anything else.   Smile ☺—still cameras were introduced with built-in flash units.   Power steering was launched by Chrysler and they marketed this feature as "Hydraguide." *Colorforms* was the hot new toy in 1951 even though it was flat and two-dimensional. More importantly for little girls (and some boys) everywhere, Mattel introduced *Barbie* in 1959. I do not know about my male peers, but Barbie never looked like any of the girls I knew... and nothing lasts forever, anyway, as Barbie and Ken have since separated.

Television was becoming the dominant mass media for communication and diminishing the role of radio.   Color television was introduced in the United States just a month before I was born—clearly one of the more critical events in my personal history. However, back then our family did not even own a black and white TV set. We watched television at our grandmother's next door on a black and white *RCA Victor*. The top opened like an old fashioned stereo to access the television controls, which to us looked like the baffling cockpit of a modern airliner. If you wanted color, you could buy a multicolored plastic screen that you placed in front of your black and white television display. It was a long time before I realized that color was not *evenly* horizontal! You could also enjoy a TV dinner in your own home in front of your television—the precursor of the dinner theater of today.

A number of classic TV shows were broadcast at the time, including *Amos 'n' Andy, Dragnet, All Star Revue, The Jack Benny Show, The Red Skelton Show, The Roy Rogers Show*, and Edward R. Murrow's *See It Now*. The television soap opera *Search for Tomorrow* and the situation comedy *I Love*

Lucy debuted. The first transcontinental television broadcast in America took place, as it televised President Truman's address to the nation. Television also broadcasted its first human birth at mid-year. Woo-hoo! So much for the age of innocence and thinking we came from the cabbage patch or whatever patch that you crawled out of as declared by your parents!

It was a time when events drove the news unlike today where the news can drive events or perhaps gives them a good push tainted with shameless bias. News coverage was ½ hour daily of local and national news back in the 1950s, not the 24/7 coverage of today. The around-the-clock coverage and *endless* analysis are strained at times to make news out of the news in order to sustain on-air coverage. You used to have reasonable time to digest the coverage and then arrive at your own conclusions. And if the news runs dry today, somebody is sure to spot *Elvis, Nessie, Big Foot, or Small Toed*!

The first videotape recorded (VTR) was invented in this decade. *An American in Paris* won the Oscar for best picture in 1951. Best Actor was awarded to Humphrey Bogart in *The African Queen* and Best Actress went to Vivian Leigh in *A Streetcar Named Desire*. Moviegoers of the time could also see *All About Eve, Alice in Wonderland, Scrooge, The Day the Earth Stood Still*, and *A Place in the Sun*.

Yul Brynner made his first appearance of many as the king of Siam in *The King and I*. Alan Freed used the term *rock 'n' roll* for the first time to describe R&B music. Top songs for 1951 blaring on jukeboxes included *Come On-A My House* (Rosemary Clooney), *If* (Perry Como), *Cold, Cold Heart* (Tony Bennett), *Too Young* (Nat King Cole), *Cry* (Johnny Ray and the Four Lads), and *Be My Love* (Mario Lanza). J. D. Salinger penned *The Catcher in the Rye*, Herman Wouk wrote *The Caine Mutiny*, James Jones penned *From Here to Eternity*, James Michener wrote *Return to Paradise*, and Tennessee

William's *The Rose Tattoo* was published.

Not in time to prevent my birth, but I suppose you readers may or may not be eternally grateful that the first oral contraceptive was developed. I think I hear snickering again. UNIVAC, the first computer to process both alphabetic and numeric data was introduced. The U.S. performed the first nuclear test in the Nevada desert as an Air Force plane dropped a one-kiloton bomb on Frenchman Flats. The U.S. Atomic Energy Commission built the first nuclear power plant, which best explains why I have a tail—but that is another beginning!

In sports, the New York Yankees defeated the New York Giants in the 1951 World Series—no doubt a commercial bonanza for the east coast. Willie Mays began playing for the New York Giants at age 20 and Joe DiMaggio announced his retirement from baseball after signing his third $100,000 contract earlier in the year. The Pro Football champion was the Los Angeles Rams—the Superbowl extravaganza was not yet envisioned. The NBA championship was won by Rochester over New York. The Toronto Maple Leafs defeated Montreal for the all Canadian Stanley Cup. The Circle City's Indianapolis 500 winner, who blazed the two and one-half oval at 126.244 miles per hour, was Lee Wallard. Ben Hogan was the U.S. Open Golf champion. At Wimbledon, Dick Savitt won the match for men and Doris Hart for women. The Kentucky Derby champion was Count Turf. Kentucky was the NCAA basketball champion and Tennessee the college football champion. Jersey Joe Walcott won the heavyweight title in boxing.

My birth aside, a number of influential and famous people were born in 1951. According to the Chinese Zodiac, this was the year of the Rabbit. Rabbit people are affectionate, obliging, and always pleasant, but they can get too sentimental and seem superficial. Being cautious and conservative, these people are successful in business but would also make a good lawyer, diplomat, or actor. I have no business sense and I am not a lawyer, diplomat, or actor—but those born in 1951 include John (Cougar) Mellencamp, Jane Seymour, Kurt Russell, Rush Limbaugh (EIB), Sally Ride (the first American woman in space flew on the space shuttle Challenger), Bonnie Pointer, Francis Ford Coppola, and Dan Fogelberg. At the same time people came into our world, others were exiting it. Those that died in 1951 include Will Kellogg, Ferdinand Porsche, John Alden Carpenter, William Randolph Hearst, Joe Jackson (of baseball's black sox scandal), and Fanny Brice. We take notice of people leaving us, as with age it becomes a measure of our own mortality. And if the reader will forgive me for jumping out of character and time, as I write this particular day of July 27, 2003, Bob Hope is dead at age 100. *Thanks for the memories, Bob*!

There were other events shaping our world and neighborhoods in the 1950s. The Immigration and Naturalization Act of 1952 made it easier *legally* for immigrants to become United States citizens. In 1953, Lucille Ball gave 'birth' to Little Ricky on the *I Love Lucy* show after having given birth to her real life son Desi Arnaz, Jr. earlier in the day. In 1954, U.S. senator Joseph McCarthy began televised hearings into alleged Communists in America. Racial barriers in the United States were attacked by several marked events. In 1954, the Supreme Court ruled in *Brown v. Board of Education of Topeka* "separate educational facilities are inherently unequal" and reaffirmed that the separation of races violated the Constitution's requirement of racial equality. In 1955 in Montgomery, Alabama, a black woman, Rosa Parks, refused to relinquish her seat on a public bus to a white person.

Transportation and beyond got its start in 1956 when the federal Highway Act was signed. This marked the beginning of projects for the interstate highway system in America and introduced *orange cones* and *barrels* to weary driven Americans everywhere; and where Midwesterners in particular eagerly awaited the arrival of the cold winter when road construction ended and those barrels disappeared. In 1958, the first domestic jet passenger service is begun between New York City and Miami and little further up in the sky, the U.S. satellite, Explorer I, orbited successfully the earth. And if America was not yet big enough, Alaska and Hawaii become the 49th and 50th states, respectively. The phrase *under God* was added to the Pledge of Allegiance in the fifties.

Not only does the decade of your *beginnings* influence your development and character, but also so does the place of birth and the laws that govern your state. I was born in Indiana. Sometimes it is difficult to comply with what one would consider *normal* and *necessary* laws mainly because there are so many of them. Laws are not written for criminals anyway because criminals do not comply with them—what would be the point?

In addition to essential regulations, there are laws on the books that seem pointless and only serve to question the sanity of the people of the state. These senseless decrees impact one's temperament if not on one's behavior. Their absurdity, however, do provide a degree of humor. One's imagination runs amuck in pondering what circumstances and turn of events had to come together to force reasonable men to create such eccentric laws:

- Your body is no longer your property once your breath leaves you [probably enacted because your estate is taxed after your death like you owe the government something for dying]

- It is illegal to bathe during the winter months from October thru March [likely enacted because deodorant was not used widely and you smelled less during the winter than summer months]

- A resort area passed a law requiring all black cats to wear bells on Friday the 13th [probably enacted because cats ate the rabbits' feet they were given]

- It is against the law for a barber to threaten to cut off a child's ears [apparently enacted because some impatient barber did so]

- It is illegal to ride public transportation or attend the movie theater in one city within four hours of eating garlic [probably enacted with the increase of Italian immigrants]

- It is illegal to make a monkey smoke a cigarette [everybody knows that pipe smoking is the method of choice for apes]

- Liquor stores may not sell milk [likely enacted because children sent to buy milk spent their milk money on booze]

- You may not back into a parking spot because it prevents the police from viewing your license plate [likely really enacted because of the increase in auto accidents, as most people do poorly in backing up in confined spaces]

- Pedestrians crossing a street at night are prohibited from wearing taillights [likely enacted because it simply was not done in the fashion world]

- No one can catch a fish with his or her bare hands [probably enacted because something was fishy for those who did]

- Men are prohibited from standing in a bar [likely enacted because they couldn't stand even if they wanted to]

- Drinks on the house are illegal [probably enacted because drinkers would fall in the gutters soon enough]

- State government officials who engage in private duels can be dismissed from their office [likely applied to the loser only]

- Mustaches are illegal if the bearer has a tendency to kiss habitually other humans [probably enacted as a way to control running the bases]

- The value of Pi is 3.2, not 3.1415 [probably enacted by some rounder who wouldn't know a good pie if he ate one]

- It is forbidden to eat watermelon in the park [likely enacted because of the increased assaults due to seed-rage]

- No one may spit on the sidewalk [likely enacted because somebody did and people who spat thought they could vomit for free too]

- No one may throw an old computer across the street at their neighbor [probably enacted after a frivolous lawsuit because nobody could pick up those heavy old computers let alone heave them]

The pressure to grow up normal and sane is harder than people think, but we were a generation of character and we generally did anyway.

So this was the backdrop of my developmental growing years. In addition to these events and decrees, family life was quite different in the 1950's than in the 21st century. Families actually ate meals together—home cooked, non-microwaved meals by your mother. In our Italian family, that meant some variety of pasta 4 days a week with meat thrown in between for good measure. Meals were the center plate of the home attended by each and every one. After all, the first countertop microwave, which most families could not afford at the time, was not introduced until 1957. The first McDonalds was opened in California in 1948, but did not proliferate in the Midwest until the late 50's and early 60's. So, family members communicated and sat at the table patiently until excused. Yet, even with such bounty you did not readily gain weight, as children's lifestyles were not terribly sedentary then as they are today. And you were not bombarded with television commercials for diet pills that boasted anecdotal histories of vast loss in weight followed by the ever present yet brief flash brought to you in minuscule, unreadable print: *Results may not be typical*—no kidding! What results?

Mealtimes, particularly the evening meal and on Sunday, were dominated with family sharing and conversation. Parents generally understood their children of the time and the children of the time generally knew something of their parents. Piercings were restricted to the ears of mature women. You did not worry if you could not remember that *left is right and right is wrong.* Two parent households were the norm rather than the exception. Few people were single at the time where single men and women occupied only 9% of homes, which today has risen to more than 25%. People married younger at the time where the median age for first marriage was 22 years for men and 20 years for women. Only 2.5 people per 1,000 were divorced in the 1950's compared to the now nearly 5 people per 1,000. Divorce was uncommon at the time and carried a stigma for those who dared to venture outside of an unhappy marriage. Same-sex marriages were not thought of at all.

During my growing years, you felt safe, sheltered, and protected by your family. Childhood symptomatology associated with anxiety, depression, hyperactivity, and other psychiatric ailments was uncommon even though in the latter part of the 20th century and now the 21st century almost every family has one or two such children with such ailments.

My family lived in a duplex designed by my father with my paternal grandmother living on the north side—in essence, two separate homes joined together in what was called a 'double' in those days. Long cement sidewalks curled from the street to their respective porches. Two brick columns and railings surrounded each cemented porch. Our families spent many evenings on these porches watching dusk turn to darkness, and neighbors going about their uncomplicated nightly lives. Two ordinary brick chimneystacks belied the ornamental marble fireplaces that were hidden inside each home. Perhaps they were just a facade anyway, as they were as marble white as the day they were built for neither side were ever lit for the warmth and ambience they could provide.

Our kitchen was white as snow, which balanced the black and white squares of the linoleum floor. Our home hosted three bedrooms. My brother and I shared the back bedroom with two windows, one facing toward the driveway and the other toward the backyard. Territorial wars were not uncommon between us, as our beds were only several feet apart. My sister had her own bedroom in the center of the hallway cattycorner from my parents' bedroom. Interestingly, that would have been my bedroom if I had two sisters—ah, the fickled finger of fate! A single air conditioner protruded from our parent's bedroom at the front of the house—not necessarily decorative, but frigidly functional. There was no central air-conditioning at the time. My sister, brother, and I often slept on our parents' bedroom floor during those long hot summer nights. There was no relief in any other room of the house when the heat and humidity were high and the evening breeze was quite still. Those were amazingly safe and uncomplicated times, as the three of us cuddled on the floor with a thin blanket and our own comfy pillows.

Oddly, it is this summer night custom from which I developed a case of arachnophobia, a fear of.... uh... itsy bitsy spiders (yuck!). After a typical night of sleeping peacefully on our parents' bedroom floor, my sister awoke and began brushing her long dark hair, as she did every morning in her attempt to straighten out her curls. In mid-stroke, what should happen to fall out of her hair and saunter away on the floor like he owned the place but a big, black, hairy spider—believe me, it was not an itsy bitsy spider. For me, this was more blood curdling than crossing paths with snakes and it left its traumatic mark. I was such an impressionable little snot!

Each side of the double had a full basement. I often played in the basement, but grew to dislike them because of the dust and bugs they seem to collect despite mother's constant cleaning. It is where friends and I skateboarded—well, we put a piece of wood on top of a roller skate and pushed ourselves along with our hands. It is where friends and I played basketball—well, we used a tennis ball and a tape recorder that counted down the minutes from five minutes, and we aimed the ball through a specified space in the cross ceiling. It is where friends and I played hide-and-go-seek—well, we tried to even though one soon learned where to find the few best hiding places.

On our side of the basement there was a separate room where my father had built an intricate train setup with original *Lionel* trains. *Lionel was* just about the best toy for a young boy. There were dinning cars and cabooses. We had train locomotives that smoked after dropping a smoke pill in their stacks. These smoke pills were later discontinued as they were found to cause cancer. We had train cars with cranes and cargo. In and around the multi-layered tracks we had signals and switches, roads and cars, people and streets, bridges and lakes, fences and buildings, barns and animals, and always something new to add every month or two.

And, when we were not good or violated limits, we were often banished to the basement, sort of an underground time-out. During the day, this was not so bad—with the darkness of night, it was a different story. We were generally good children, but mother did almost all the parenting in the house. Even good children go bad once in awhile and tax even their most patient caretakers.

My grandmother's basement had a separate room that included kitchen appliances. She also had a separate room right off the backdoor. It was not uncommon for grandmother to take in a single female border who would use her basement as a kitchen. This was somewhat confusing in that our Italian family, especially and particularly our grandmother, was more than just a little bit suspicious of strangers outside our family or our Italian heritage. *A famiglia!*

In the center of the large front yard spanning the doubles was a birdbath sculptured by my paternal grandfather, who was no longer alive at the time. I spent many moments kicking footballs and batting baseballs from our front yard to my friend Rick's front yard across the street, especially on Sunday evenings after dinner when our homework was done and school seemed such a long time away. The driveway was covered with rock, doublewide, and quite straight until it made the right-hand turn to the double garage. Opening each garage door was manual labor, as there were no automatic garage door openers in those days. For many years, only our father's car inhabited the garage. Our grandmother and mother never drove. It stayed this way for a long time until the three of us began driving our own automobiles. In a recent visit, the driveway is now cement with a below ground swimming pool crowding the backyard.

A hedgerow along the driveway divided our property line from our neighbors. We spent much time moving the rocks here and there looking for those special quartz rocks or any rock that was shinny or out of the ordinary. There seemed to be an abundance of them in our young lives. There was an alley to one side of the garage where one could take shortcuts to friends and places. Yard fences were not common then—we did not know anybody that we wanted to keep out—and we often had a straight shot to anywhere we wanted to go. Bush upon bush circled the house—a trimmer's nightmare. Nature's insects and tiny creatures were in abundance back then, but in today's cities, you hardly see a one even with focused scrutiny. While growing up, a multitude of cocoons dangled from the bushes and inside each cocoon was a caterpillar waiting to burst out... and sometimes we prematurely helped them. Butterflies, grasshoppers, praying mantises, bumble bees, and yellow jackets were more common than people on our street. Nature's mix was in full bloom before overrun by suburbia.

You did not lock your doors to your home when you left during the day or slept at night. You left your keys in your car. Sleeping on the porch or in the backyard was not uncommon. You could walk after dark without fear of becoming a blot on the local police blotter. Not that in 1951 there were no murders, child abuse, rapes, robberies and other insidious crimes. Our parents and neighbors protected us from those kinds of events and they did not occur naturally in our community.

In our town, the civil defense sirens always shrieked at 11:00 am every Friday. In our neighborhood, the emergency siren was located outside the old family owned *Stop 'N' Shop* grocery store. Mother often walked us to the store… and everywhere. When marketing with our mother, we often found ourselves covering our ears in a vain attempt to banish the noise. We did not understand what the howling was all about or all the nuances and dangers that made up civil defense. The wailing of the civil defense siren in our town has changed neither the day nor the time in over a half of century. I always thought this would be a good time for foreign invaders to attack our town, as the citizens are complacent to its pleaful warning each and every Friday morning.

Your newspaper was delivered to your front door, not the end of your driveway, in the street, on the roof, or not at all. Mail was delivered to your mailbox on the porch or swallowed by the mail slot of your home. Siblings often fought one another to be the one to extend their arms up the mail slot to see if more mail lingered outside. You enjoyed talking to your letter carrier and he not only had time to talk to you, but also enjoyed a glass of water or a cookie. Going postal was not a phenomenon. Milk in glass bottles, butter, and other dairy products were brought to your door—well, actually to your porch and placed in your family's milk box. You did not pay immediately for these products, but you were extended credit even before credit cards became commonplace—you were trusted and charged no interest. You left the money you owed *in cash* in the company's envelope and placed it *securely* in the milk box until tomorrow's delivery. I still have a metal *Roberts* milk box trying not to rust away in the garage like many forgotten things of the past.

A big yellow truck hauling three men collected the neighborhood trash like clockwork every Wednesday in our neighborhood. Recycling was not in vogue. There were no plastic trash bags, only aluminum or metal trashcans. Each and early every Wednesday morning during the summer, Mark, my back door friend and I, sifted through the trashcans of the neighborhood looking for discarded *Stokely van Camp* company canned vegetables, fruits, etc. Armed with our trusty razor blade cutters with no thought of malice, delinquency or terrorism, we slashed the can labels that could be mailed to the packing company and bartered for prizes—just as magnificent as Battlecreek, Michigan. It was a time when you did not fear sticking your hands into somebody else's trash of life.

As a child, you really enjoyed the summer because you were actually out of school for at least three months because the next school year did not commence until after Labor Day. Schools did not legislate wholesale group testing, 185 days of attendance, or made-up snow days—and yet, children of the time did not grow up uncouth and stupid! Summer days were long back then and summer evenings seemed forever endless. You had time to decompress from the school year and enjoy a good part of the summer before thoughts of schooling reentered consciousness. What you forgot over the summer usually was something you were not going to use as adults anyway. As a young child, it was your most favorite time of life that you hoped would never end even though year by year you knowingly felt it slip away, as being childlike gave way to maturity.

Summer ice cream cost a nickel or a dime, as the ringing bells or music of the *Mr. Softy* truck or the three-wheeled bicycle with the icebox lodged in front of the handlebars beckoned you. Children searched their family's couches and chairs, or begged for coins as others ran into the street ready to make their purchases. You rode your bicycles everywhere, especially to the local prescription or drug store where ice cream and sodas were on tap. You played baseball or football in adjoining yards and did your best, albeit not always successfully, at not breaking glass—what a pane!

My parents were proud of their Italian heritage and participated in the Italian celebrations at the time. The annual *Little Italy* festival occurred each summer at a local parish south of downtown. The sites, sounds, and foods of Italy filled one's senses and brought familiarity and comfort to first generation Italians. Also, there was an army camp in the southern part of the state that played a major role in U.S. efforts during World War II. This camp was constructed early in 1942 when the American government purchased tracts of land to build a key military installation in our state. During World War II, the camp was home to some 15,000 Italian and German prisoners of war. During their internment, the Italian prisoners of war built the *Chapel in the Meadow*, in part due to their appreciation for their humane treatment at the hand of their captors. Every year thereafter in late summer, Italians gather at the army camp to celebrate the Mass outside of the *Chapel in the Meadow* before joining each other for Italian food, drink, and fun.

Well, those are the sum of my parts that I remember today and shared with the peers of my yesterday. These are the experiences that influenced my parents and, in turn, impacted on my life choices.

Now, let me tell you about another *beginning* in my life...

Chapter 2

The Melting Pot

This *beginning* was some 22 years ago. Charly and I were married on a cold January morn in 1984 having proposed to her six months earlier. We had many discussions about our marriage, as I am Roman Catholic; Charly is not being a generalized Christian. Catholicism is steep in deep ritual, rules, and Canon Law. Doctrine dictates that a Catholic can indeed marry a non-Catholic Christian; however, permission from our region's Bishop would be required. Also, Charly must learn and accept the teachings of the Catholic Church on Christian marriage. In turn, I, with Charly's knowledge, must promise to continue practicing my faith *and* to bring up our children in the Catholic faith. Although Charly did not summarily reject out of hand the conditions of faith, she was never one who wanted her choices to be predetermined. After much discussion, we opted to have a civil marriage recognizing that a more proper Catholic or Christian wedding was a future prospect. Ironically, Charly participated in Catholic instruction and was baptized into the Catholic Church one year later.

So, our wedding day was not a particularly enchanting day—at least from the point of view of ritual, pomp, and ceremony. We were not blessed with a grand church wedding attended by all the relatives and friends of the bride and groom; instead, an everyday Justice of the Peace 'gave up his good life' just to unite us. The wedding sanctuary was a sterile office setting with row upon row of desks and filing cabinets. The mechanical taps of electronic typewriters forced by the fingering of hurried clerks echoed in the background. Neither the tune nor the cadence produced was remotely reminiscent of the wedding march.

Fortunately, not everyone was a stranger as there were several people present that Charly and I knew. My brother Rick, and his family stood by our sides as witnesses to our formal mating. As we waited for the Honorable Justice, the kids became restless and pranced around the well-worn wooden chairs. Twenty minutes after our date with destiny, the Justice arrived and introduced himself as the "Honorable Justice Justin Justwill." After we exchanged customary pleasantries, the Honorable Justice's opening remarks were notable, steeped in tradition, and forever etched in our minds: "I can make this as short or long as you want. You don't even need me. You have your marriage license." With such fiery passion and ritualism, Charly and I were overcome with wedded bliss . . . and tradition be damned!

The ceremony continued long enough for a single wedding picture to be snapped. It was not your ordinary wedding picture for it accentuated the incomparable marriage motif in the background: the American flag and unending rows of mundane-colored filing cabinets. In a very short time, Charly and I were *certified* man and wife. For a moment, I was uncertain as whether to kiss the bride or salute the flag! Since I am not one to tempt fate, I ended up doing both. We had nobody's blessing in particular—neither God nor church—but we were just as married and just as happy. Why not? After all, we were completely in love and cared deeply about each other.

Charly and I met several years before our wedding. I frequented a local toy store for though I had no children, they were very much a part of my every day life—nephews, nieces, kids of close friends, and children seen in my professional contacts. My parents lived far away at a distance separated by five states. The children of friends were considered my family—at least I often thought of them that way. Sometimes "feeling" part of their family can be a painful experience. You share in the family experience, but these experiences unkindly remind you from time to time that you are not a family member. You care and you are cared about. You give and they give back. You love and they love back. The cold realization, however, is that eventually you leave as everyone else stays. Even your friends can at times be unkind without intending to do so and they typically have no awareness or knowledge of their silent transgressions.

Having said all that, children and having a childlike nature were the common threads that brought Charly and me together. Being immature or I believe the politically correct identification of being maturationally challenged can have its benefits. Charly was the assistant manager of a local family-owned toy and hobby store. Although it was a very large store, the owners were quite family oriented. They took interest and pride in serving the shopper, including the smallest ones who otherwise were typically admonished for touching, dropping, breaking, or innocently staring at amazingly awesome store merchandise. Charly was perceptibly charming and accommodating. I attributed her charm to her kind temperament and warm smile. If love at first sight exists, Charly's impact on me lends credence to that romantic idiom. She had, excuse the cliché, the kind of smile that made your troubles melt away as soon as you walked in the store. Charly paid attention to detail and her compulsiveness showed in the assistance that she provided you. It was not long before I shopped at the toy store for self-serving reasons. I shopped more often than needed. Charly seemed aware of this, but she did not appear to mind, complain, or file a protective restraining order.

I was surprised, fortunate, and content to have met somebody like Charly, let alone fall in love with her.

Surprised? Well, yes. You see, I went through a period in my life during which time dating was frowned upon—actually, I was not permitted to date... did not consider dating... and willing accepting it. I later found myself in the position of *catching up* with my male counterparts in the social arena. However, I am getting ahead of myself once again . . .

Let me start at another *beginning*. This is the *beginning of the end* that we all share in common, the universal type: the day of delivery... Deliverance? Do you hear a banjo or two? I was born in October of 1951. My beginning of the end was, of course, linked historically to my parents. That goes without saying, but I decided to say it anyway. My mother was born in Carrara, Italy in May 1924. My father was of strong Italian heritage, but born in Memphis, Tennessee in June 1914. My father was in the armed services and they met during the waning years of World War II. Well, "met" is not exactly true. A mutual friend introduced my mother and father the old fashioned European way. My parents later married in New York in May 1948.

It would be less than candid to say I remembered anything about my entrance into this world, and based on the unfolding events of the time, quite fortunate as well. As my birth approached, my parents were experiencing a devastating *beginning of the end* coinciding with my *beginning*: the illness and subsequent death of my paternal grandfather several months before my birth. Grandpa Edgar was an Italian sculptor who worked in marble and stone, as he created many sculptures for buildings and museums that are still exhibited today around America. He was born in Southern Italy in 1884 and immigrated to the United States in 1909. According to the American Family Immigration Center at Ellis Island (http://www.ellisisland.org), more than 22 million immigrants, passengers and crew passed through Ellis Island and the Port of

New York between 1892 and 1924. The Center documents that my grandfather traveled on the ship Barbarossa built in Hamburg, Germany in 1897. The Barbarossa had a service speed of 14.5 knots and carried 2,392 passengers. Historically, the Barbarossa was seized by the United States Navy for a troop transport in 1917 and renamed the USS Mercury. It was reportedly scrapped in 1924. Interestingly, World War II history buffs will recall that *Barbarossa* was the code name given by Adolph Hitler to the German attack on the Soviet Union in June 1941. Historians have referred to this attack as Hitler's worst single military blunder because of the massive conflict that he unleashed ended four years later, in May 1945, with his reported suicide in his Berlin bunker.

The registry indicates that my grandfather traveled under the first name of Egisto. His port of departure was Genoa, Liguria, Italy. My grandfather immigrated to America in 1909 at the age of 26 stating that he was visiting his uncle Catozzie at 400 Bay Street, San Francisco. He arrived at Ellis Island on March 19, 1909 and received his certificate of naturalization in the United States on June 16, 1944 at the age of 61. At the time of his immigration, grandpa was described as having dark hair, brown eyes, and a stature of 5 feet, 6 inches. The ship's manifest identified my grandfather's marital status as 'married.'

My paternal grandmother was born in February 1806. Why my grandmother, who called herself Adunia in Italy but changed her name to Antonetta in America, did not voyage with grandfather at that time is another story. I will only say that she immigrated to the United States some five years later in 1914 when, as it was told to me, grandfather demanded that she span the Atlantic soon or he would find a new life partner. Five other married men from Carrara, Italy traveled with my grandfather. Curiously, they also traveled without their spouses—well, that's also another story.

Grandpa Edgar was said to be a kind man, spry in his old age and full of youth. I never met him, of course, but I saw my elderly grandfather laughing and running swiftly in several vintage black and white 8 MM home movies. Grandpa Edgar developed emphysema and other respiratory problems, which were attributed to the dust from his carvings that progressively hardened in his lungs over the years. He was bedridden for several years and weakened steadily until his death at age 67. His sculptures adorn many museums and buildings throughout the United States. Among his works are a bust of Abraham Lincoln, which stands in the Nancy Hanks Lincoln Memorial, and a bust of our state's ex-governor at a state university. Grandpa also sculpted statuary in the state's federal building and local high school. I was unaware of my parents' struggle with their bipolar feelings of happiness and sadness as these two events collided horridly. I was safely protected in my mother's womb, as my grandfather died on August 30th, several months before my birth. Perhaps coming along at the time that I did eased or distracted the ache of my parents and grandmother. I do not know because my family never discussed this tragedy.

My mother recently gave me a photograph snapped shortly after my birth. It was an old black and white photo that you knew with immediate confidence was taken with an original *Brownie* camera. In the photo, a nurse draped in hospital white held somberly my 19 ¼ inch frame and 7-pound, 11¼-ounce body. The nurse wore a white gown, white cap and white surgical mask across her mouth. She appeared as sterile as her uniform. I was wrapped in a white cloth and looked quite bored. The occasion apparently did not impact on me as a particularly invigorating one. I was giving the new world in which I found myself a big, wide yawn as my little fingers covered what they could of my mouth. The photo documented that good manners are as much instinctual as they are learned. God only knew what I thought about being held by this masked stranger, but I guessed that *Tonto* must not have been far away! I was a cute baby, and obviously destined to grow up and do great things... at least that was my subjective take of the photograph.

My earliest recollections begin at about age three years. My older sister came before me and my younger brother was born after me just like clockwork. Yes, I can hear you again with that 'hmm... the middle child..." Diplomatic? Manipulative? Chip on the shoulder? Tired of being left out of things? Why doesn't anybody listen to me? Why doesn't anyone understand me? It is said that one can escape the effects of birth order. Even if I cannot, I am in good company with other middle children: Dwight Eisenhower, Jack Kennedy, George Bush, and Tony Blair. Perhaps I missed my real calling and should have gone into politics! But I digress...

I remember that our father drove to work early in the morning. We often accompanied him since my mother liked shopping downtown... or perhaps she liked escaping the boundaries of our home to which she was confined 24/7 with us three munchkins. At that time, women were not career minded and homemaking with its many care-taking responsibilities was the singular career of "choice," especially for European women. "Keep them barefoot and pregnant" was not just an idle idiom. It was certain that we three musketeers shattered our mother's nerves now and then, maybe even more often than that. We unquestionably frazzled each other's nerves and resolved our differences rather bluntly. The physical approach to conflict resolution is not uncommon among young children as an initial response and our behavior was no exception.

Unfortunately, my father began work at the state's highway department several hours before the customary time for store openings. The impact of these early risings stayed with me as I am still cursed with rising with or before the roosters, and crowing just as loudly because of it. The downtown ritual was unbending. My father dropped off mother and her brood in front of a little church. The church was built in the early 1900s and neatly tucked away on a circular, brick road that identified the center of the city; hence, 'The Circle.' The church doors were opened 24/7 back in those days. Vandalism against a church, of all things, was unheard of at the time. Churches were the center of miracles, not the victims of sin. I was raised Roman Catholic and always thought it ironic that God's home is now opened only certain hours of the day. It is like a realtor purchased the hallowed property and prayer is by appointment only, or 2 to 4 on Sundays as always!

I admired tremendously my mother for taking care of three mildly hyperactive preschoolers in a confined place, holy or not, for two solid hours. I do not recall specifically what we did and I am sure God will remind us at some point, but I can only imagine we were neither religious zealots nor prayerful. We probably ran amuck through the church, touching things that were considered holy and screaming loudly enough to wake up the saintly dead. God must still shutter to this day when we make ourselves known in his presence. I understand His memory goes back a long time!

We eventually made our way to the stores as sleepy downtown became alive. Mom never missed going to the city market where the staples of life were fresh and emitting an aroma I can still recall by memory. My mother is an Italian immigrant who always looked forward to this rather European experience as the market was stocked primarily by Italian vendors. The farmers' market was a sight to behold for a young child and the sights and smells were as breathtaking as any carnival. Everything was fresh and the pasta was homemade. Meat, fish, pasta, fruits, vegetables, cookies, candies and other sweets filled the stands. Chickens were slaughtered and plucked on the spot. We laughed as they persisted with their contorted dance without their heads—after all, we were preschoolers.

A multi-layered sugar wafer cookie was our favorite treat at the city market and mother seldom disappointed us. We were admonished to "be good" to receive our treats. Mom was an expert at applying contingencies to our behavior long before such techniques were formalized in psychology textbooks. And best of all, the layered sugar wafers cost only about 25 cents a pound. Mother knew how to stretch a dollar. What a cheap token behavior management program our mother created and implemented!

We walked from store-to-store following our mother like imprinted ducklings. Mother did more window-shopping than buying. Men riding three-wheeled bicycles hawked ice cream and other novelties. Blind men and men maimed in war having lost their legs were often seen sitting on boards with roller wheels pushing themselves along sidewalks and across streets. They often sold pencils and brooms to help support themselves and their families. To wee little ones, downtown seemed to have an endless number of stores, and like the state fair, we would not be able to visit each and every one of them. One store had a horseshoe shaped walkthrough with a large scale located at the center of its curve. We all took turns weighing ourselves for it was free and in those days *free* meant *free*— even our mother did so when we were not looking. The 'five and dime' store was a favorite of our family's, not only because goods were incredibly cheap, but also the 'five and dime' had a dinner counter with a long single row of twirling bar stools. One could rest and order your favorite ice cream or sandwich. You could watch your order being prepared by women dressed in white because the stoves and other equipment were just on the other side of the counter. I think my mother liked it so much because it was a rare moment where she could watch somebody else do the cooking! And when were done with lunch, we could twirl the tops of the dinner stools making them higher and lower in an autistic-like way for no particular reason or goal.

Somehow time passed and my mother always managed to survive until lunch, a meal that she always prepared for us before leaving home. Mom did her best to skimp, save and cut corners in those days. She was better than my father at applied home economics. The family income was low even by the standards of the 1950s. Money indeed must have been the root of all evil because our family did its best to stay away from it! Whatever could be stretched was stretched. Our family seldom used condiments. We grew skeptical of everything in liquid form, as the staple was apt to be diluted by half or more with water. Although my mother does not receive patent monies, I am sure that she invented skimmed milk. Until I was an adult, I did not realize that products such as milk, ketchup, tomato sauce and shampoo were so rich in color, taste, and texture! Mother economized where she could. Anything that could be branded as a staple in our every day family life that was not nailed down became fair game. Mom "borrowed" just about everything she could from local department stores, restaurants and restrooms, sometimes even toilet paper. Mother was also very practical and sensible. Although I did not appreciate it at the time—um, this would be an understatement—my mother exchanged a birthday gift from my aunt, a stamp album, for something that every little boy would be overjoyed about—a pair of pants. My mother was a shrewd businesswoman who did not need a degree in economics to be savvy. For my part, I licked those pants for several months every time I put them on just out of childhood spite!

Then there were those special times of the year that going downtown captured the young and those young at heart. Christmas is a time of awe, miracles, and imagination for children. In the heart of downtown, a 284-foot limestone monument dedicated in 1902 to soldiers in the armed forces who died in the Civil War, was transformed magically into the world's tallest Christmas tree. The strands of Christmas lights boasted nearly 5000 multicolored lights.

One prominent corner store had its beginnings in the late 1800s. A clock with eight foot illuminated dials faced in all four directions. Each holiday season, a cherub miraculously appeared on the top of this clock. The store dressed up its ordinary window fashions with seasonal scenes, most of which were animated and enchanted us beyond expression. Watching Santa laying gifts underneath the tree, carolers holding hymnals and singing, and reindeer pulling the sleigh captivated us and captured our hearts, as we pressed our noses to the glassed enclosures. In the basement of the store was Santa's Toyland equipped with a small train that transported wide-eyed children throughout the land of magical toys.

Our family participated in any form of entertainment in which little or no funds were expended. We usually visited the cemetery after church on Sundays. Dead people neither charged for visitors nor seemed to mind their presence. Had we been older, this would have been a rather morbid experience. My grandparents were laid to rest in the cemetery's above ground mausoleum and my parents purchased their own vaults beside them many years ago. One of the most fiscally appropriate judgments made by my father who paid $300.00 a plot. In making pre-planning arrangements I was informed by a credible source that it will cost $500.00 to open each vault by unscrewing 4 screws and applying leverage with a pry bar. Upon hearing this, I believe I was hit over the head by the latter and only one screw was involved.

This particular mausoleum hosted row upon row of marbled compartments stacked a half dozen high. I remember trying to peer between the bordered cracks of my grandparents' vaults only to see what I thought was an eye staring back. This always spooked my brother, sister and me, as did a showing of *The Wizard of* Oz, especially the part where the stripped stocking feet of the wicked witch of the east curled and were sucked under the house that fell upon her—*be gone before somebody drops a house on you*! After our family paid their respects to the departed, we fed the ducks in the cemetery's pond. The ducks always seemed happy to have contact with *living* people even the three of us with stale bread. It was generally a pleasant experience for such a morose edifice. Besides telling our friends, the only other drawback was that swans occasionally chased us around the lake. They were apparently unimpressed and impatient at how fast our little hands could dispense stale old bread. How rude!

As adults, we paid increasingly more respect at the cemetery as our paternal grandmother Antonetta and our beloved uncle and aunt, Joseph and Edna, were laid to rest. Grandma died in 1971. Aunt Edna lost her battle with cancer and slipped away at the age of 71. Uncle Joe died at the age of 80. Our father was lovingly taken care of at home by our mother and passed away at the age of 89.

On many Sundays, we had the double treat of not only visiting the cemetery, but also appraising new model homes. The suburbs were growing immeasurably at the time. The boundaries of natural woods, a ready free source for landscaping dirt and soil according to my father, were in constant flux and being driven away long before environmentalists complained of manmade erosion. Local and television personalities were often hired to help market the homes. I particularly remember meeting Leo Carillo one Sunday at one of the model home openings. He was best known for his role as *Pancho*, partner of the *Cisco Kid* from the 1950's television western action series, *The Cisco Kid*. *Pancho* sat on his horse, gun drawn, smiling and waving to the crowd. We children were very pleased.

As a family, we also more or less went to see drive-in movies. Father parked the family green Plymouth off the shoulder of the road that was perpendicular to the movie screen. The three of us were huddled in the backseat with little room to spare. We would squint our eyes and did our best to peer at the distant screen. Drive-in theater owners of the time did not see a need to build tall walls to conceal the screen from view. We watched the movie in silence, as for some inexplicable reason theater owners also did not see the need to run speakers beyond the drive-in's fenced boundaries. We followed the movie dialogue as best we could, which left much to our emerging imaginations. If nothing else, the three of us became visual learners and developed the art of lip reading at a very early age. This will serve us well in our old age as our hearing declines. Best of all, our trips to—well, near the drive-in—always included the iniquitous sharing of one nickel ice cream cone from a local and original *Dairy Queen*, and one bag of popcorn recently homemade by our mother, who stood by the stove and shook the kernels in a pan until their tiny bits of water exploded into popcorn. Family togetherness has never been the same!

During our downtown trips, we sometimes consumed lunch at this particular department store that had a restaurant-like dining area for paying customers on the second floor. A balcony and railing provided an engaging view of the main floor below. The decor was excessively white: white tables, white chairs, a white floor and a white railing. As our mother sat at the table, we were often kneeling on the floor peering through the white railing. The railing kept us from falling on unsuspected shoppers below, although not necessarily our food. We often amused ourselves by making less than flattering remarks about people who innocently milled below us. Bald men and balding men in particular were vulnerable targets of our unflattering critiques and giggles. We were young children after all and easily amused... and it was free!

Time passed and depending on how much effort in parenting we three young-uns forced out of our mother, we either went home earlier than planned *via* the public transportation system (bus) or we waited until early evening for our father to pick up his then tired and cranky family for the return trip home to suburbia.

Growing up second-generation Italian in America was often a challenge. We were all part of the great "melting pot" at mid-century except somebody forgot to tell *those of us who were not the main ingredients that assimilation had its price*. There were choices to be made as American and Italian cultures often clashed and clashed unrepentantly. Such differences in cultural experiences created mild discord between parents and children. Mom and dad strived to maintain what they knew: **TRA-DI-TION**! (Kind of feel a musical coming on...) We children on the other hand wanted to be like our contemporary peers in dress, speech and behavior. In essence, we were faced with two-generation gaps—a cultural one and the time-honored parent/child gap. Such was the predictable friction that stewed in our home as part of the "melting pot" of the 1950s.

Assimilation aside, things were not futile back then. We experienced customs curious and unique to our family and Italian heritage. There were a host of superstitions that impacted on my parents and intruded indiscriminately on our family life. What dictated our parents' behavior dictated ours, as families were bonded units in the 1950s. The list of superstitions that concerned our parents seemed endless and unforgiving. We were forever admonished if we did not heed them for they would bring "bad luck" not only to us, but also to all family members, and perhaps to an entire generation of Italians. Family guilt was inherent and instilled early in our lives. Although we never really understood what all the fuss was about, we perceptively learned collective guilt.

You and your parents may have shared in some of the superstitions that consumed much of my parents' waking hours and invaded ours:

- Never travel or visit a friend on a Friday
- Never visit a new place you have never been to before on a Friday
- Never place a hat or purse on the bed
- Never break a mirror unless 7 years of bad luck appeals to you
- Never open an umbrella in the house
- Never walk under a ladder
- Never let a jet-black cat cross your path
- Be careful about what you do on calendar days of the "13th"
- Be careful of places and events with the number "13" in them (do not live in a house with an address like 1310; if you have 13 people at a dinner party, set a 14th chair anyway at the table; if you were born on the 13th, dig your grave early)

- Never put on clothing backwards
- Never visit someone's house after visiting a mortuary or attending a funeral for that brings bad luck to the person you visit
- Never send a card or gift to someone that bears crosses or birds—the cross thing was a tough one given our Catholic affiliation. For the birds, do you realize how few greeting cards exist without these feathered friends?

If superfluous superstitions were not sufficient, our parents were consumed with other events that were said to bring us bad luck:

- Spilling salt, milk, rice and especially olive oil brought sickness to the family

- Seeing a lady with a hump back (rather amusing and discriminatory since viewing a man with a hump back was said to bring you good luck)

- Seeing bound straw in a field or a flatbed truck carrying straw meant that news was heading your way, presumably awful news

- For the paranoid among you, people were said to be talking about you if you have two eggs in your hand and they break—break a dozen eggs and you experienced delusions of paranoia!

To be fair-minded, there were a few things, albeit a very few things, that supposedly brought you and your family good fortune:

- Seeing a man with a hump back (people who saw the *Disney* movie, *Hunchback of Notre Dame*, undoubtedly were infinitely blessed)

- Seeing a white horse, which was not often seen in the suburbs

- Seeing a man first on the first day of the year is said to bring you good luck all year round—don't even want to think how to accomplish that feat

The Italian tellers of fortunes were apparently male-dominated. Other good fortune came from a medal that was very popular in Italy as a good luck charm. It actually was two distinct medals made out of gold. The number 13 made up one of the medals and a small horn made up the other. Wearing these two medals together was presumed to bring you good luck all your life. I guess the horn cancelled out the ill luck of the number 13. A small price indeed to pay for eternal prosperity!

Is there more? Yes. There were a myriad of proverbs and sayings that were suppose to influence how Italians lived. These adages, in my mother's tongue and dialect, included:

- *Non puoi avere porcho e St. Antonio* (You cannot have pork and St. Anthony—something similar to you cannot have your cake and eat it too)

- *Ne di nartede, ne di venerdi, non si taglia e non si porte* (Not on Tuesday and not on Friday, you can cut and you can travel)

38

- *Paese voi usanza trovi* (The town you go, the way you do it—whatever town you go to, you do things the way the people do them in that town)

- *Sono gentile e son cortese ma pagatemi le spese* (I am gentle and I am courteous, but I leave the check to you-- typically a really bad tipper)

- *Sono nato stanco percio vivo per riposarsni* (I was born tired, so I live to relax—an aphorism I have very much taken to heart in my own life as my badge of honor)

- *Se una donna per sbajlio mette il suo vestito al rovesceio, per quel georno tutto lva male* (If a woman puts her dress on the wrong side, for that day everything goes wrong—I assume a man could wear a dress in any manner without ill effects—well, maybe)

- *Si crede di prendere il prete perla barba* (If you think that you can touch a priest by his beard—this loses much in the translation, but basically suggests that if you are waiting for something great to happen, do not; it is not going to happen or what happens will be small—sort of a precursor I think to the modern day lottery experience)

- *Ne di Manzo ne di Maggione, none ti levare il pedizoine* (In March or May, never take off your heavy underwear— linked to the crazy Italian weather in March and May)

- *Tutte le pecore vanno alla chiesa a portare I soldi al prete* (All sheep go to church and bring all the money to the priest—it is a ridicule in that people are called 'sheep')

Is there still more? Yes, there is more! If the superstitions and proverbs did not overshadow family living, then "folk" remedies aimed to maintain our good health and ward off enemies of the family further stewed the pot:

- Rubbing garlic on your chest to cure a cold (and drive away your friends)

- Wearing garlic on a string around your neck (or many women pinned it to their bras) keeps you safe

- Curing a cold by warming up bricks in the fireplace and then placing them between two pieces of wool—these were placed upon your chest to keep you warn until the cold went away

- Picking flowers called *Comomila* (looked similar to dandelions) eased a sour stomach by placing them in a pot of water to brew and then drinking the hot juice

- The cure all of cure alls—a teaspoon of olive oil will cure just about anything, genuine or imagined.

The ultimate folk remedy for a sick person or to keep a person from becoming ill in an Italian family was the *Evil Eye*. When my grandmother determined that it was time to practice the ritual, she insisted that you drop immediately anything and everything that you were doing. This remedy involved placing a bowl of water on the unfortunate person's head. She then placed three drops of oil in the water and a small prayer was spoken three times: "Rotta e finochio, Leva il malochio." My grandmother continued the ritual while the oil in the water remained visible. If the oil drops dispersed, your sickness was thought caused by people wishing you bad luck. In essence, it was a method of determining whether your illness was caused by the ill wishes of others or by the common microorganisms of the day. It must have tarnished the friendships my parents fostered as they were in a state of wondering which friend or friends among them were wishing them ill will. On top of all that, imagine trying to explain to your playmates why you called time-out in the middle of a game. Having to pee was not only a better excuse, but a face-saver as well. Fortunately, my parents did not continue the practice and this gypsy ritual died with the death of our paternal grandmother in May 1971.

If all the home remedies and cures did not ward off bad luck or sickness, my father's faith did—not in Catholicism as you might have thought to a good Italian, but in the leading evangelist of the time. From my father's perspective, I could not always tell whether the Reverend sat to the right of God or God sat to the right of the Reverend. In the 1950s the Reverend celebrated his healing ministry on weekly television. At 9:00 a.m. (Indiana East time) each Sunday, the evangelist stepped into our living room as the five of us sat quietly in front of the television. He ended each service the same way by asking the home viewers, like us, to touch the television screen, as he prayed for our healing. Our family did as he requested at our father's insistence. And there we were with our five hands pushed flatly against the television screen. I often thought how our whole family could have been incinerated in an instant by a well-timed electrical storm. However, we were spared for some reason obviously for some greater mission. Father brought us to see the evangelist in person at the local Coliseum. We were herded in line like cattle by our father and waited for several hours. The Reverend eventually appeared and placed his hands on our heads in passing. Father seemed happy—at best, we were confused and a trifle bored.

Growing-up Catholic and Italian also presented many rituals, ceremonies, and festivals whose essence impacted on our family life. Most festivals celebrate the feast of a patron saint of a city or town. When the feast of the saint is upon us, a great procession is held in the city with the townspeople carrying a statue of the saint through the streets of the city. All the windows are decorated with the best-colored blankets. All the young girls of the city wear white dresses and follow the procession scattering flowers through the streets. When the procession is over, the people return home to dinner, music, and dance, especially the *Tarantella*. This is an old dance that reminds the elderly of the city of their earlier days. The remembrance is brought about because of the old style of the dance.

In another celebration, the Easter period is filled with many activities. Beginning with Palm Sunday, all the children dress in their best clothing and prepare for the days activities by constructing a large palm. This was accomplished by holding together many small palms or branches of the olive tree. After the palm was constructed, the children placed homemade ornaments such as cookies and chocolate eggs on the palms. They then brought their palms to church and had them blessed during the Mass. After the children returned home, they placed the blessed palms in their bedrooms usually behind a picture of the Blessed Virgin Mary or Jesus, and kept them there until the next year. At that time, they are burned and replaced by new palms.

On *Holy Thursday*, the people visited all the churches in the city—my mother had 7 churches in her city—to see the sepulcher where Jesus laid. The sepulchers were made of mosaic or colored rocks. Mosaic rocks and flowers are also used to celebrate beautiful sceneries of our Lord's passion and death.

On *Good Friday*, the *maceleries*—stores in which only meat was sold—are the view of the city. The best meat, especially lamb, was displayed in the window decorated by much greenery and flowers waiting to be sold on *Holy Saturday*.

On *Holy Saturday*, people gathered in Florence, Italy to see one of the largest processions, which included many city officials dressed in old style costumes. The procession went to one church after the other all through the city.

On *Easter Sunday*, millions of people gathered in St. Peter's Square in Rome to hear and see the pontiff give his papal blessing. My mother took part in many of these ceremonies in her birth city of Carrara.

The city of Viarreggio was famous for another procession, the Viarreggio Carnival. Throughout the month of February, people came from all parts of Italy to enjoy a historical procession that included floats, great flower displays, people dressed in costume and masks, and dancing in the streets. This carnival is much like Mardi Gras in New Orleans.

The city of Venice also celebrated a similar carnival except that it is said the festivity was much more beautiful because it took place at night. A parade of gondolas with multicolored lanterns are loaded with food, musicians, and people who all enjoy themselves by eating, drinking, and singing through the Grand Canal. The carnival, which lasted all night, also included a display of fireworks. The next day, the *Regata*, a race between two gondolas, took place. It was considered a sport and included prizes of money and flags of the city. There was also a main prize: the *Trofee Marciano*, a trophy that became a permanent possession of a three-time winner.

Food is at the heart of all of Italy and the center of many festivals. Many food experts believe that the greatest chefs come from Bolgno. During the months of May and June, the Bolgnese people enjoyed a festival of food in the *Parco della Montagnola*. This festival attracted many people who came to admire some of the best specialties of Bolgno: Tortellini (ravioli) and Lasagnette (lasagna). The food was placed on large tables similar to picnic tables and served to the people who came to the festival.

Another festival, *Festa del' Uva*, the Feast of Grapes, took place in Tuscany, which is in northern Italy. In Tuscany, the month of September is called *Vendenia*, which is also called the *Festa del' Uva*. During September, all the people get together to pick grapes by hand and place them in a large barrel. While they picked grapes, they sang folksongs or *stornelli*, told jokes, and did anything else that would make people laugh. At night, when the day's work was completed, the grape growers (owners) gave a dance for the young people while the elderly sat around and watched the young dancers. Sometimes it took three or four days to pick all the grapes from the groves. However, once they are all picked, they are placed in a large barrel. The young girls of the village then wash their feet and climb in the barrel to mash the grapes. The juice of the grapes dripped out of the faucet at the bottom of the barrel and drained into a smaller barrel. Then the wine was bottled and set aside for fermentation.

On a more personal note, we always had productive grapevines on our property. Both my grandmother and mother picked grapes every summer and mashed them down with their bare feet in a large bucket into their own wine... and we did not sell any wine before its time—actually, our family consumed what little wine we made.

What happened is that our family had apparently more good fortune than bad. We all survived the superstitions, proverbs, and remedies. The historic rituals and ceremonies enriched our lives. We confused our friends perhaps a little, but survived nonetheless with no apparent ill effects. Well, for the most part... I work hard at not spilling milk or salt and never, ever spill olive oil. I don't even go near the stuff!

Chapter 3

Living History

The early childhood years passed without much fanfare or notice. Another *beginning* entered our lives as mandatory formal education soon beckoned at our door. Mother was overjoyed for some reason—a reason we never clearly understood until our later years. Attending parochial school left me with many memories, most of them fond and sentimental ones. These memories are often brought sharply into focus by fleeting scenes on television and the movies, or by nostalgic song lyrics. By now, you may be wondering where this is going, but stay with me. I am still leading up to why I was unable to date formally.

In 1957, I and 119 other neighborhood six-year-old children were entering parochial school for the first time. Those of us who were born during the term of President Harry Truman were known as the *Korean War Babies*—at least that was how we were described by the newspapers of the time. There was no kindergarten in parochial schools in that era. All 120 of us wide-eyed and curious entered the first grade at St. Therese of the Infant Jesus.

In 1957, a World War II hero, Dwight D. Eisenhower was serving as president. It was the year in his term that he was to suffer a serious illness only to recover and serve three more years. In America then we were laughing at a Cuban named Castro and the French were losing a war in some far away country we never heard of—Vietnam. Our own nation and people were at reasonable peace.

As many young Catholic girls and boys, we learned about God and the teachings of our Church *via* the dark blue covered

Baltimore Catechism dated pre-Vatican II. The *Catechism* taught us the faith of the Catholic Church in 37 lessons using question/answer format, and included the learning of standard prayers. Well, at least *drilled* us for our conceptual thinking and abstract understanding were limited due to our young ages and much of what we learned was rote memory. For those of you half-baked Catholics with poor memories, some of the questions for the first two lessons went like this...

From Lesson 1, *"On the End of Man"*

- Who made the world?
- Who is God?
- What is man?
- How is the soul like to God?
- Why did God make you?
- What must we do to save our souls?

From Lesson 2, *"God and His Perfections"*

- Who is God?
- Had God a beginning?
- Where is God?
- If God is everywhere, why do we not see Him?
- Does God see us?
- Does God know all things?

My first grade class received one of the seven Catholic sacraments, first Holy Communion, on May 2, 1958, and back in those days later that same evening, another sacrament, Confirmation. The sacrament of Confirmation is a mature Christian commitment and faith in God's fidelity to us. Again, we were too young to understand fully or even moderately appreciate the significance of these sacraments.

As a second grader in 1959, I remember the beginning of several visits each year from missionaries known as the Maryknoll Fathers. For some reason, their spirit and presentations mesmerized me or the Holy Spirit was stirring me at a young age. They always included a film about their missionary work in some remote country that I had no idea existed let alone know its geographic relationship to our country. Hell, I did not even know where our state was located. I did not really understand in any great detail the importance of the films, but the passing scenes of the plight of third-world countries and narration made the message clear: those who have more help those who have less. God was marketed as a big part of that message and it seemed a clear, simple message at the time. Little did I know how much it would both enhance and complicate my life, by choice or otherwise, and in some ways alter my unfolding adolescent years.

A less fond memory of my second grade year was receiving a spanking from a relatively mean spirited Spanish nun. My transgression? I was the last student out of the classroom during a fire drill and forgot to close the classroom door. My punishment was meted out when we returned as El Nun took me by the hand to the front of class and gave me several smacks across my butt. It was only after this embarrassing incident did she relate my hideous misdeed and forewarned others that they would receive the same castigation if their 7 year old brains committed the same sin of omission. To this day, I am not particularly fond of doors, which ruled out any future careers as an Amway salesman or as a Jehovah Witness.

Hindsight dictates that the assimilation of these life experiences had a considerable impact on my being. I recall playing with trucks, cars, pick-up-stix, slinkies, tinkertoys, cowboys and Indians, GI Joe, erector sets, and other gender-specific toys of the day. We played outdoor games such as hide-and-go-seek, kick the can, lawn darts (encouraging children to throw sharp metal things toward each other was a rather insidious invention), and backyard golf. Backyard golf was most annoying to my parents not due to burying a tin can to simulate the golf hole, but mowing the yard at three different levels to simulate the fairway, rough, and green. This seemed to annoy my mother a great deal even though to me it was just grass. Needless to say, they did not encourage my participation in the sport of golf—another Tiger Woods-maybe was lost to the world!

In outdoor games, like all children, we did not always play fairly. I recall a particular game of "kick the can"—the object of which is to kick the can placed in the middle of the yard before the person identified as 'it' can touch the can while calling out your name. Five of us convinced our unsuspecting friend that there was safety in numbers. We all decided to run toward the can as a group agreeing that all our names could not be called out before one of us kicked the can. We encouraged our gullible friend to lead the pack, but what he did not know is that although we would scream with him, we would remain at our veiled location. Needless to say he was caught easily— apparently there is no safety in 'one.' Laughing so hard at our friend's predicament, however, justice was served as we were all subsequently caught.

Unlike most of my agemates, however, I also remember

donning the role of the celebrant at home saying the Catholic Mass. Any piece of furniture was always accessible for the altar and one of my parents' wine glasses served as the chalice or cup. Bread was forever abundant, and cutting circles out of the bread and smashing the circles flat represented the unleavened sacramental hosts. A blanket, sheet, or towel always served as the blessed cassock or cape.

Grabbing any family member formed the congregation as did any pet that was willing to be part of the congregation or by happenstance was at the right place at the wrong time. Bribery was often involved in building my congregation and seemed to work better than putting the fear of God into my perpetual flock. On many occasions there was no congregation at all, but the virtual celebration of the Eucharist went undaunted by empty pews. Even my imaginary friends at the time would not attend—I know this because they told my parents they did not want to play with me!

I survived my parochial school days, in part, because there was an abundance of holidays and vacations during the grade school years. Remember, "I live to relax." Parochial students had many free days celebrating the lives of saints or biblical moments in history. We had many more saints back then because removing the celebration of their sainthood was unheard of at the time. Schools were not concerned with a 184-day schedule or statewide group testing, and we welcomed as many snow days as the heavens would bestow upon us. Snow days in our Midwestern state did not have to be woven back into the school year schedule. They were one of few things that were truly free in life—well, in a child's life.

In grade school, free days for events other than sainthood and biblical festivities were bestowed happily upon us. As a fifth grader in 1961, a new church was built and the old church became a gymnasium—a rather holy one at that! All 900 of us, grades 1-8, went outside to watch the crowning of the church with its steeple. It was midmorning and for whatever construction reasons, the steeple could not be properly fitted. We were sent home anyway as parents were notified the night before of our early dismissal and made the necessary arrangements for our care. We returned the next day to watch the steeple topping once again. It took several hours to accomplish the task, but this time there was nothing left to chance. Perhaps some divine intervention was requested. After all, even our gracious pastor was not about to let us miss school for three consecutive days. We applauded the crowning event before being sent home midmorning for yet another unscheduled holiday. Gosh, those were indeed the good old days!

When a boy entered the sixth grade, he could choose or be chosen as an "altar boy." I realize that "altar boy" is now considered sexist language, but altar persons were not in vogue at the time and girls did not serve Mass as they do today. As the altar boy of a given week, I arrived at the church by 6:00 a.m. for early Mass. During the winter months, I remember trudging through the snow that arose above my waist; well, I was a short 11 year old. It is amusing now because we all say something like that when we get older, but it really did happen—but we all say that too. Despite such dedication, the priest and I were usually alone in celebrating the Eucharist. God, after all, resided in the hearts of people. The multitudes had sufficient common sense to stay home where it was warm, dry, and safe. The site of prayer mattered less than the spirit of invocation.

As much as going home from school unexpectedly was a great thing for a kid in those days—only to be outdone by spending time in front of a new black and white television—it was not a pleasant one for a seventh grader of the time. It was

November 22nd of 1963, a particularly cold day in November in Indiana, but unseasonably warm in the state of Texas. President Kennedy traveled to Dallas in hopes of resolving a feud between the then Governor Tom Connally and then senior senator Ralph Yarborough. President Kennedy believed that he would be unable to carry the state of Texas in the 1964 presidential election if the feud was not abated. The motorcade showcased an open-air limousine for President and Mrs. Kennedy given the unseasonably warm weather in Dallas. President Kennedy was reportedly shot near a book depository building. We all walked from the school to the adjacent church to pray for our Catholic president who was trying to survive an attempted assassination. We prayed. He died anyway. And then we sadly went home.

People of our generation always say that this is one day we remember not only where we were, but also what we were doing. The generation before remembered Pearl Harbor on December 7, 1941, and the generation after remembered their circumstances following the terrorist attack on the World Trade Center in New York on September 11, 2001.

I do remember clearly the presidential assassination. I recall watching television with my family when Walter Cronkite announced President Kennedy's death. He took off his glasses and for one of the few times exposed his tearing vulnerability as he spoke these brief, haunting words: *From Dallas, Texas, the flash apparently official, President Kennedy died at 1:00 p.m. central standard time, 2:00 p.m. eastern standard time, some 38 minutes ago.* What we thought of as Camelot vanished in a horrifying instant. There was no longer *...a more congenial spot for happy ever-aftering than here in Camelot.*

On a less somber note, it was in that same year that I recall witnessing Catholic nuns "out of place," that is, not in the roles

52

in which we inflexibly restricted them. In the late fifties and early sixties, nuns were habitually in habit and we assumed wrongfully that they probably slept and showered in them as well. There was both a mystique and admiration about priests and nuns back then that blinded us about their human condition and human frailties. We did not attribute normal human actions and daily functions to nuns. We assumed that they had no hair, and never left the confines of their convent. After all, they were stay-at-home nuns on house arrest for God. Most of us did not even think that nuns used restrooms! I do not know why; we just did not attribute normal bodily functions to women of God.

We knew that nuns did not drive or go shopping. I am not sure how we thought that they purchased food or other commodities. I guess we thought such merchandise miraculous appeared—if they had water, they could make wine! Anyway, the aura about nuns was shattered one day when I caught a glimpse of a Sister shopping at the local grocery store. I was dumbfounded and astonished. I remember asking myself, "What is she doing here? How could this be?" The event was unordinary and the experience surreal. Something was obviously out of place and it was not I!

It was Sister Modestrine whom we called unaffectionately "Mighty Moe." She was thin in frame and all of four feet tall. Her short stature was inconsistent with her gruff presentation. She was tougher than any drill sergeant you could imagine or would want to experience. Her reputation preceded her in a Bondian sort of way, or the demented ravings of her past pupils exposed her. The *Incredible Hulk* had nothing over her. Progressing from the third to fourth grade became known as hell's rite of passage for some students. You found out your assigned teacher several weeks before the start of school on a Sunday morning. Students who were entering the fourth grade scanned wearily the classroom lists posted on the main door of school. You prayed that your name was not identified below the envisioned title of "Mighty Moe." Like many students before me, I hesitantly ran my finger down the classroom list as I peered through the fingers of my other hand... and there it was! No doubt about it. Many are called, but few are chosen. And I was chosen. There was no escape as my baptized name betrayed me and did not protect me from perceivable harm and horror. A prayer, a novena, not even a trip to Lourdes, France or joining the foreign legion would make a difference now. Although reality did not set in immediately, the dye was cast. But I digress once again...

I was startled to see a nun shopping at the local grocery store; never mind that it was "Mighty Moe." Her head was not much higher than the top of the cart and you wondered how she steered the darn thing. I thought it best to stay at a discreet distance and observe her from afar. I was flabbergasted that Sister was placing items in her cart that were similar to those mother placed in ours. How could this be? We eat the same foods and use the same products as "Mighty Moe?" All of a sudden the theory of parallel universes made good sense because this Sister certainly was not sharing the same time and space as my mother!

Outside of school, somewhere around the third grade, my friends Bob, Skip and I decided to start a local newsletter in our neighborhood. We entitled the newsletter *LuCinDa*, which was named after who we believed were our 'girlfriends' at the time. My girlfriend was Lucy, Bob's was Cindy, and Skip's was Diane. I do not remember whether they were flattered or not, but I assume they were; or perhaps they preferred roses or jewelry.

The newsletter shared much about nothing that occurred in the neighborhood. There were no computers or copy machines at the time. So we typed the newsletter on our *Smith-Coronas* portable typewriters using 10-12 sheets of carbon paper. Now, for those of you who precede carbon paper, it had the interesting quality that the more you used, the fatter, duller, and less readable the type became. You were not sure whether you were reading something or analyzing psychological ink blots. We almost felt guilty about selling these latter copies of the paper to our neighbors for the full 25 cents... almost, for this would cut into our ice cream and soda money; after all, the "profits" had to be split three ways. The neighbors did not seem to mind and enjoyed reading about the going-ons in a very narrow slice of the community while they were working or busy being homemakers. The reader is spared the *breaking* news events shared in our neighborhood paper, as no known copies have survived the passage of time.

Beyond our community, more noteworthy events occurred in the world from 1957-1965 during our eight years of what was then identified as "grammar school." Indeed, unbeknown to us at the time, we were living history as much as studying it. There were three chief executives serving our country: Presidents Eisenhower, Kennedy and Johnson. The coronation of three popes as heads of the world's Roman Catholics also occurred: Popes Pius XII, John XXIII, and Paul VI. The Second Vatican Ecumenical Council (Vatican II), dedicated to *The Immaculate*, was convened. The First Vatican Council was adjourned way back in 1870. Vatican II was declared open under Pope John XXIII in 1962 and closed under Pope Paul VI in 1965. Pope John hoped that the Council would "...increase the fervor and energy of Catholics, to serve the needs of Christian people." Locally, two of the worst disasters occurred in our state during that period: a gas explosion blew up the local Coliseum and killed 75 people; and 135 victims lost their lives to a tornado.

By 1964, we all entered our last year in grade school. We were now maturing into young adults—well, a good many of us anyway. This was a year of work that was to prepare us for high school. Boys finally discovered girls and girls seemed to like the idea. Being the less mature of the sexes, there were still some boys whose chief concern about relating to girls was contracting *cooties*.

At the end of these long eight years, I *chose* what I thought was my life's calling and in all honestly had not thought about much else since the second grade. To my family's surprise, I decided to enroll in a Catholic seminary with the intention to be ordained a Roman Catholic priest. How did I know that at age 13 I was too young to decide what to do with the rest of my life? Yet, it seemed naively simplistic, but so reassuring at the time.

As a young man with a pastoral focus, I spent almost as much time at the parish rectory as I did at home. The rectory is where priests lived and the parish business was transacted. My transportation back and forth to home, which was less than a mile away, was initially by bicycle, then by car when I became of legal age. This worked out rather well until one evening when somebody broke into my car and lifted my cassette stereo deck—right in front of the church! Such incidents were unheard of at the time in this neighborhood. Neither the culprit nor the deck was ever found; however, I suspect the person progressed to bigger crimes and is surely rotting in a jail cell or hell today. At least I hope so because I do not feel particularly forgiving.

Typical tasks that were entrusted to the seminarians at the rectory included answering the door and telephones during the evening hours, and printing the parish Sunday bulletins, newsletters, etc. In turn, we also had free run, more or less, of watching television and raiding the icebox. There was a group of five of us seminarians who were honored with these responsibilities. They were a large part of my life at the time, an important part of my forming adolescent years. Bob, Jim, Joe and Tom (Gris) hold a special place in my heart even though we rarely see each other now as our roads have traveled diverse paths and what relationally bound us then has weakened.

Bob was the bright, intelligent seminarian keen in theological wisdom and Canon Law. Jim was the caring seminarian with a kind and inviting smile for anybody from anywhere. Joe had the most angelic voice whose singing did more for one's peace of mind than Prozac ever could. Gris—well, we spent so much time together because of our duties and friendship. I was closest to Gris in age and deeply miss those times we had together. Yet, all these men generously shared their friendship and their guidance at a formative time in my young life.

During the years, we saw a number of parish priests come and go from the rectory. Some went because priests were reassigned generally about every five years. Some went because they chose a different path and abandoned their chosen vocation—some to marry. Some went because they were assigned only temporarily to the parish to 'dry out' from the alcoholic demons that devoured them.

We also developed relationships with the good sisters of the parish who lived in the nearby convent. Parishes did not have coed dorms that housed both priests and nuns. These relationships, beyond our peer relationships, were highly treasured ones. It was difficult to see them go after being such a big part of our young lives. It was during this period that I could remember first experiencing personal feelings of loss.

Graduating from grade school was another one of those *beginnings of the end* that most of us commonly share. It was a time when you first gained awareness that you are not just kids anymore. Playtime neither reigned supreme nor could you get away with just playing all the time even if you wanted to do so. This thought was reflected in the address to our graduating class of 1965: "Now you must enter high school, a time only half as long as grade school. This is your preparation for tomorrow that will be here much sooner than you think. Your parents spent the last eight years begging you to study and will probably continue for another four years... The tomorrow has arrived. You soon will be on your way to a career. The years will seem to pass quicker now so enjoy them as you progress through this fine part of your life..." Responsibilities came to the forefront and thoughts about life, life's goals, and careers became more defined—truly, a *beginning of the end.*

Chapter 4

Amo, Amas, Amat...

In Midwestern Indiana, the seminary high school, college and graduate theology school for young men were all located on one campus in the southern part of our state. The seminary high school was scheduled for closing the fall of the year that I planned to attend. Instead of leaving home and beginning my residential stay there, a seminary high school opened in our city and I remained in my home nest.

The seminary high school, Latin School, was part of Holy Rosary Church and located on the near-southeast side of the city in the part of the city known as "Little Italy." Many Italian immigrants settled in "Little Italy," including my paternal grandparents, father, and aunt. The foundation for Holy Rosary Church was laid in 1911, but the structure was not completed and the dedication did not occur until May 1925 due to limited funds. The Church features twin campaniles or church towers. The parishioners donated the massive bells for the campaniles.

The seminary secondary school was the only one of its kind in the state. Holy Rosary parish continues to this day, but the high school was closed in 1977. The property is now used for meetings and youth activities. However, the annual Italian festival, which was revived in 1984, continues to this day—a time for celebrating, sharing, and consuming the greatest sampling authentic Italian cuisine.

Latin School came into existence at a time in the sixties when the world was changing and the church's role was trying to adapt to the shifting social environment. Simply withdrawing from the world and developing some sort of individual fulfillment no longer achieved spiritualism. Personal spiritualism provided guidance and strength of character that would serve as a catalyst to inspire others to channel their lives for the good of all. Seminary student life expanded our activities to face modern experiences and opened the doors to the social environment of the time. Students for Community Services created a fresh spirit of communal effort in students as they attempted to spread Christian love and charity. The high school was located adjacent to a leading pharmaceutical company that encompasses much of that side of our town. The mere act of breathing on some days was a labored experience back in the '60s. The interaction between the burn-off of chemicals and by-products and the heavy air of summer's end produced a truly indescribable, undesirable weighty odor. Moreover, this perfumed unpleasantness was intensified by the heat and intense humidity of any late summer day.

The seminary's ambition was to prepare young men for Christian leadership. The Liturgy served as the core of our seminary community, as it was the source of Christian life and energy. Religious activities were the basic foundation for all individual and school activities. I was not alone. My friendships with my mentors Bob and Jim migrated with me from grammar school to my secondary years where I met Joe and Gris.

The accredited seminary high school, like many college-prep institutions, held very high academic standards. For those of you who have not had such an experience, high academic standards translated to 3-4 hours of homework every night and typically more on the weekends. Academics were considered to encourage personal initiative and growth. The good fathers believed that as a person in the right environment grows in knowledge, he grows in responsibility and maturity as well.

Striving for the ideal, the seminary experimented with these personal changes, which stimulated further individual initiative for development.

Well, more than one person has said: "Knowledge is good." I know this because I said it and it was also carved in stone in a movie where academic endeavors were not primary concern—or concern at all for that matter. I suspect that the pursuit of knowledge was indeed the major goal of such daily toil. I also think that such drudgery had a hidden agenda for enforcing the school's number one rule for young seminary men: **NO DATING!** The learned priests of the school probably were quite aware of the need to counteract the biological urges that surge in adolescence; namely, hormones! You had to admit, it was not only clever, but clearly legal as well. If you let your studies slide due to *extra curricular activities*, your grades gradually decreased leading to academic failure and expulsion. Then you would be a free man and could date all you wanted. Straight-*A* students tended to be simultaneously celibate and smart. Of course, there were others like me who was not only celibate, but also average more or less.

All work and no play makes one a dull seminarian. In addition to academic endeavors, our more artistic students performed in a number of plays, dramas, and musicals much like any other high school. Well-known plays such as *A Game of Chess* and *The Hobbit*, and musicals such as *Finian's Rainbow* and *The Music Man* were performed during my high school years.

I guess I was somewhat naive as an emerging adolescent. Sex education then was not as it is today, especially in a seminary. In fact, there simply was none, nodda, zip... Although most of you know or have heard about the 10 Commandments, the good Fathers convinced us of the existence of the lost *11th* Commandment: *Thou shall not have sex.* We generally accepted that Commandment without challenge, lost or not—sort of within the context of infallibility. I cannot say I particularly miss the *good old days*, but I often miss the clarity of the period.

This is not to say that we did not notice girls or they us, because we did. And being adolescent boys, we sometimes... well often... well almost always tried to impress adolescent girls. I recall one time when a girl whose identity I did not know was standing outside of the rectory basement window. I was working on printing the church bulletin for the Sunday services. Our eyes met. She smiled. I smiled. She winked. I nodded my head. She lit a cigarette. I lit a cigarette. She took one long puff and definitely inhaled. Being my first cigarette, I took a long puff and inhaled. She exhaled a plum of smoke with a satisfying smile. I gag and coughed like there was no tomorrow. She smiled that sophisticated way and sauntered out of sight. I extinguished my first and only cigarette of my life. We were just two smokes passing in the night.

Beyond noticing girls, seminarians were part of the social arena of life and did involve themselves in social activities. Such activities occurred pretty much with each other, sort of early male bonding you might say and more difficult to achieve these days without perceived sexual overtones. We did many things in our feeble endeavor to manage are biological urges and avoid young women and dating. We socialized through such activities as cookouts, ping-pong, pool, putt-putt, cards, table games, sports, masturbation, watching television, praying, and community activities. Seminarians worried needlessly about developing facial acne and going blind! What we did not worry about was *breaking* anything since we assumed there was no future productive sexual use of that particular part of our anatomies. We did not realize that as men, we would soon be reaching our sexual or physical peak at around age 19. But wait! The age of 19 is too soon to reach a peak at anything! No wonder that most freshmen college dropouts are men. And what's this? Women do not reach their physical or sexual peak until around their mid-to-late 40s. Hmmm... So let me see if I got this figured out. Men begin reaching their psychological peak around age 50 when hormone levels drop; so at about the time men start losing their sexual interest, women are reaching their sexual peak. Of course, we know that many women are relieved that their mates no longer had sexual desire in their later years, and many of these same women filed for divorce in their old age when synthetic medications changed the natural scheme of things and brought desire back to old men—at the dismay of old women, of course. Although it escapes me at this time, there is a lesson in here somewhere!

Well, enough sex! There was some inherent security and comfort in the structure and routine of seminary school. The uniform of the day was a white shirt, tie—geeky slender in those days and customarily fake—dress pants, and dress shoes. They preferred that your socks matched as well. Selling bibles or other products would not be a far stretched observation in such attire. The seminary high school was south of downtown in the city and certainly not within walking distance. Our parents typically took turns transporting us to school, and when they could not, public transportation served its purpose. In riding the city bus, it was necessary to fend off the unfortunate and harmless winos of the time that paced the downtown street corners begging for quarters to support their habits.

Our daily routine had us arrive at 6:30 a.m. and the first order of business, I kid you not, was choir practice. Now, there were two phenomenons about choir practice. First, unlike the amateur shower singer, carrying a tune as a group in the very early morning hours takes considerable fortitude, perhaps even intestinal fortitude. We mustered such grit with varied success on any given day. Although many of us sang with our voices lifted in joyful praise to the Lord, a good number of us also mumbled incoherently and sung off-key. Second, and the early morning hours aside, have you ever wondered how a group of young men sounded whose voices were in various states of maturational change? Not only is it not a pretty sight or sound, even the tone deaf took perceptible umbrage! It was the only time of day that I recall that the pigeons refused to perch at the top of the large columns supporting the church.

I am reminded of a similar "sounding" incident that occurred at the time. My brother attempted to teach me how to use a clutch for the first time. He was brave enough to allow me in the driver's seat as he sat next to me. This was uncommonly characteristic of my brother to allow somebody not only close to his car, but also actually to sit inside his Fairlane Ford convertible. Not only did he permit me inside the car, I was in the driver's seat. The honor and horror of the episode was all mine. It was truly a *Kodak* moment—well, it was certainly some kind of moment!

In our family driveway, my brother instructed me explicitly how to put his car in reverse. He went into great detail on the finesse of how to use a clutch. Although I thought I followed his directions with unusual precision, the gears screeched and screamed—for mercy I guessed. The car traveled about 3 feet, if that far, and my brother yelled in his best-controlled anger, "Get out!" I did so and to this day have never learned how to drive a clutch. Well, that screeching sound was similar to how 103 young men differentially phasing through puberty harmonized. If there was anything dead around the school, we surely woke them and drove their spirits away. I only hope that our choir instructor had the good sense to wear cotton in his ears!

Whether we personally benefited from early morning choir practice over four years is a matter of opinion—and as you know, every one has an opinion. The significance of such a practice will be left in each student's heart and theologians to ponder through the ages. I'm not a professional singer and friends typically ask what the cackling is all about when we burst into song at various gatherings. If nothing else, we learned to be wide awake by 7:00 each morning and ready to go! Academics began and the morning was completed with the celebration of Mass. Squeezed between choir practice and Mass was voted our least favorite class, Latin-lab. *Amo, Amas, Amat* . . . I love, You... uh, well, whatever.

Seminarians studied Latin each year of high school: four long, excruciating years. For those of you who are not aware of Roman Catholic history, Latin at that time was the *official* language used in celebrating Mass. This tradition changed in the late 1960's when the language of the respective people became the official language of celebration. In America, it seemed to make perfect sense for people to understand what was being said *via* English. However, the change in language met with opposition and anger by many people reinforcing the adage of being careful when messing with...**TRA-DI-TION**! Perhaps the people took some comfort in not understanding completely what was going on during the Eucharistic celebration, or change—whether good or bad—is always difficult to accept and usually better for somebody else.

In Latin-lab, each of us sat in front of this extraterrestrial contraption. No, we were not abducted or controlled by aliens. Each device was labeled with a large, white number that permitted an individual to be singled out or *targeted* as I recall, the latter being more aptly descriptive. Out of a stand of this device grew two slender sides appearing much like a magnet. We placed our heads between the two extending arms and spoke into the device—hardly a flattering look yet quite controlling, as our head movement was restricted and reduced the gawking factor (*gf*). We were not sure if we were being radiated at the time.

The lab device incorporated microphones and speakers. Each device was hardwired into a central switchboard controlled by the instructor. The switchboard allowed the instructor to speak to one or several students at the same time. Unfortunately, it also allowed the instructor to listen to one or more students recite Latin or what our less conversant students considered a reasonable facsimile. Now, I do not need to remind you that adolescents, even seminarians, are known for doing the unusual or strive for novel experiences. The dear Father often heard more than Latin and, if identified, you paid the price for your indiscretion.

For those of us who did not properly study our Latin assignment the previous evening, what the instructor heard was more of a mixture of Latin-English—the *Dominoe Nabisco* interpretation of classic works. It was sometimes difficult for the instructor to determine whether we were reciting Latin or some other twaddle. Much mumbling was heard and we prayed that Father did not *dial* us in or at least did not tarry while listening to us to understand what we did not understand. That was a false hope, however, much like animals in the wild pouncing upon an injured beast of burden. There was no way out. The queried face of the instructor in and of itself disclosed to you that either he did not understand what language you were using or he understood quite clearly what was unclear to you. If you did not quickly recover and make reasonable Latin sense (carpe diem), your reward was doubled the assignment for the next evening. Woo-hoo!

Of course, the nature of the setting lent itself to seminarians saying things that had nothing to do with Latin recitation. The slang of the time was often uttered along with attempts at *formal* pig Latin. The instructor was sure to hear: "If you are really listening, Father, I owe you a pack of cigarettes" [smoking was good for you at the time] or "Father, Father, if you can hear, you know I have not studied Latin since last year!" The device also lent itself to utterances common to traffic controllers in training ("Father, you are clear to land on runway seven" or "Father, you'd better jettison your excess wine"). Still, other seminarians simply moved their lips without saying anything with the hope that dear Father assumed it was an electrical problem or that he was growing a bit deaf in his old age.

I remember one of many times that I did not study or study well my Latin from the evening before and called upon one of my tried and true routines. There usually was enough Latin-sounding Italian words that I hoped that a quick 'hit and run' by the language padre would result in a triumphant deception. The instructor was typically too experienced, however, and in these situations often chose to come to your station—*up close and personal* if you will—to listen to you *live at the Coliseum*! Ah, there was no escaping Father death! *Amo, Amas, Amat...*

Well, having survived Latin-lab more or less each morning, the afternoon schedule at the seminary high school was pretty much the same as morning academics. We were educated in the classic literature; well, educated to the extent that our young minds would allow—reading, trying our best to understand their undercurrents, and writing critical book reports on such classics as: *The Scarlet Letter* by Hawthorne; *The Sound and the Fury* by William Faulkner; *Lord Jim* by Joseph Conrad; *Kidnapped* by Louis Stevenson; *The Red Badge of Courage* by Stephen Crane; *The Red Pony* by John Steinbeck; *Robinson Crusoe* by Daniel Defoe; *Oliver Twist* by Charles Dickens; *Romeo and Juliet, The Merchant of Venice,* and *Much Ado About Nothing*, and many more by Shakespeare; and my personal all-time favorite, *To Kill a Mockingbird* by Harper Lee.

The exception to our daily schedule was reserved for the uppermost of upper classmen—seniors, that is. Seniors had access to a partially enclosed area in what was called the "Rec Room." The Rec Room contained the recreational equipment of the time, including ping-pong and pool tables, card tables, etc. The partially enclosed room was the holiest and reserved for upper classmen: the "Senior Room." The Senior Room boasted of the only television in the school. Seniors gained passes to their sanctuary during their free periods. The Rec Room was off limits to other students until after school. History always has found itself difficult to shed instances of class societies and a seminary dedicated to holiness was no exception. The lot of your station in life, in part, dictated what you got or didn't get.

The priests who taught us had their own mystiques and endearing personalities. Through their interactions with seminarians, they had developed, earned, or had thrust upon them some special names, *most* of which were affectionate in nature. Monsignor was the rector of the seminary. There was "Old Smokey" who often could not resist a fine cigar. "Shorty" was less than five feet tall. The "Dough Boy" coached most of us in sports. In the wake of his prominence and black cape, "Zoro" often left his mark. "Inky" took care of the school's printing needs. These dedicated men and others shared their knowledge and life with us. They were our mentors and guided or jostled us through the tumultuous years of adolescence.

"Inky" and I grew particularly close over four years, as we along with Gris took care of the offset printing needs for the school and local parish. Church bulletins, newsletters, directories, programs for staged high school musicals, special notices, and yearbooks all required our special skills. Inky was my mentor. Desktop publishing was not in vogue back then. He trained my emerging offset printing skills and guided me spiritually. Inky was a rock, focused in his mind and emotions. I admired his stability and forthright approach to life.

Inky was a compassionate man. I recall printing some invitation cards using an old stamp press. It was powered by the pedaling of one's feet much like the sewing machines of old. You controlled its speed, as the jaws of its mouth opened and closed repetitively like a huge clam. There was little room for error, as the rhythm of placing a sheet of paper in its opened jaws must be followed quickly by the removal of one's hand. Well, I do not have rhythm—cannot dance or sing—and cannot jump either! One day, my timing was off and the jaws of the stamp press were unrelenting, as they smashed my fingers of my dominant hand slightly above the knuckles. I saw it happen. I heard it happen. I felt it happen. Then I fainted heroically. Inky revived me and took me to a nearby hospital emergency room. He continually assured me and attempted to take my mind off the pain caused by my well-bloodied hand. I can still remember the nurse asking me despite the visibly bandaged hand, "Where does it hurt?" I was fortunate that my fingers were only smashed. My skin was broken, fingers were bleeding, and several nails were pushed out of place, but no broken bones were visible on the x-rays. To this day, I am very careful when I make waffles for breakfast!

The high school years were much like the experiences of other adolescents not attending the seminary. The temperament and behavior of seminarians covered the range typical for the age group except for the limited, open contact with the opposite gender. We participated in the fads of the period, even the less desirable ones from an adult perspective. I recall that several students "mooned" passer-byes from the school windows. Unbeknownst to them, one of the "moonees" was the father in charge of physical education and athletics. The two students *earned* numerous demerits for their feat and are probably still participating in detention to this day—oh, the agony of de-feat! Certainly by now their problems are all behind them! As seminarians, we were expected to bare our souls, but the rest of what we were or had was expected to remain veiled. There were many revelations by God and church, but this was not one of them!

Seminarians were often involved in activities on holy days at various settings around the city. On one such Good Friday, my best friend Gris and I participated in the Way of the Cross at a local convent (or "nunnery" to lay people). The sisters at this particular convent were of the holy order that took a vow of silence in addition to their vows of poverty and celibacy. They did not interact with the outside world. The sisters neither communicated directly to persons beyond the convent walls nor did they have face-to-face contact with them. Information was exchanged *via* a rotating cylindrical wooden tube that measured about four feet tall and two feet in diameter. This was long before modems and the Internet. The desired material(s) for transfer were placed in the cylinder and a pull of a rope rang a bell signaling that the material(s) were ready for transfer—pre-transporters to you trekies out there... and you know who you are!

Now my friend Gris and I were curious as to whether or not a person could actually fit inside the tube. After much serious debate between the two of us, he decided on the direct approach to scientific inquiry and jumped into the cylinder. Carpe Diem! As my friend crouched in the tube, I pulled the rope and the bell clanged. A good sister must have sensed our shenanigans because the cylinder immediately began rotating and my friend disappeared gradually with no escape, as if swallowed by the walls of the convent.

A glimpse of Gris' face as he rotated away suggested some horror and a silent cry for help; but there was nothing that could be done. Besides, I was laughing too hard inside and out to be of much help. Events were set into motion that could not be halted. My friend was gone. I could not beam Gris back! The tube stopped eventually with its wooden back facing me. After several long minutes which seemed to last several days, the cylinder rotated slowly once again. My friend slowly reappeared and blushed more radiant than a red ripe tomato. I will never forget the hue of Gris' face. He did not speak about what he saw and undoubtedly very few people had seen, but then again, I did not ask. There was no sense in inviting evil into our lives, or bad luck at the very least. Gris jumped out of the cylinder and we hightailed out of the area to prepare for the upcoming services. The possibility of being struck dead for invading the privacy of the sisters' sanctuary did not appeal to us, and it laid heavily on our minds for a period of time.

We lived despite our misadventure. Gris and I survived four years of seminary high school. Many others did not. There were 103 young men in our freshman class four years ago. By our senior year in 1969, there were left only 45 mostly celibate, mostly smart young men. Out of our senior class, five of us chose to continue our religious studies. Yes, Gris and I were two of the five. I again found myself facing a *beginning of the end*. It was the transition from adolescence to adulthood. It was a time when you started looking more ahead and less behind. You really began to believe that you had the "calling." You became more certain of your life's direction and perhaps why you were on earth. Well, at least that was what you thought at the time...

Also impacting our decisions was the events and social changes in the United States in the 1960s. Historically, the sixties have been described as the age of youth—youth dominated the culture of the 60s. It is estimated that 70 million children from the post-war baby boom were now teenagers and young adults. Long hair was not worn just by women, which often confused the casual onlooker. Debates on college campuses became more intensive and decisive for the youth of the day. The United States became increasingly involved in the Vietnam War with massive troop buildups ordered in 1965 in an unsuccessful attempt to put an end to the conflict. As the war grew, so did the draft and anti-war sentiment. Many draft dodgers fled to Canada rather than join the armed forces. The Civil Rights movement, which evolved *via* peaceful protests, headed social change in our country. Nonviolent sit-ins were lead by Martin Luther King and Stokely Carmichael. The National Organization of Women took center stage in questioning the unequal treatment of women (the glass ceiling), and Women's Lib was born. The hippie movement supported the use of drugs, particularly marijuana and LSD, rock 'n' roll, and sexual freedom. These were celebrated, reaching their peak in expression and culminating in the Woodstock Festival. The sixties were indeed the decade of experimentation, freedom... and inherent confusion.

Lyndon B. Johnson, president at the time, declined to run for reelection in 1968 with his heavy heart and all. This left the door open for JFK's brother, Robert Kennedy, to campaign for President. However, fanatics assassinated Robert Kennedy, Martin Luther King, and Malcolm X in the mid-to-late sixties.

The space dream began by John Kennedy and the space race with the Russians intensified. Alan Shepherd was the first American in space in 1961 and John Glenn first orbited the earth two years later in 1963. The Apollo space program culminated in 1969 when Neil Armstrong and Buzz Aldrin walked on the moon in Apollo XI. President Kennedy's dream of landing a man on the moon before the end of the decade was realized, even though he himself was never conscious of this extraordinary event given his assassination in 1963. As Elvis was to the teenagers of the fifties, the Beatles set the scene and the fashion for young people around the world in the 1960's. The Beatles, notably many say the most successful singers of all time, had their humble beginnings as the *Quarry Men* in May 1960 in Liverpool, England. They changed their name to the *Silver Beatles* before becoming the *Beatles*. It took awhile for them to cross the Atlantic, but they eventually exploded onto the American scene on February 9, 1964 as guests on the *Ed Sullivan Show*—a really big 'shoe' indeed!

Back in my corner of the world, graduation ceremonies for my class of '69 were held on June 1, 1969. The Archbishop of the city offered the Baccalaureate Mass. Commencement exercises, including the presentation of school rings and diplomas, occurred later in the day. Upon receiving my diploma, it was certified that I "...satisfactorily completed the course of study prescribed by this institution and by the State Board of Education and is entitled to this diploma...." It was the first time in my life that I was *entitled* to anything. The decade was ending and my classmates and me were at another *beginning of the end...*

Chapter 5

Sorry, Wrong Number

The college years were another *beginning of the end*. The first time I would live away from home had arrived. Just about at the time you sort of believed that you were emancipated and a man, dependency arrived quickly and abruptly when you were in need financially or emotionally. It was a time to prove that you could stand on your own, that you could make decisions. You were going to live by the sword or die by the sword—or you were going to call your mommy!

I found it difficult to leave for the seminary, but not in the separation sense. Family is family no matter how far apart life brings you. You become comfortable in a routine, a routine that provides you safety and pleasure. It is rather predictable, and it is this constancy that gives you the false sense that life will be this way forever. Then that "end" comes around and almost in a blink of the eye, predictability is gone. Routine is gone. Security is gone. You are gone. But don't go! I am getting ahead of myself...

The seminary college of St. Meinrad was set in a peaceful pastoral setting. Unlike the central part of the state, the southern counties provided a welcomed change from the flatland where I grew up. The roads gradually became hilly and curvy, like an endless but gentle roller coaster. As you approached the college, you passed through the small town, which lay at the bottom of *The Hill*. The seminary shared the same name of the town. We called it *The Hill* because the college was majestically placed on top of a hill and the town was nestled below. It reminded you of scenes from the *Sound of Music* except of course they were no women or nuns on *The*

Hill. Curiously, the time in the town below was one hour ahead of the time on the campus above. Being out of sync was commonplace.

This Midwestern town was quite small, but provided the necessities of the simple life. After all, that was what we were supposed to live at the time: the simple, monastic life. The town had a small grocery store, a post office, and Mama's place. Mama was a very kind, grandmother-ish lady whose sprightliness belied her 75 years of age. She was always vibrant, florid, and very kind to the seminarians. It seems that she knew just what complexities we faced just above her quiet part of town. Mama's was the hub of the town, a place to socialize off *The Hill.* Well, at least you could socialize more there than at the grocery store or post office—the only other two businesses in town at the time.

It was surprising if people less familiar with the geographic area were able to find *The Hill* at all. For one of our pastimes involved pilfering city mile and directional markers. Go figure what seminarians will do! Such trophies adorned the walls of the residence and for whatever reasons generally went unnoticed by those in spiritual and legal authority. In my later years, I discovered that missing city and mile markers were more than just annoying and made it difficult to arrive at one's destination in a timely fashion—if at all. If you were fortunate to stumble upon the seminary, driving up *The Hill* was a rather European experience as your car grind slowly up the steep, spiraling road. The steep cliffs cradled you as you floated upwards to the seminary.

The day of student arrival was a cool, crisp day. The skies were clear and deep blue. The sunshine was bright and bathed you with relaxing warmth. You thought absolutely nothing was wrong in the world. Trees and flowers of all kinds were changing with the season, as autumn signaled the start of the school year—and back in those days, the start of school was in September after Labor Day. The splendor of the experience leads you to believe that Disneyland was at the top of *The Hill.* And when you arrived, indeed it was... and more.

The college was a castle-like structure built in the mid-1800s with towers and turrets straining toward the sky. Like many structures in Europe, you gazed in awe, oblivious for the moment to others and movement around you. You placed yourself temporarily back in time wondering how people lived and the things about which they cared. As you approached the seminary, tall pine trees aligned the road. These trees looked exalted, a rich green and very old. They turned your thoughts to the time of Christmas. Such trees easily stimulated your imagination, as you envisioned them decorated in lights and tinsel with angels on their pointed crests.

As your gaze turned toward the monastery itself, a structure standing tall and supported by burnt-orange brick, its variable heights dotted the skyline. The curved doorways and windows balanced the round towers at the pinnacle. Old red brick roof tiles capped the structure and added to the prominence of the towers. Pigeons and other foul appeared quite comfortable, as they seemingly mused smugly and stared below at the latest crop of geeky looking seminarians. The thrust of the experience was similar to 'wishing upon a star.'

The inside of the monastery was no less awe-inspiring. The inner sanctum was as majestic as the outer blanket. Solid oak wood banisters, marble stairways, and a golden altar adorned the monastery. The warmth that they exuded helped you forget the cold drafts that permeated the hallways. The beauty and care taken in maintaining the sanctum were apparent and very pleasing to the eye.

As one went through the monastery and approached the building that housed the freshmen, an apt label I might add, our awe almost turned to disdain. Unlike upper classmen, you had no decorated rooms with furniture—no decorum whatsoever. You instead encountered a large, open-styled dormitory, with cement floors and paint peeling from the walls. Talk about culture shock! Row upon row of bunk beds filled your vision. Of course, you did not expect those early regal feelings to continue; but now, the king indeed was wearing no clothes. "You are in the army now" may best familiarize you to the experience.

Despite such monastic dwellings, we were each given our own desk and mine was fortunately by a window. I needed stimulation, as I did not tolerate well the silence of sound and blindness of sight. The window provided a reprieve from such monotony. I remember the first time I gazed out beyond the dormitory walls. It was a very beautiful and sunny day on campus. As I glanced away from my study books, for the first time I took notice of the countryside that lay before me. A few cows grazing in the distance on a hill immediately caught my eye. A cow path was beaten and worn in the grass. Other cow stuff was evident as well, but I will spare your sensibilities and not go into great detail about the nature of cow chips. Looking upward, other farm animals were grazing on a plateau, with small hills above and below the plateau. A white fence enclosed the cows and immediately to the left were two red houses. On the other side stood a weather worn red, wooden barn with a gray roof. The blue horizon and radiant sun crested beyond the barn and the trees.

Many trees lined the bottom hill. Most of the leaves were a beautiful red and yellow. However, it was still early autumn and leaves of green remained unchanging among the trees. A handball court with its huge, grayish cement wall was located in the foreground of the trees. The court was cluttered with leaves, decaying, and in need of attention; yet seemingly functional. Through an opening in the trees, one could see the gymnasium with its gray-black roof and red brick siding. Beyond the gym, the backstop of the baseball diamond was visible although a forest of trees hid the ball diamond itself.

I took a number of religious and secular courses that first semester in 1969, including a psychology course. One of our first assignments in psychology was to complete a vocational interest test, which I took in October 1969. The purpose of a vocational interest inventory is to, well, to see what interests you have in common with various vocations or careers. The inventory has two scales, basic interest and occupational scales. In 1969, my interests that were in the high-to-very high range were: public speaking; science; mechanical; adventure; social service; religious activities; and writing. Now, this matched my actual interests very well at the time because I often wet my pants during public speaking, never understood science, could and can do nothing mechanical except perhaps pull a beer tab, and was too mainstreamed to wish for an extraordinary adventure beyond the 'adventure in moving' hailed by *U-Haul*. However, at least I was interested in religious and social activities, and I did become a writer. Of course, you the reader may wish to debate this writer thing, but it's early in this book—so fight off your desire to rush to judgment and keep reading!

In 1969, the low-to-very low range of interests were: business management; sales; merchandizing; military activities; technical supervision; nature; and agriculture. These really matched my non-interests well because I have no business sense—couldn't sell you oxygen if I was the only source of this life sustaining merchandise, would trip on our own mines before I ever saw the whites of the enemies' eyes, known to eat agriculture and not grow it, and have no desire to be part of nature unless it's catered under a comfortable canopy. For the latter, it must be my Italian blood or there is a virtual sign on my back in buggese that says 'bite me,' as insects, bugs, and sometime humans center their attack on me as if I were a lone carrier in a sea of destroyers! I remember when at drive-in movies—some of you oldsters will remember what those were—I would be under a barrage of attacks and doing the disco dance of the seventies while my unaffected friends sat motionless enjoying the movie.

On the 1969 occupational scales of the interest inventory, I scored similar likes to these occupations: physician; psychiatrist; psychologist; biologist; musician performer; and author-journalist. Well, those are pretty close because I faint at the site of blood, you can find me on at least 10 pages of the *Diagnostic and Statistical Manual of Mental Disorders – Fourth Edition*, I had no children at this time—at least nobody came knocking at my door on Father's Day claiming so, and I can't sing a note—not even in the shower! And then there is that author thing again!

Despite my interest or lack thereof, the daily regimen of college life in the seminary was not much different from that of my secondary years. Those main requirements and traditions continued. Living away from home was an adjustment and dormitory life was rather sterile. Yet, American society was changing in the 1970's and so was the Church. The thrust of the documents of Vatican II of the previous decade had begun to trickle down to the Catholic rank and file.

The Church and the secular world have their own centers of change. In the secular world, what is innovative often begins in the universities and training centers. In the Church, the centers of theology—the seminarians—are often the faces of change. The social activism in the secular world had its impact on the Church's desire to reach out to others, or perhaps was simply part of the Church's own survival at the time.

Community action programs sprouted in an attempt to help the disadvantaged. We were no different and I became involved in tutoring disadvantaged youth in a nearby town, a community service that I had begun in my last year of high school. I was caught up in the times and developed gradually a desire to work with children. My focus was changing from living the monastic life to integrating into the secular world. Thoughts of family and children crept slowly into my preoccupied mind. The security of the past was eroding and what I had envisioned for my life began fading with it.

Well, after having the "calling" for five years in grade school, two years in junior high, four years in high school and one year of college, I was beginning to get a busy signal. Maybe I was not being "called" after all. Maybe it was a wrong number. It was another *beginning of the end*, but an unexpected one, an unplanned one, and perhaps an unnatural one. It was not suppose to happen. Yet, the end happened. It came like a freight train even though it started 12 years ago in the second grade. How could this be? You thought such experiences and events were enduring. A vocation was supposed to be forever. You once again needed to face change, adapt and adjust to it, then put it into perspective; or regress and be compromised.

Having graduated from high school in 1969, the Vietnam War years were building and U.S. troops in increasing numbers were being sent to that country. I dutifully registered with the Selective Service System in October of 1969. My selective service number was A12-208-51-1312BBC. At the time, I had brown eyes, black hair, was 5'11" in height and weighed 150 pounds. Unfortunately, only one of these demographics is true today and how I wish the others were too. Damn old age!

I carried my obligatory draft card which proclaimed: "The law requires you to have this certificate in your personal possession at all times and to surrender it upon entering active duty in the Armed Forces." I never understood why it was to be in our possession at all times. It was not like we would be snatched up from the city streets, as in countries with dictatorships. While attending the seminary high school and college, I had a deferment: *4-F.* No, I did not earn four failing grades in school... well, at least not to the best of my recollection. Class *4-F* indicated that the "registrant is not qualified for military service."

It was funny. We never consider government agencies as particularly efficient or quick acting. Our perception is generally that they are slow moving, fraught with errors, and typically the right brain never knows what the left hand is up to. Right? Wrong! When I voluntarily left the seminary and transferred to a local university, it was necessary by law for the monastic administration to notify the U.S. Government of my status. I knew my deferment status would change, but I never gave much thought to it.

What I did not expect was that within two weeks, I received a letter from the U.S. Government. No, it did not say "Greetings." In large, dark letters, the return address inscribed was the **SELECTIVE SERVICE**. The envelope proclaimed it was "official business" and under "penalty for private use." I recall half-smiling to myself at the time and wondering, "How much of a penalty could there be beyond the requirement of its contents?"

I did not move and was frozen by the anticipated contents of the envelope. I knew I was possibly at a turning point in my life, another *beginning of the end.* Upon opening the envelope, there it was. You knew it was there, but its impact was unlike any other when you first saw it in writing: *1-A.* Yep, that was it. There was no mistake. Now the "registrant was available for military service."

It was fate! For me, fate was my random number. My random number was 318 out of 365. I was not going to be one of the first called and perhaps not called at all. And that is what happened. In May of 1972, my classification was changed to *1-H*, that is, "registrant not currently subject to processing for induction." At the young age of 20, I already was too old for the armed forces. Not only had I passed my sexual peak, I peaked in another category—even the armed forces did not want me! As of the writing of this book, of course, I am too old for anything! Yet, fate pushed me into a new *beginning of the end* that began with the transfer from the seminary college to a local university. Then, Lucy entered my life...

Chapter 6

The First Time?

This *beginning of the end* thrust upon me by fate had little to do with the local university other than being the setting for a common meeting ground. I was no longer a seminarian. I know you know that. However, it also meant that I was free from certain restrictions imposed upon me and accepted by me at the time given my vocation. Do you need a hint? Do you really need a hint? Are you sure you need a hint? I did not think so: *dating, romance,* and *sex*! Until this time in my life, I had accepted celibacy and had not considered relationships, physical or otherwise, other than in fleeting fantasy. After all, I assumed, rather unprofessionally so, that my parishioners would be involved in indiscretions and old fashion guilt would drive them to confess their sins in the shrouded darkness and privacy of the confessional. What was said in the confessional had the same protection and privilege as what was said between an attorney and his client—what was said in the dark, stayed in the dark.

I suppose it is no surprise to acknowledge that at that time I was, shall I really say it? Do you really want me to say it? Are you sure? I was a virgin. The attitude toward virginity was more juvenile and less responsible in the 60's and 70's than it is now for it was sex and drugs and drugs and sex, and then somewhere more productive in between. I was 20 years old, a virgin, and I was already passing my sexual peak. How can you peak at something you have yet to experience? I was over the hill and Viagra had not yet been discovered; yet another 23 years would pass before our female counterparts would reach their sexual peaks.

Sex instruction was not provided and questions were not answered clearly, even if you summoned up all the blushing courage to dare ask one question or almost ask part of one. Sex education was neither practiced nor preached. As a youngster, the only "instruction" that I can recall was presented by the local pastor during my seventh grade year. The boys in my parochial grade school were sharing with the girls, shall we say, euphemisms for standard male and female anatomy. I recall all the boys and all the girls in junior high were sorted, separated, and escorted to the church as a group. I do not know what the pastor said to the girls. I assumed it was much the same as he told us. What our pastor told us was that the slang names we were using were inappropriate to identify the male penis and female vagina—and he identified what seemed like all of them of which many I had never heard. That was pretty much it. It was a lecture, a scolding, and **HELL**, I recall, was mentioned at least once if not on more than one occasion. It did little to expand our sexual knowledge base or sensitivity toward the opposite sex, but I suppose that was not our pastor's intent. After all, we did not want to spend an eternity in hell for uttering every Tom, Dick, and Harry!

It was now the 1970s and Richard Nixon, Gerald Ford, and Jimmy Carter shared the presidency. This decade would see a continuance of the social change and attitudes of the 1960s. Civil rights, the women's movement, and space exploration continued to press forward. The stalemate and failures of the Vietnam War caused younger adults to become disenchanted with politicians and those in the government. Watergate forced Nixon to resign in face of impeachment. The disillusionment triggered by the fallout of Watergate was keenly visible and expressed largely on university campuses.

The Apollo space missions had successfully landed man on the moon in 1969 and future missions were viewed as commonplace. In April 1970, astronauts James Lovell, Jack Swigert, and Fred Haise were speeding to the moon in their Service Module on the Apollo 13 mission when Lovell uttered to the Houston Space Center, "Houston, we've had a problem." People around the world prayed and were glued to their television sets even before news aired 24/7 to watch the life and death struggle of the astronauts, and prayed for their safe return, as they eventually splashdown safely.

Back on earth, it was May 4, 1970 when four students were gunned down by the Ohio National Guard in an effort to calm antiwar demonstrations and became known as the Kent State Massacre. In January 1974, the Paris Peace Accords ended military participation in Vietnam. The conflict would eventually take the lives of some 58,175 soldiers.

Intel introduced the microprocessor chip in 1971. *Roe v. Wade* legalized abortion in January 1973. The first test tube baby was born. The 1975 Education of All Handicapped Children Act was passed by Congress to guarantee equal educational access to the handicapped. Forced busing in public schools was begun to achieve racial integration and balance. America celebrated its 200th birthday on July 4, 1976—truly a history of independence.

In the swirl of these events, my *beginning* finds the local university as the common gathering ground where I met Lucy. Yes, I know I started talking about Charly, and I married Charly. I knew Lucy before I knew Charly. This was the memorable young male experience and Lucy was the traditional *older woman*. The year was 1972. Lucy was about 10 years older than I. We met at the university in an abnormal psychology class, which should tell the more insightful of you something about our relationship right off the bat. The course descriptions for such classes typically go like this: Abnormal psychology involves the discipline and principles of psychology and human behavior in understanding the etiology, nature, development, and treatment of mental illness. Class topics might include models of abnormal behavior, research, diagnosis, and assessment of abnormal behavior, affective disorders, personality disorders, sexual disorders, substance abuse disorders, childhood disorders, etc. The mid-term exam includes identifying those specific pages in the *Statistical Manual for Mental Disorders* that describe your personal disorders from which you suffer. You only hoped and prayed that the *Manual* did not have your picture printed beside your alleged disorder!

Well, not really. However, it did help if you were a little crazy—empathy and all that crap. We all are a little crazy, but there is a fine line between creativity and psychosis! Creativity is the ability to generate ideas and to solve problems that are worth solving. Psychosis prevents people from being able to distinguish between the real world and the imaginary world. So you see, if you cannot tell the difference between reality and fantasy you are a very, very busy person in that every problem is in need of solving, even problems that do not exist. Never mind... it is kind of like proving philosophically that you exist... I am! Are you?

Back at the local university, Lucy often sat next to me in class and we usually both arrived early. It was not love then. My excuse or perhaps rationalization was that I arrived early to avoid rush-hour traffic. And this must be the truth in that this habit of mine is still annoyingly practiced today. I have never been fond of traffic and on occasion fantasized driving a tank, without a clutch of course, to compensate for the rudeness and ineptness of others on the road. Arriving early was a way to avoid the maniac drivers pouring out of the downtown area and lashing out their pent-up frustration on other unsuspecting motorists. And this was before *road rage* became in vogue.

You know the type. You can see the look in their eyes, as they appear oblivious to others around them. They impulsively take the shortest route to their respective homes for yet another pleasant or miserable evening with their loved ones, even if they have to cut you off on their way.

For Lucy and I, arriving early and sitting next to one another eased the art of conversation. She had the personality that made communication easy. Lucy was also pleasant to the eye for an *older* woman of her 30s. Her facial features called you to her as she always carried a warm smile. She had dark brown eyes and shoulder length black hair. Lucy's figure was shapely and her frame trim. The contours of her breasts were obvious and pointedly outlined by the sweaters she often wore. Though I was young and relationally deprived, or relationally challenged to be politically correct, it was clear even to me that Lucy was indeed a beautiful woman—inside and out.

I met Lucy at a time when she was recently separated from her husband and had filed for divorce. She had two children, Jake and Amanda. Lucy lived in a large country home in a small, rural town about 30 minutes northeast of the big city. It was an old wooden-framed home, well-kept, freshly painted in white, and complete with a picket fence—everything a family would want. Lucy was married for 10 years and was trying to renew her life. She was planning a career in the area of social work. She enjoyed helping others and her interest and care seemed genuine. At the time, I was planning a career in counseling. We appeared to have many things in common and also seemed physically attracted to each other.

After several months of innocent conversation and sharing *normal* topics in an *abnormal* class, Lucy invited me to her home. For whatever reasons, we never met at my apartment. When I left the seminary and returned to the local university, I did not return home to live with my family much to my parents chagrin. In fact, I took a priest friend from the seminary with me the day I told my parents I was not moving back home. I do not know why I thought that was needed, but after trying to explain why I needed to be on my own, which persisted for almost 5 minutes, I left my priest friend alone with my parents to accomplish what I could not accomplish, and then exited, stage right. To this day I do not know what was said. My priestly friend never told me and he died unfortunately and unexpectantly a year later.

I was too young to sign my apartment lease and had to find a cosigner. It was much easier to find friends who would risk fiscal responsibility in those days than now. My apartment was nothing fancy, and it had the required beads of the time hanging down from one doorway—it was as hip[pie] as I would apparently become. The apartment was otherwise a plain one bedroom on the second floor and less than a mile from my family home...and that's all my old age allows me to remember about it. The apartment complex still offers people a place to rest their heads, although it has deteriorated physically over time.

My first invitation from Lucy came on a Friday evening. Her children were visiting their father as they apparently did—say it altogether men—"every other weekend!" We talked—that came easy, and often watched the relationship-oriented sitcoms of the time on television such as the *Mary Tyler Moore* Show. After several visits, Lucy and I sat together on the family room couch and she began kissing and cuddling. I was uncertain where all of this was heading, had no conscious expectations, and was probably more than a little bit hesitant; yet the experience was certainly pleasurable and welcomed. With such shyness and great lack of assertiveness, Lucy often took the lead and I followed, hesitantly but willingly. I say hesitantly, because that must have been how Lucy perceived me. Our relationship progressed at a snail's pace, very slowly and deliberately. Lucy cautiously fostered the relationship and perhaps thought she might scare me away if she became too dominant or assertive. I do not really remember and we never talked about the experience. I do recall paging through Lucy's family album with her and reviewing her ten years of memories. I felt uneasy like I was intruding on the sacred lives that two people built over a decade. I was in awe of all the tangible and intangible events generated by two people in love over a relatively short period of time, not to mention the gift of their two children. I had no similar long-standing relationships, experiences, or memories to share—not even a household of collected possessions.

I also mistakenly perceived our relationship as growing. Hindsight, being what it is, tells me that Lucy probably never meant for the relationship to grow at all let alone into something special. It was not meant to be extraordinary. It was a sharing that was not going to lead to growth or maturity even though that is what I foolishly believed. In looking back, I'm kind of smiling in that half-embarrassed way. Our physical relationship did grow—very slowly—in that our conversations were increasingly becoming augmented with touching and cuddling. In my mind, it was another *beginning of the end.* I thought my "pure and natural" state would be ending. AIDS had not yet devoured the continent and cautioned sexual relationships. Lucy was woman. I was man. We were about to roar!

About four months into our relationship, Lucy and I were watching our typical shows on television, the ones that poignantly dealt with relationships in a comedic way. No matter what happened, those shows always left us feeling good at the end of their half hour run. Problems that developed and crises that evolved were solved all within the scope of those thirty minutes less commercials, just like in real life. We were cuddling, kissing, and probing as we always did, but something different was about to happen. And Lucy made it happen.

Lucy arose from the couch and turned off the television. She commented that she never liked the upcoming program as well as the others and asked somewhat rhetorically if I wanted to go upstairs. We did. She softly took me by the hand and led me up the creaky, curvy stairway to her bedroom, much like Scarlet in *Gone with the Wind*. Other than a tour on the first day I came to Lucy's home, I had not been upstairs. The upstairs bedrooms were carpeted in a deep shag light blue in color. Shag was in back then. There were three bedrooms, one for each of Lucy's two children and the master bedroom. She entered her bedroom slowly, still leading me, as our hands remain clenched to each other. I was soon to find out why this was called the master bedroom.

At the foot of Lucy's bed, we slowly uncoupled and she gently lay down on one side. She patted the pillow softly not saying a word; of course, words were not needed. Lucy's shining eyes and warm smile were very inviting, a beacon to nature's course. And there it was. I lay beside her. We began kissing, cuddling and embracing as we had many times before except we were now horizontal to each other for the first time. We were no longer vertically challenged. Lucy and I were both cautious and deliberate in our actions. Time seemed endless and past unnoticed. Conversation was sparse to none at all. Lucy and I caressed for a long time, neither of us shedding any clothing. That is how the evening faded: in a tepid embrace sharing bodily warmth that melted away concerns of any unfolding events of the outside world.

If I was the follower, then Lucy was the conscious leader, although not necessarily by choice. For weekends to follow, our sexual desire evolved, albeit slowly. I was unaware that

Lucy was on the *pill*, a fact to which she confided to me much later. Hell, I did not know what I was doing. I was concerned or perhaps scared about pregnancy although not exactly sure how that might occur or how to prevent it. In the Catholic faith, there are two recognized contraceptive practices that are not considered sinful: the "rhythm" method and abstinence— much like the lottery and just saying 'no.' I cannot recall whether I was aware what a condom actually was at the time. I knew it was not related to a condominium and you did not live in it. I knew it was neither ketchup nor mustard. I suspected that this compounded my own sense of hesitancy and I relied on Lucy to forge the way.

Lucy appeared in harmony with my indecisiveness although she may not have known exactly the reasons behind it. The next weekend visit began the same as many weekends before it. We talked, watched some television, cuddled each other . . . and then went upstairs. As we lay on the bed, somehow we decided that this time it was *OK* if we each took off our shirts, that we begin exposing ourselves to each other. We did. Lucy and I stared briefly at each other; ironically, my breasts exposed and her full, rounded breasts still hidden by her lingerie. We kissed, cuddled and embraced much as we did before, but something was definitely different. Oddly, it was not the near-exposure of Lucy's breasts. It was the touching and caressing of our skin-to-skin. The softness and warmth of Lucy's skin stirred feelings in me that were somehow different, perhaps more intense than those experienced previously. I felt closer to Lucy and happier than I had been, oblivious to everything else happening in the world as if time stood frozen and it matter not what was occurring outside her bedroom.

Our physical relationship progressed again during the following weekend visit. Lucy and I shed both our shirts and pants. I was in my underwear—chique boxer shorts to be exact. Lucy was a very beautiful woman and she glowed in my eyes. She stood at the side of her bed wearing her bra, panties, and hose. She removed her panty hose. Lucy apparently felt the need to justify her further undressing by remarking that her panty hose and underwear together placed undo pressure on her abdomen. Not being a connoisseur of women's clothing and lingerie, I accepted her pronouncement without remark.

Our hands now caressed more freely and intensely than before with our increased exposure of skin. Our private areas were no longer private to each other's direct touch. Lucy removed her bra and I gazed at the fullness of her breasts for the first time. What inhibitions that existed previously between us were now fading rapidly. Sensual touching now took nature's course. Touching was turning into groping and suckling, more pleasing and exciting than ever before. Our bodies moved and jerked more intensely to each other's touch. Lucy and I began massaging our most private areas that until now were left unexplored. At each other hands, I slowly burst into ecstasy followed by Lucy's orgasm. We fell asleep entangled in each other's arms and remained enmeshed until dawn, oblivious again to the world and events emerging around us.

Lucy and I repeated these sensual encounters over the following weekends fully unclothed, but another *beginning of the end* was approaching. Our relationship was drawing to a close and my "pure and natural" state remained unchanged. Perhaps it was my own uncertainty, my own hesitancy, or Lucy's dawning realization about what was occurring in our relationship. I had entered her life on the rebound and apparently accomplished what I was supposed to achieve. What Lucy wanted in her life then was not what was occurring between us. She was recovering and maturing, and our relationship gradually ended before I was discarded. We saw each other several times later, but the physical closeness was gone and the emotional growth arrested. I really did not understand why at the time nor did I realize the complexity of our relationship. It was almost a year when our relationship ended. Perplexed at the time, I later realized that the relationship had ended as expected. My *Summer of '42* experience was regretfully over. My reminiscences are very vivid and pleasing to this day, but I never saw Lucy again. Besides those memories, Christmas and Valentine's Day cards lovingly given to me by Lucy are stored away safely with other life's treasures.

Chapter 7

The Love of My Life

Ten years passed between Lucy and Charly. I was involved in a number of dating relationships during that period, but they did not mature into anything substantial, including marriage, a live-in significant other, or a long-term dating relationship. I think that covers about all of the possibilities, does it not? I believe that this was the first time I grew to hate the phrase, "Let's just be friends" although it was not the last time I was to hear it.

I completed my undergraduate work at the local university and decided to continue my studies in graduate school. I attended Indiana State University, which was about 120 miles due west of my home in Indianapolis. The graduate program was accredited nationally. I was pleased and fortunate to be accepted, as it was only one of seven graduate programs in the country at the time that was so accredited.

The town had a lingering odor on some days, which was said by the locals to be due to factory waste. I thought that was putting it mildly. In midsummer of 1974, I took residence in the "Quad," a university housing area of the time, where four separate bedrooms opened into the main living area of the residence. I was excited and looking forward to another stage in my life. Apparently I was too excited for I had packed my books and some necessities—like a TV set—but had brought not a stitch of clothing except what was on my back. My fellow residents appeared quite amused at my omission, as the word *dork* seemed to hang on their lips and no doubt was stamped indelibly on my forehead for everyone to see. So far I was off to a great start! But dork or not, I needed clothes since graduate classes started the very next morning. *Country roads, take me home...* I unpacked what little I remembered to bring and returned home to pickup my clothes. My parents did not seem eager to see me so soon and were also amused with my plight. I found the clothes neatly packed away in my bedroom where I had left them hours earlier.

I received some financial aid and worked various assistantships to help support my way through graduate school. My parents helped where they could. I checked frequently the innards of the couch for food money, as some of these times were desperate ones. In the fall, I moved to the university's 30-floor high-rise student building. The floors alternated male and female residents with males on the odd floor. I surmised that putting guys on *odd* floors was more than simple coincidence. To my dismay and very poor casting, I was provided a room on one of the odd male dominated floors. I have a long history of not getting *even*! If that was not bad enough, my fellow dormy was a political major (or liability) from New York. Jack hated our state and constantly whined about our limitations compared with the Big Apple. Not to say that there was not some truth to that; but, hey, nobody was forcing him to come to our lowly state and attend school here. There must have been plenty of schools of political thought in New York, or at the very least he could have changed his major.

Well, I took all the bitching and arrogance that I could from the easterner. By the end of the first semester, I pursued housing in the university town and found a small, old duplex. I was not refunded money by the university (I had paid for a full year), but thought that the loss of funds was a small price to pay for peace of mind. So I left the state ambassador from New York and the high rise behind me. I gave up apples for oranges. The transition was facilitated by the fact that one of the many local bars was one block away. After all, it was vital to soothe the savage beast. Today, the high-rise student building contains offices for teaching professors and classrooms. The building is waiting to be razed, as the university can no longer maintain its infrastructure.

Though I was rid of the human eastern influence, my cousin Toni mistakenly thought I needed some company. Although I preferred the two-footed kind of the female persuasion, instead she gave me a little kitten from a little litter of her cat. Toni was fond of cats and I have not known her to be without one or two or three with at least one of them named *Elvis*. Poor thing. It was bad enough that he was forced to live in the same town with me, but to add insult to injury I named him *IQ*. It was really quite innocent—at least it seemed so at the time. I was taking a course in psychometrics and the class was focusing on ability measures. Well, at least it seemed logical at the time. IQ was a black cat except for his white paws, underbelly and face. He was a playful kitten who did not always live up to his name. Live up to his name? You would think his name was two words—*I* and *Q*.

I did well at the university, at least for the major reason I was there—academics. I finished the coursework for an advanced degree in the spring of 1977. I experienced no difficulty with the decision to leave town and complete my dissertation elsewhere. I accepted my first position at a community school corporation as an elementary guidance counselor with ABD status ("all but dissertation" or "all but dead" if you do not complete it). This status allowed you to be called "doctor" although you really were not one. Once the doctoral degree (Ph.D.) was achieved, most people referred to you in less flattering terms. Such titles included "*P*ost *H*ole *D*igger," "*P*lenty *H*elp *D*esired," and "*P*iled *H*igher and *D*eeper" among others—not exactly what higher education considered in the acronym. It did not matter for I was not a *real* doctor who had an unlimited license to practice anything. I was soon to discover that I could not even make a dinner reservation. After all, I am not a real doctor. I just play one at school.

Despite it all, I completed my dissertation. It was entitled, *An Investigation of the Relationship Between Self-Concept and Others-Concept of Regular Class Children and Student and Teacher Perceptions of Classroom Environment.* The abstract summarized the findings of the study (you may yawn in advance): "This study investigated the relationship between self-concept and others-concept of children and student and teacher perceptions of classroom environment. Previous research suggests that...

Well, although you might find how incredulous this amounted to anything, the bottom line was that I received my doctorate in the winter of 1978. I will tell you that the dissertation was 88 pages in length, but was summarized to 10 pages when it was published formally in a professional journal. Could it really be that there were at least 78 pages of unnecessary or unimportant fluff? Oh, nay. Certainly not! Yet, people say that higher education is more of a matter of persistence than intelligence! Hmm, could be.

At a professional level, the Elementary School Counseling Organization defines the role of school counselors. They assert that the elementary school years set the tone for developing the skills, knowledge, and attitudes necessary for children to become healthy, productive adults. Counselors are part of the team of administrators, educators, and school psychologists working together to create a caring atmosphere where children's needs are met by prevention, early identification, and direct intervention. The Organization continued that students need encouragement to develop positive attitudes toward themselves, school, peers, family and the community. The role of the counselor is to provide an environment of safety, trust, and positive regard.

As a counselor, I moved from position-to-position and city-to-city to gain broad experiences that would later allow me to make critical career choices. I became much more involved in work and much less involved in relationships. I enjoyed my professional life and was quickly becoming a borderline workaholic. Of course, this collided head on with my philosophy of life: "Live to relax." My personal and social lives both became rather predictable. I hated it. Then I met Charly and together our lives changed and grew with what we brought to each other.

The decade of the 1980s was fondly and aptly called the "ME-GREED" generation. It was a status seekers delight and a millionaire's playground. "If you got it, flaunt it" was the tone of the decade. People had to have the best of whatever they wanted, including designer labels for their children, pets, and themselves. I can honestly tell you, however, that IQ never wore designer clothes—or any other kind of clothes for that matter. He was a free-spirited feline who took his orders from nobody, especially from his 'master.'

Overindulgent buying and credit cards balances came to the forefront in the 80's. Personal computers were everywhere—home, offices, schools, and libraries. Sadly, the space shuttle Challenger exploded shortly after liftoff in January 1986 killing its crew, including the first teacher in space. AIDS was killing more people and putting a dent into the sexual revolution of previous decades. Sandra Day O'Connor was the first woman on the U.S. Supreme Court. The Vietnam War Memorial inscribed with the names of fallen soldiers was at long last dedicated. Ronald Regan and George Bush carried the presidency. The Berlin Wall collapsed on November 9,

1989. The cry, "Tear that wall down" was taken literally.

Back in my world, I met Charly in 1982. Charly was younger than me by some eight years and I suspect, in all honesty, that I was almost as mature as she. Charly was modest in build and slightly shorter than me. She dressed informally and often wore long or short pants rather than dresses or skirts. Her long flowing black hair glistened in the light. Charly had deep blue eyes, short lashes, thin eyebrows, and a small nose in perfect proportion. Her facial features were highlighted by her pleasing smile and this encouraged meaningful eye contact from those conversing with her as well as distant onlookers. Charly knew no enemies or strangers and showed kindness to all those who crossed her path. She always maintained her focus on others and her attentiveness was apparent to those who met her.

Charly and I were opposites as far as signs go under the Zodiac. She was born in April near the day of fools. I was born in October near the day of witches. Fools and witches we were and celestial opposites under the Zodiac. Charly was born under Taurus and I was a Scorpio. As a Taurus, Charly *should* be patient, reliable, persistent, determined, warmhearted, and loving. They can also be jealous, possessive, resentful, inflexible, self-indulgent, and greedy. As a Scorpio, I *should* be determined, forceful, emotional, intuitive, exciting, magnetic, passionate, and powerful. They can also be jealous, resentful, secretive, obstinate, compulsive, and obsessive... or is that obsessive compulsive?

We were astrological opposites according to the Zodiac. As a Taurus, Charly's harmonious signs were Cancer, Virgo, Capricorn, and Pisces. As a Scorpio, my harmonious signs were Cancer, Virgo, Capricorn, and Pisces. We were opposites, but our harmonious signs were the same. Actually, according to astrologers, Taurus and Scorpio are sexual opposites, and as we all know, opposites attract. Together, the union of our signs should produce money, power, and families. What more would we want?

At the time that we met, Charly was the head sales clerk at a regional toy store located in the historical downtown section of the city. Like many urban centers, our city was revitalizing the downtown through its architecture and landscaping. Within three years, she became the regional manager for Totsie Toys. Totsie Toys began in 1898 and architecturally represented the buildings of that era. The storefront boasted a series of three large panes of glass, each framed in dark, well-worn wood, and each shaded by the overhang of red, white, and blue tarpaulins. Through the expansive windows, an onlooker could see boy and girl toys of every kind placed precisely on flat shelves; and if that was not sufficient, bicycles and other toys were hung invitingly from the ceiling. The inside of the store was as large as a grocery store with sections separated by individual rooms or walls, and each section stocked by themes: dolls; models; electronics; holidays; etc.

I was the elementary guidance director for a public school system. We had a great time in *trying out* new toys at Charly's employ, educationally speaking of course. Christmas was certainly a great time of year at our house! We received generally more enjoyment from her career than we did from mine. Her kids were happy and trying to have fun. My kids were sad and trying to cope. Yet, kids are kids and their happiness and resiliency are equally amazing.

Like many young couples that were newly married, we rented an apartment in hopes that our scrimping and saving would lead eventually to our own perpetually binding mortgage. A mortgage is something in which you go into debt knowing that you will probably not pay it off. I must admit Charly was much better at economizing. I was more of an impulsive buyer who could rationalize almost any purchase and detail vaguely why our lives could not do without this or that. If not impulsive buying, I knew what I wanted and where to get it. I did not have to comparison shop; instead I made a beeline to the store and aisle where I knew I could find it. Women shop. Men don't shop... Men buy. I loved guy-toys too—computers and electronic stuff. I also was generous with money and gave readily to others, a trait that Charly came to regard with mixed feelings. The fact there was now two of us, and perhaps we would add to the two of us was a notion that I had not yet fully appreciated.

Charly and I were both happy with most things we each brought to our marriage. To say she was not enamored with IQ was a gross understatement. IQ was by then nine years old, used to not sharing me with anyone, as much as cats share, and worked hard at being standoffish and independently feline. Unfortunately, IQ did not really live up to his name and this further did not enamor him to Charly. He did not always like what you fed him. IQ's meal stance was an ongoing challenge to Charly and the ultimate battle of wills—from "her will" to "his will not." Of course, as pet owners will attest, uneaten pet food dries and hardens within several days to such a consistency that it makes fine mortar for construction purposes... and it holds bricks together much longer than standard cement. In any case, IQ ultimately won each battle as Charly's warm-heartedness changed the hardened mortar to moist feed once again.

Charly and I had thought about children, but we mutually agreed that we were not quite ready at the time to add to the populous of the world. Shortly after our marriage and based on repetitive experiences with IQ that were less than nurturing, we (that is, singular she) purchased a dog. The puppy was a Golden Retriever, AKA registered of course, and priced at only

$250.00 in those days. We named him Disney. Disney was like most golden retrievers—golden brown, cute, and retrieved nothing. He was playful, cuddly and naively friendly. He was fearless in the face of danger. Disney loved the water and whatever mud he could roll onto his puppy frame. He liked anybody and every one. By design, we named him Disney because Charly and I had never traveled to Disneyland and it was our hope to do so for our second honeymoon. That was our hope.

IQ and Disney got along as well as a cat and dog fatally could. Disney was always trying to be friendly and IQ never really understood why this beast ten times his size was slobbering over him. You could see the discouraging look in Disney's eyes as he cocked his head toward us as if to say, "Am I doing something wrong here?" At times, this friendship was also stressful for IQ. He would occasionally let go with a hiss and the strike of his paw against Disney's nose as if to underscore nature's intended differences. Disney took such aggression in good nature and was always the first to try to make up. IQ did not avail himself to these friendly overtures. Be it ever so humble, that was our family—Charly, Disney, IQ and me—and pretty much in that order!

Oh, me? That is right. I have yet to formally introduce myself to you. I am Greg—Gregory—and my wife, in her infinite wisdom, decided not to keep or hyphenate her name, thus avoiding a nebulous link with her family of origin. This was no great sacrifice on Charly's part, as her family name was Stinkwater. The four of us were known as the family Edwards.

Chapter 8

The Ever Deepening Love

Charly and I often emailed each other from work or left letters around the house expressing our feelings for each other and ever deepening love...

Dear Charly,

Sometimes the right words don't always come to us at the right time in trying to express how we feel. If they did, I would have described to you the depth of my feeling for you the first time our eyes met and I held you in my arms. That night is forever etched in my memory—the beauty I saw, the sensual voice I heard, the soft touch of your body, the scent of your perfume, and the taste of your lips. Seeing you every day I realize I'm not just imagining you; that I'm not just dreaming. Your love for me makes me feel special. I will forever love you, Greg.

Dear Greg,

The best thing that has ever happened to me is having your love. I have not loved anybody as much as I love you, and around you I feel so loved. Being apart all day, I'm like a child at Christmas at the end of the day full of excitement, hope, and affection. I can't wait to throw my arms around you and to feel the security of your arms around me. Touching each other brings me such joy and calmness. The many miles between us during the day melt away when I see you and we embrace. Thank you for loving me the way you do. Charly.

Dear Charly,

You are always lighting up my heart with the kindly things you do and say. I have to be careful because every time I think about you, my heart skips a beat and a smile is drawn to my face. Those around me here at work don't understand the smile, but you are the love of my life. Every moment we share together we grow closer and our love ever deepens. I can't imagine life without you or your love. Greg

Dear Greg,

I need only to think of you and my troubles melt away or they seem less stressful. Don't you dare go anywhere 'cause I plan on spending my whole life with you. You know and understand all the little things that mean so much to me. Sometimes it's just telepathy—you have a sixth sense of what I want and what I need. It makes it so easy to understand you and our hearts have come to dwell together as one... our love is one. With all my heart I'm forever yours. Love, Charly

Dear Charly,

My love for you grows each day, which gives me a peek into your soul. If I could marry your soul, I would. You are beauty inside and out. Loving you comes easy. Being apart from you does not. It's wonderful that our minds can hold images and memories, for it is memories and images of you that makes my day pass until I can hold you once again in my arms. I promise that you are always in my heart and that I will love you until the end of days. Greg

Dear Greg,

You've peeked every place else, why not my soul? □ Sorry, honey. I am feeling a bit naughty today... and I know there are days when you like me to be a bit naughty! I enjoy our times together when we are having fun. Sometimes you are so silly I don't know what to do with you, but don't ever stop being silly. You make me laugh and our laughter brings us closer together. Charly

Dear Charly,
    I get silly because when I get silly, you usually get frisky… and I love it when you are frisky. Greg

Dear Greg,
    Have I told you today how much I love you? The day we met was fate and now you are my destiny. I love you more today than I did yesterday, and I will love you more tomorrow than I loved you today. Our days together will go on forever, as will our love for each other. Charly

Dear Charly,
    I'm sitting at my desk thinking about all the times we've spent together and the things we've done for each other. Being in love with you brings out the best in me. I cannot remember what my life was like before you and I cannot imagine what life would be without you. I love you more than life itself. Greg

Dear Greg,
    I'm sitting at my desk thinking about all the times we've spent together and the things we've done for each other. Being in love with you brings out the best in me. Life would not be life if not shared with you. Charly

Dear Charly,
    Our love for each other is so strong that I am sure that we can weather any storm that harbors are way, as long as we are

together. We will never drift apart no matter what curves are in the road, as that would bring out the worst in each other. How we feel about each other is a little bit crazy, but that's the way our love is. Greg

Chapter 9

Needling IQ

Back at the home front, Charly and I were married for two years when IQ began changing. Although in our ever deepening love we were growing closer to each other, I cannot say the same for Charly and IQ. Another *beginning of the end* obtrusively entered our lives. IQ was 11 years old at the time. We noticed he had developed a ravenous appetite; yet, he was losing weight. He never appeared to have sufficient food no matter how much we fed him. IQ began jumping on the kitchen table during our family meals. He helped himself to whatever he could with or without our knowledge or permission. He was neither apologetic nor thankful during the time when his voracious hunger dominating his life. IQ deteriorated rapidly and became increasingly aggressive in his quest for nutrients. It was not uncommon for IQ to hiss, snarl, and claw his way to our food... and if our food were not available, Disney's food would serve just as well thank you.

We made an emergency appointment with our veterinarian. Dr. Trout Tev was a gentle man who exercised a great deal of common sense in his treatment of animals. Having told him the symptoms and following several tests, the findings were unmistakable and quite surprising: diabetes. We knew animals were sometimes afflicted with human disease, but we never considered that our family cat had diabetes. Ironically, diabetes ran on Charly's side of the family. I guess we were even more astounded by the prescribed treatment: insulin shots.

People say you can find some degree of humor hiding behind most tragedies if you look long and hard enough.

Humor can be one's release in coping with tragic events. This seems particularly common in the mental health profession—a type of safety valve for helping to maintain one's own health and peace of mind while trying to help others reclaim theirs.

Picture this if you can: administering insulin shots to a cat. Charly and I soon found out that giving a shot was the easy part. What do you think was the hard part? Imagine repetitive attempts at coddling your cat to urinate on a 4-inch by ¼-inch litmus strip to find out how much insulin to administer. "Here kitty, kitty, kitty . . ." does not even begin to depict the procedure or the outcome. For his part, Disney simply wanted no part of the process and scampered away. Worse yet, IQ became conditioned to the routine, as did Pavlov's dog. He associated the deranged approach of large man holding a slim, pale paper sword with the subsequent painful prick of a needle delivering life-sustaining insulin. Tragic, yes; but, it brought a shake-of-the-head smile to an unfortunate experience. Charly and I maintained our motivation by telling each other we only needed *one* drop of IQ's urine... and how many people in hell want ice water?

Charly and I were not sure we were making headway. Actually, I was not sure. Charly chose to pretty much detach herself from the situation. She had an apprehension about needles. Besides, IQ was my cat. Disney was her dog. That dichotomy was obvious and if not clear, Charly made it clear more often than once. IQ seemed better on some days than others. His appetite was in check for part or most of the day; then his appetite seemed to have no limits. IQ's voiding became more random and he increasingly forgot the foremost purpose of his litter box. He determined that our home was equivalent to the wide opened spaces, sand or not, and treated it as such. If IQ was not peeing, dumping or spraying in the house, he was snarling, hissing and scratching those of us who shared his kingdom. And I, his long time friend, trusty scout, companion and *kemosabe*, was not spared his wrath. It no longer became necessary or desirable for Charly and me to visit the local zoo. The sounds and smells in our home became undifferentiated from the scents of any animal habitat. Disney seemed the only living thing in our home that was immune to these unfolding events and he may just like the habitat el naturale.

The inevitable turning point soon came as I arrived home one day to find Charly standing on a kitchen chair and screaming frantically. Tears flowed down her anguished face. IQ was hissing and helping himself to anything within his reach. I could see the long and thin red scratches on Charly's face and arms. Her expression was one of devastation. It was quite clear that the end was swiftly approaching. Something had to be done and somebody had to be elected to do it.

It was a Saturday morning as Charly and I took IQ to Dr. Tev. It did not take our veterinarian very long to size up the situation. For even to the untrained eye, it could be seen that IQ's ribs protruded from the contour of his thin, deteriorating frame. Increasing dosages of insulin could not impede death's grip on IQ. Dr. Tev glanced toward us and without uttering a word had said what nobody needed to say. It was not a human life, but pet owners know the strength of bonds between man and animal. We began blubbering like small children and Charly put her arms around me. Dr. Tev left us alone with IQ after he gave him a sedative. IQ was resting comfortably on the cold, metal plated examination table. And we cried.

Dr. Tev soon returned to the examining room. He assured Charly and I that IQ would feel no pain from the drug that would end his suffering. We were told he would simply drift into unconsciousness and sleep. Dr. Tev asked me if I wanted to hold IQ in my arms during his last moments. I wept again and mumbled, "No." Somehow, I did not have the courage to watch IQ die, even supposedly a painless, fading death. I wanted to remember him in other ways. I even made Dr. Tev promise not to begin the process before we left his office. I knew that IQ would be dead soon and his lifeless carcass would be incinerated. Dr. Tev assured us that he would wait until we left. Charly grabbed me by the hand and we both wept as we slowly left the office. We drove away quickly, wanting to put as much distance between the veterinarian office and us that we could; but we were running away from something we could not escape. As with the beginning of life, death is always around the corner and leaves its mark on the living.

Chapter 10

The Family Oaks

Three years into our marriage was a happy time for us. Thanks much to Charly's steadfast saving and pinching, we purchased our first home together in 1987. We—Charly, Disney and I—lived on the suburban eastside of Indianapolis, a large metropolitan city in the Midwest. Charly and I spent most of our growing years on this side of town. Living in suburbia provided us tranquility and belied the real insecurities of residing in a large urban city.

Our home sat on 1-½ acres of land. It was warm in appearance and gave off a radiance that framed our marriage. There were tall ceilings and the living room was framed in dark walnut beams crossing at the midline. The rich, brown carpet was also framed in similar dark woodwork. In the dining area, a bronze chandelier extended from the ceiling and bathed the table in a yellow glow beaming from the tinted glass. In the main area, a ceiling fan ventilated our home with a mild breeze. The fireplace flamed our romance during the cold, dreary winter seasons. A natural wooden stairway climbed upward to the family bedrooms.

The family room patio door consisted of two large doors with full panes of glass. It, too, was framed in dark walnut and mini blinds decorated the doors. The view from the patio door was that of small timber, like a mini-forest complete with four-legged critters and chirping birds. Charly particularly enjoyed feeding the local vermin and some she trained to eat out of her hand. Squirrels seemed notably comfortable in their physical closeness to Charly; or as I told Charly, "You're probably the biggest nut they have ever seen!" She always laughed at my tired jokes. The rule of the house gradually evolved that the critters, including Disney, were fed before the humans; and so it goes...

The kitchen was unusually large as far as kitchens go. Charly loved cooking, particularly cooking foods and meals that were "original." Being married, she now had an in-house tester of what we came to call "C.O.s"—Charly originals. This did not require hazard pay, as she was really a good cook. In the center of the kitchen were a chopping block and little sink area. Immediately above the center block was a rectangular wooden frame mounted in the ceiling with pots, pans, and other kitchen utensils hanging from silver hooks. I swear that for some of these utensils, I neither could identify their names nor their functions in life. I sometimes thought some of the utensils were probably not of this world, that parallel universes somehow crossed and confused both realities. That amused Charly although she was somewhat dumbfounded in that she found me to be so dumb about culinary stuff. The kitchen cabinets framed the kitchen on the top and bottom, two rows of walnut shelving and plenty of storage. Off to the side, a large walk-in pantry stored our food and supplies, neatly arranged by variety and size.

It was a four-bedroom home purposely chosen by us because we had mutually envisioned little boy and girl Edwards' pitter-pattering down the hallways. The master bedroom reflected primarily a feminine motif although I was permitted, after considerable beseeching, to add one masculine piece of furniture to the mix: a *Roy Rogers* table, otherwise known as a stagecoach wagon wheel with cowboy boot legs on the bottom and a plate of glass on the top. Even though it was located in a very remote corner of the room, Charly constantly reminded me of her extreme sacrifice and embarrassment at conceding my request. It was a gag on my part anyway and to her elation the furniture was removed within a week. Charly told me she was forever grateful, as I raised my eyebrows wondering just how grateful she would be.

Charly was adept at decorating and quite handy with a hammer—somewhat of a Mrs. *Home Improvement.* Now there were definitely three things that Charly was better at than me. She was always matching and decorating, fixing and painting, and moving furniture until she achieved just the proper balance in each room—even if the room was returned to its original state before she started an hour before. I must admit that recognizing such a balance sometimes escaped me and on occasion I traded honesty for reassurance and support—not to mention my next meal! Charly was usually right in these matters as often confirmed by the opinions of our friends who complimented her taste and decorum. I helped where I could, but supervising seemed to suit me best. I recall that Charly often asked, "Don't you have something else to do?" Obviously I did not or I would be doing it. Right? If I were the self-conscious type, I would have taken umbrage or an umbrella or something. We took pride in our home and it gave us a sense of accomplishment, a place to call our own. Our home projected to others what we professed in ourselves— well, at least the better half of ourselves.

Charly and I lived in a quiet neighborhood; yet, it was alive with children who attended the community elementary school down the road. We lived in the corner house on a cul-de-sac. The Oaks family, with whom Charly and I grew very close, lived next door. I warmly recall when I first met the Oaks. Charly and I had moved during the cold, wintry days of February. Ice hung precariously from our house, glistening in the cold sunlight and coming to a sharp, dangerous point. It was a particularly bad winter that year and neither we nor our neighbors met each other until the start of the spring thaw.

That is when I went to work outside the home. I attempted to do the great male thing and accomplish outdoors what Charly had effectively attained inside our home. Yes, you're right— she still had a better 'innie' than I had 'outtie.'

It was a wonderful spring day and I was preparing to mow our lawn for the first time. It was the kind of day where you could feel the warmth of the sun, but did not become uncomfortably hot. An almost perfect day—the warm sunshine, blue skies and streaks of clouds—the kind of day often caught on an artist's canvas. Someone in the neighborhood was doing his, her or their laundry and you could smell the faint scent of the dryer as the softener permeated the air. For some reason, such fragrance always incited a pleasing sense, much like the aroma of burning leaves in the dwindling days of autumn.

Mrs. Oaks was outside tending to her flowers that she had woven on both sides of their sidewalk and bilaterally down their driveway almost in military precision. Life experiences taught me in an ugly way that discerning the difference between pregnancy and obesity was not my strong suit. However, even I, a sensitive male person who could get into touch with my feminine side, could tell that she was not merely pleasingly plump, but just blossoming in motherhood. Mrs. Wendy Oaks wore a blue dress and further covered herself with a dark brown sweater. She was kneeling on a worn rubber-like board and spading between flowers. I kept glancing in Wendy's direction until our eyes met.

Dropping my *Sears* appropriated lawn tools I walked toward her and introduced myself. Mrs. Oaks greeted me with her large green eyes and a pleasant smile. We quickly began the kind of small talk common for such interchanges and she was forever Wendy from that moment. Wendy's husband, I found out, was Fred Oaks. He was the assistant editor of the local newspaper. Wendy was an assistant manager at a local department store and now working part-time with her pregnancy. Fred and Wendy had one daughter, Carrie, who was two years old at the time we met. Wendy was five months pregnant with their second child, a boy, whose chosen name was Craig.

Our conversation turned to sharing backgrounds and we found out much about each other's families in a short amount of time. The Oaks were married for six years at the time that Charly and I met them. They were originally from a medium-sized town 90 miles north of our metropolitan city. The Oaks first met while attending college and married in 1980. They moved to the big city shortly after their marriage and lived in an apartment building before purchasing their home. I was to find out that Fred and Wendy always had a horror tale or three to tell about their experiences as apartment dwellers.

The Oaks lived in their home for about four years. They put much effort into molding their home and highlighted it with their own special touches and accents. Fred and Wendy took pride in what they had accomplished. Photographs shown to us of their home at the time of their purchase warranted their pride.

Fred and Wendy were simple people who led uncomplicated lives. Fred was a short, balding man who wore glasses and maintained a beard even through the hot summer months. He was trim in weight for his short stature and muscular. Fred was more distant than his wife and his occasional shortness in disposition may be interpreted as rudeness or aloofness to those who did not know him. Wendy was a short, slender woman with green eyes and flowing red hair. She had a common, pleasant face with proportional features. Unlike her husband, Wendy typically smiled and easily conversed with others. The Oaks' daughter, Carrie, was a cute, quiet two year old with long brown hair. She often spoke in a soft, high-pitched voice, yet talked up a storm or perhaps more precisely, a tornado, once she warmed up to you.

The Oaks did not contaminate their lives with the trimmings that many of us take for granted and would not know how to live without—cable television, a VCR, dishwasher, garage door opener, telephone answering machine, etc. More importantly, Fred and Wendy were good planners. They thought of their future and the future of their children. The Oaks routinely purchased government bonds to finance their children's future college education even though Carrie was not yet in preschool and Craig was still in Wendy's womb. They were a loving family and their children were very fortunate indeed.

Charly and I admired the Oaks and envisioned us with similar family values and ambitions. We saw ourselves as the *Ricardo's'* and *Mertz*. Charly and I cherished the time that we lived next door to the Oaks. We grew close quickly, shared our lives with each other, and never envisioned a separation in our friendship. As our relationship with the Oaks grew, so did our desire to start a family. We wanted to give back to our own children what God had blessed in us and in our relationship.

What Fred and Wendy gave us through their family lifestyle and friendship was immeasurable. It was not very easy to give back to them, but we did in our own way. Without a family, other than Disney, Charly and I were pretty much into each other—and I was told on more than one occasion that I could be more selfish and self-centered than the dog. Sometimes I just don't get no respect! Woof!

We tried giving back to the Oaks in little ways. We helped where we could and tried to be there when we were needed. Friday evenings were particularly enjoyable for us as we began the habit of bringing a VCR over to the Oaks. We shared the evening watching recently released movies, conversing, and commenting late into the night. Now you might think it odd that we brought the VCR to the Oaks' home rather than the Oaks visiting us next door. However, it was much easier for Charly and me to make the short trip across the driveway, VCR in tow, rather than have the Oaks gather their belongings with baby paraphernalia in tow. It was no sacrifice for us as we enjoyed immensely their company and they seemed to genuinely enjoy ours.

Charly and I also liked babysitting. When Craig was born, watching the two children was good experience for us. We learned about the ways of the newborn as well as the toddler. Carrie and Craig were always well behaved. They had been taught well as Fred and Wendy fine-tuned praise and disappointment to an art. From abundant praise to gentle commands to the bad girl/boy chair, the eventual outcome was to find two well-behaved children who were respectful of their elders and each other. Carrie being the eldest sibling had an eager listener and follower in Craig, not to mention a "gofer." Like most elder siblings, Craig's sister quickly learned how to manipulate the relationship to her advantage. Yet, Carrie and Craig were inseparable buddies and one might suspect that their sibling relationship will be a source of strength for them in their adult lives. They enjoyed uncomplicated activities, as it was less important as to what they were doing than with whom they were doing it. To underscore this point, I once found Carrie and Craig sitting on their kitchen floor and wrestling with a plastic kitchen bag full of everyday garbage. They both tugged at the bag like it was actually worth something—perhaps like grabbing the golden ring on a carnival merry-go-round; but it was worth something to them. We have a photo of them in our family album tugging at the priceless bag on their kitchen floor with their coloring book art adorning their kitchen wall.

Chapter 11

Everlasting Bliss

Early on in our marriage, Charly and I were imaginative in demonstrating our affection for each other, highlighted by whatever surprises our respective creativities could originate. After all, we were a young couple very much in love. We tried to stay one step ahead of each other, not in competition, but in that true happiness of watching the other experience something new, different, and pleasurable. We loved giving to each other. This often occurred on the holidays and special days like birthdays. Yet, surprises are just that—so there were no rules about how or when we did what we did to celebrate our relationship—for we grew to be the best of friends with a long life of giving ahead with those wonderful surprises potentially around every corner.

Charly and I were married in January 1984. I remember for Valentine's Day that year, I wrote a special children's story for Charly in multiple parts that narrated my Valentine's surprise for her. I left the story under her pillow one week before Valentine's Day. The instructions asked her not only to read the story, but also to do what her namesake did in the story. I am not known for making a long story short, so here is Charly's special Valentine's Day story...

"Greg and Charly have lived next door to each other, they will tell you, for all their lives. Now, in dog years, that would be a long time. However, in human years, it has not been that many. Greg and Charly ride their bikes and fly their kites. They attend the same school where learning is first rate and they read books into the night until quite late. At the same church they always pray and stay with their families the rest of the day. Charly and Greg share the same friends in the neighborhood and go to summer camp at Fort Hood. They quickly glide down water slides and enjoy bumpy rides on roller coasters that fly!

Greg and Charly for Christmas dress like elves and in karate class they defend themselves. They play ball on many teams and then order out their favorite pizza supreme! When at home Charly and Greg on their computers roam for while on the World Wide Web they are often fed. And you may not believe that this is so, but their favorite ice cream is chocolate chip cookie dough! Yes, Greg and Charly were forever friends from before dusk to after dawn. That is the way it has been for almost all of Greg and Charly's years.

Valentine's Day was fast approaching. Greg and Charly have exchanged Valentine cards since the second grade. This year, Greg wanted to do something extra special in appreciation of his friendship with Charly, but what to do? Greg thought and thought and then thought some more. When he was done thinking he thought even more. How could he surprise Charly?

Greg knew that Charly liked mystery and adventure. He decided to give her both: a mysterious adventure and an adventurous mystery! Valentine's Day was just one week away—7 days. Greg began his quest by leaving Charly the following message and a map in the knot of the big oak tree that she visited daily:

> *If you follow this map*
> *And find the spot exact;*
> *You will be pleased to find*
> *Something rare and divine!*

Charly smiled and looked for a signature, but she found

none.   She opened the map and began walking off the directions one-by-one. Charly stepped 15 paces to the right of the big oak tree.   She took 10 giant steps that lead her to the backyard of her family home.   Charly completed the directions by walking left 20 teeny steps.   She found herself at the birdbath in the backyard.   Charly looked down to find a small box wrapped in aluminum foil.   She removed the foil and opened the box.   Inside the box was a tiny doll wearing a big red heart and a golden necklace around her neck.   A brief message was also in the box that said to return at the birdbath tomorrow.   Charly sat down near the birdbath.   She gazed at the doll and wondered who left her such a precious surprise and gift.

Charly was determined to find out who left the map and gift.   She decided to keep an eye on the birdbath as she could see it clearly out of her bedroom window.   As darkness grew, Charly told herself that she was not going to sleep until she found out who is leaving her the mysterious messages.   She looked and watched and watched and looked.   Her eyes grew tired and began to close.   Charly shook her head to awaken her eyes but found that they were closing to no surprise.

Charly awoke the next morning in her bed; apparently, her mother or father had put her there.   She remembered quickly what yesterday's message had said.   She flew out of her room down the stairs saying a quick "Hi" to her family as she fled.

Out the back door to the birdbath Charly ran and looked down near the flowers to find a message in the sand.   She opened it quickly and read what it said:

> *By the rose bush near the garage,*
> *You will find your second surprise.*
> *There you will uncover no mirage,*
> *But instead something that's just your size!*

Charly ran toward the side of the house where the garage and rose bush were plainly in sight. She searched on the ground here and there, but found nothing anywhere. Charly reviewed the message once more and looked up at the roses blooming galore.

Tied to one rose was a small box covered in newspaper. Charly removed the ribbon being careful not to prick herself with the thorns of the bush. She removed the old newspaper and opened the box. Inside was a rose encased in a glass snowball. Charly shook the ball and snow drifted around and around. The rose sparkled as the snow settled to the bottom. There was no signature and no note this time; but Charly guessed that the next surprise would be here in time.

Charly saw Greg later that day. She showed him the messages and gifts that she found. Greg acted surprised and denied leaving the gifts when questioned by his friend. He said, "Really, not me. You know I wouldn't give a girl gifts! Yuck!" Charly was not completely satisfied, but never knew Greg to give her or any other girl gifts. The thought left her mind and they went to the park to play.

The next morning could not come fast enough for Charly. Her parents were accustomed to her flight out the back door and the inevitable quick "Hi" or "Bye." Charly ran toward the family garage and bush of roses. She carefully looked around the thorny plant, but did not see anything but black ants crawling around the bush. Charly looked and looked and looked some more when out of the corner of her eye she spied the note she was looking for. Charly swiftly untied the note and read to herself the following quote:

> *This is day three*
> *Of gifts to you from me.*
> *I hope that you are enjoying*
> *Solving clues that can be annoying!*

Charly read the word "over" and turned to find a map on the other side of the note. She read the directions and followed them at the same time. Charly walked to the front porch of the family home and read to walk up the steps near the little gnome. Charly knew where the ornamental gnome decorated their home. She climbed the stairs and headed to the gnome. Charly saw nothing nearby and wondered where was her surprise.

In a flash, Charly remembered that the head of the gnome was like the top of a cookie jar. She twisted the head and off it came. She looked deep inside and found her next surprise. Charly reached in and grabbed a chocolate chip cookie baked in the shape of a heart. It was wrapped in plastic and still quite warm—perhaps a clue that her secret admirer lived nearby. Hum?

Greg and Charly went to the zoo later that day. There were many things to look at and learn as the zoo was always fun. They had a great day, but grew quite tired in the afternoon. Greg and Charly returned home and both rested before supper.

It was now the morning of the fourth day leaving three mornings left until Valentine's Day. Like every morning this week, Charly ran out the door barely able to speak. Out the front door she quickly walked and went to the gnome whose head she did pop. As before and without surprise, Charly read this note from inside:

We're halfway to Valentine's Day
But please don't you cry;
For still headed your way
Is another big surprise!

Charly found another map with directions that started at the gazebo in their backyard. She loved the gazebo, which was painted yellow and white. Flowers of every color grew by its side. Birds, squirrels and chipmunks played all around the gazebo.

Charly arrived at the gazebo as birds and animals moved away. The directions told her to walk around the gazebo five times starting at the open gate. On her fifth time around, Charly read to face the direction of the shed and walk 10 paces straight ahead. Charly did as she read and found herself at the back of their shed. She looked around and soon found a large box. Charly open the box, as was her part to find a special poem framed in wood and glass:

The Angel and the Lighthouse

An Angel looks down from clouds above,
A lighthouse peers through foggy mist off the sea.
One is Divine, the other manmade with care and love;
Protecting us, keeping us safe and free.

An Angel's mission we honestly don't know.
The lighthouse reaches out to us in the dark of night.
Yet, both comfort us, protecting us from foes;
One rather mysteriously, the other a beaconed light.

When facing thunder from others—even daughters and friends,
Or storms brew from within;
When our heart aches and seems not to mend,
Or our past confuses us as to where we've been.

When life's trails lead us in, but not out;
Or we desire a lower berth and get an upper loft.
When we want to still the spinning and just shout:
"Stop this world I want to get off!"

Take heart—the Angel and the lighthouse are forever there;
We're vigilant for one—the other we solemnly beseech.
Both lighten the load that we bear,
We take our comfort, profess faith in each.

I know you don't need another heartbreak.
So, Charly, my wish for you is a simple, caring one:

When the world and it's troubles become too much to bear,
When you just don't know which way to turn;
When you're alone and feel no one is there;
Trust in your Guardian Angel and beacons that burn.

Angels and lighthouses always were and will be;
They shield and guard you in every way.
They watch over you and your daughters you see,
Guiding your lives each moment of the day.

Next to gold, you see, angels and lighthouses are dear to Charly's heart. She collected both, as one glance of the mantle above the hearth revealed. A tearful smile came to her face as she ran back home and placed the framed poem in a special place.

Charly was very excited and could hardly wait for Valentine's Day in hopes that she will find who left her such gifts divine. The fifth day of Charly's mysterious adventure arrived. She ran once again out the back door to the shed to find another message near the fox's head. She opened the note and read with surprise:

> *Today it will not be hard,*
> *To find your surprise.*
> *Just run to the front yard,*
> *Look for something that cries!*

Not hard? Find something that cries? Charly scratched her head and said, "What is in the front yard that cries?" She walked steadily toward the front of her house as she rubbed her cheeks like a teeny mouse. Charly stood still and then turned around. She slowly turned full circle over and over again. "Something that cries?" she thought. Suddenly, Charly stopped dead in her tracks and faced a weeping willow tree, an undeniable fact.

Charly raced to the weeping willow and looked all around, but found nothing anywhere even on the ground. She eyed the bark and looked between the roots then all of a sudden jumped right out of her boots. Tied to the first fork up in the tree was a box wrapped in cloth really easy to see. Charly climbed the tree and grabbed the box. Charly opened the box and inside did find a golden wrist bracelet from somebody kind. Charly placed it on her wrist and it fit just fine. She saw Greg riding his bike and ran to show him what she got. Greg looked surprised and told Charly it was really "awesome." Charly eyed him carefully, but did not utter a word. She had her suspicions and wanted to query, but decided not to question her friend.

The day ended leaving two days left until Valentine's Day. Charly was excited and could hardly sleep that night. She knew that when the morning sun rose and she left her bed, straight for the weeping willow tree she would head.

Morning came like the others and Charly bound from her bed. She said a short "Hi" to her family who had grown accustomed to her fleeting out the door. Charly ran outside in the front yard toward the weeping willow tree. She looked upward toward the fork in the tree and saw a familiar sight—a message tied to a limb.

Charly climbed up to retrieve the message and opened it up to read what was writ:

> *T'is the day before Valentine's*
> *And the latest surprise you will find;*
> *Near the tree of cherry blossoms*
> *If you are not all thumbs!*

Charly ran toward the backyard screaming with glee. Bird and squirrels and other living things moved out of her way as she did flee. Charly approached the cherry tree and looked up and down it as far as she could see. She saw cherries and blossoms and limbs and leaves, but nothing that looked like a message if you please.

Charly was stumped for she saw nothing. She looked up and down one more time when she spotted a bird holding a piece of paper. "Oh, no" she cried. "What am I going to do?" Charly clamored and hollered and yelled and screamed, but the bird did not seem to mind anything. Then the bird had enough and flew away with message in tow. Charly was disappointed and turned away when all of a sudden she saw her prey. He flew up above her and dropped from his beak, the message he was holding so she could take a peek.

Charly grabbed the paper in midair and opened it hurriedly. She laughed out loud as she read:

> *If a bird did not take*
> *This message from you.*
> *Then it's not too late*
> *To read this clue!*

On the back of the message wet with bird beak stuff was the following clue: "What you seek you will find behind something that tells you the time." "Tells the time" Charly repeated. Clocks tell time she thought and so do watches; but there were no clocks or watches outside. "Oh!" Charly screamed. "Yes there is. The sundial in the corner of the yard!" Charly ran as fast as she could to the far corner of the yard. She stopped in front of the sundial and found another box as before wrapped in aluminum foil. Charly unwrapped the foil and opened the box. Inside she found two passes to the local cinema. "Hum?" she thought. "I wonder what I shall do with these. Perhaps my secret admirer and I will go to the movies if you please!"

It was the eve of Valentine's Day now and Charly lay in bed thinking happily of the mystery and adventure of the past 6 days. She smiled as she recalled the surprises she discovered: a tiny doll wearing a red heart and golden necklace; a rose encased in a glass snowball; a heart-shaped chocolate chip cookie; a poem of angels and lighthouses; a golden wrist bracelet; and now two passes to the local movie theater.

Charly felt very special for the attention shown her by her secret admirer. She wondered, "Will I ever find out who is giving me these surprises?" Charly was lost in her thoughts and drifted off to sleep.

It was February 14th: Valentine's Day. Charly wondered if the days of past were simply a dream; a big, wonderful dream. She jumped from her bed, dressed quickly and ran outside with yet another brief "Hi" to her mother. Charly ran toward the sundial not really caring what time it was; yet, this is where the last adventure will begin. She also hoped that this is where the mystery will be solved.

Charly approached the sundial bubbling with excitement and a little anxious. What if there was nothing there? What if she never finds out who has surprised her all week long? What if...

It was time to meet the "what ifs" head on. Charly looked around the sundial upon which the morning sun was shining bright. At its base she found the final clue. Charly nervously opened the message and read with some concern:

> *Today is Valentine's Day*
> *And this is what I have to say:*
> *Go back in the direction you started*
> *Under the bed from which you parted!*

Charly was somewhat bewildered as to how her secret admirer got into her bedroom. Charly ran back into the house greeting her mother "Hi" once again as she warped by. Up the stairs she ran just as she ran down the stairs a moment before. Charly turned sharply into her room and slid to the floor. She stopped right to the side of her bed. Charly did not have to raise her covers because, as usual, her bed was not yet made.

Charly saw a little box near one of the legs of her bed. She stretched her arm as far as it would reach and grabbed the box with the tips of her fingers. Once in her grasp, Charly stood up and hoped on her bed. This box was neatly wrapped with a ribbon and a bow. Charly gently unwrapped the box to reveal a golden locket on a chain. There was no note, which saddened Charly. Now she will never know who went through all that effort and left her so many wonderful gifts and memories. Charly then noticed an inscription on the locket: "Friends and Lovers Forever." She opened the locket to find pictures of Greg and herself."

Charly turned the table on me later that year on my birthday. She always found my Italian heritage curious given native folklore and shared stories of my growing-up in an Italian household. She often made me swear on an Italian bible that my experiences were indeed true—*De Biblio Italiano of the Early Evening Saints*. On my birthday, Charly left an envelope on my dresser, and I could feel the love and hanker as I read her letter:

Ciao Greggorio,

Maya I calla you Greggorio, Greggorio? Itta mei, again... Charlyio. Si, Charlyio... gondola Charlyio... from Venezia. I knowa you thinka you never heara from mei again—sucha wilda woman. You remember? Mei gondola, she was very dry for you. I piddled on my gondola all over Venice for you. Oh, dio mio... Mei paddled you here and piddled there... the day, she over, I coulda nonna piddle no more! Mei go to this, a, coma disch, HBO clinic? I walka up to le doctora and tolda him, mei canna no piddle no more. Le doctora, speaka Englesa; he no understanda me... he tella me, drinka lotta aqua if I wanna piddle... I tella him he no understando.

I remember last month I arriva from Italia to your smalla town, Smallaville. Everybody in town who speaka Englesa, they calla me a sonna ma bitch. The hotella waitress calla me a sonna ma bitch. The hotella clerk calla me a sonna ma bitch... even the hotella manager, he calla me a sonna ma bitch. Mei, with sucha grandiose gondola, a sonna ma bitch. So I saya to doctore, you sonna ma bitch... He gava mei a glezza of aqua anda, coma disch, prozacca? Le doctore, he saya, this will take cara of youra piddling and youra sonna ma bitch. I don't even knowa the doctor and he calla me a sonna ma bitch!

Mei decida to comma back to America... If mei gonna be calla a sonna ma bitch in mei Italia, mei comma back to America to seea you. So, I tooka the airplano from Carrara, bella Carrara, to youra country. I yella at your statua of, coma disch, liberpee? Libertee? You knowa, big statua in New Yorka with her hand stucka in the air lika putting on deorderante. I yella, YOU SOMMA MA BITCH! I yella real louda, ya know, I wanna ita to heara me. Before I step onea toe on youra country, mei calla alla of your country a sonna ma bitch! HA! You sonna ma bitch! Excusa mei. I taka me water and prozacca.

So, I arriva in a town neara you. Me tella you, I no staya at the Motella Sixo... I was gonna to, but I saw thema damn lights... them dama lights were stilla on. Boy, they really lika to leava lights onna for you. I nonna get it. Why leava them dama lights on? Nonna sleepa with damma lights on. The sunna, she nonna should shinea at night. I remember my piss of toast, my fock on the table and my sheet on the bed. I knocka on the Motella Sixo manager door and runna away yelling, YOU SONNA MA BITCHES! Boy, I feela really gooda after that.

It's late at nighta now and I canna no calla you. I knowa u needa your sleep. I thinka they calla you a, a coma disch, a doosie? A boozie? A snoozie? I donna know. I just knowa you needa lots of sleepa. But, mei Charlyio, mei comma to town and looka for adventure in Smallaville. I nonna needa sleep. I sleepa back in Italy. Then, mei seea this bigga sign. A real bigga sign. It saya, "U-Move... A Great Adventure." I donna knowa what a "U-Move" is, butta mei looking for adventure. So I walka insida and mei thinka and mei remember; you knowa what I thinka: he's gonna calla me a sonna ma bitch. I was gonna calla him that first, but I donna do that.

So, I wenna inside and aska him, "U-Movea?" He nodda his testa, coma disch, his heada and saya to mei, "U-Move." I saya, "No, nonna U Movea... mei Charlyio. Mei gondola you. U Movea?" Anda I donna understanda. He clima over the counter and grabba mei by my blouse. He saya, "Stick your gondola where it don't shine and get out of here whop." Ima looking for adventure and he wanna ride my gondola in the shada. Mei donna understand 'whop,' but hey, mei lika him 'causa he nonna calla me a sonna ma bitch. I trya to explaina to himma that I donnna bringa my gondola with mei. I donna worka now. I tella him mei comma to youra country and looka for bigga adventure. He letta me goa and saya, "That's it." He comma arounda the counter and grabba me again and shova mei out the door. I coulda nonna believe it. He yella at mei, "Stay out of here you sonna ma bitch." I don't even know the man and he calla me sonna ma bitch. Mei backa in youra country just one nighta and already mei called a sonna ma bitch.

Thats itta. Mei nonna staya with you. Nonna body understanda mei. I go backa to Italy. I wanna you come with me, Greggorio, comma with mea to Venezia. Comma staya with meo on mea gondola.

Tiamo,

Your Charlyio

Stapled to the last page of Charly's letter were two tickets to Italy. They were dated for three weeks in July during my summer break from school. Charly coordinated her vacation time accordingly—her OCD way. We would not only have time to see Venice, Rome and other beautiful Italian cities, but also would have time to visit my mother's native Carrara. This was a treasured gift for both of us, as to date we had little time to travel. Charly and I did a pretty good job of balancing each other out in a give-and-take way. We had our troubles and disagreements like other young couples, but we managed to eventually put them aside. I cannot say we never went to bed angry, and I still have the extra pillow and blanket in the living room closet to attest to those disagreements; but what we meant to each other eventually prevailed over the trials and tribulations we experienced. Making-up was such good fun.

Chapter 12

Bello Italia

This summer was full of anticipated excitement as Charly and I flew across the Atlantic and landed in Rome on a late July evening. Italy, the Italian Republic, is in southeastern Europe and is shaped like a boot. If it were in Germany, it would be known as *Das Boot*. To provide the reader with a geographical perspective, Italy is about the size of North Carolina... before the hurricanes. Rome has two airports, Leonardo Da Vinci – Fiumicino Airport and Ciampino Airport. We flew into Leonardo Da Vinci Airport *via Delta Airlines*. We were first struck by the multitude of red tiled roofs that one finds throughout the cities of Italy and shamelessly copied in the United States for apartment dwellings with an Italian motif, or is that an Italian moeteef?

Uncharacteristic of Charly and our budget, she purchased a room with a fireplace at a five star hotel in Rome, the Majestic Hotel, located on *Via Veneto*. Still, Charly budgeted our money and booked us in hotel splendor for only 4 days as we visited the sites in Rome and Vatican City. The Majestic, built in 1889, is the oldest hotel on the world famous *Via Veneto*, home of Fellini's *La dolce Vita*. Charly chose the Majestic because it was located in the center of Rome's historical sites and only 1 km away from the main railway station, Termini. It boasts of the elegant La Veranda Restaurant, which overlooks the *Via Veneto*. Although we plan to travel more than dine, we expected to sample much regional cuisine. We also decided to see as much as we could of Italy even though we might sacrifice *quality time*. Charly and I knew that it would be a long time before we would have the opportunity to repeat our adventure. We did a great deal of traveling by trains in Rome. The *direct* route from Rome to Carrara is about 150 miles. During our three-week world wind tour we will travel through Naples, Florence, Bologna, Venice, Milan, Turin, Genoa, and my mother's native Carrara. Then, my relatives in Carrara will escort us to Pisa before returning to America.

While in Rome, Charly and I visited the traditional sites of most tourists. One of the best-preserved monuments of earliest Rome, the Colosseum, was breath taking. The marble structured arena held over 50,000 spectators who observed the killing of Christians and the mighty battles of gladiators. We expected the ground to be tainted a bland red in light of the much blood that was spilt in the stadium, but it was not. Charly and I also visited the Pantheon, which the Romans devoted to the seven planetary divinities. The Pantheon is circular in architecture and enclosed in marble. Then Charly and I headed back to The Majestic Hotel. We were very tired but very hungry. Upon returning to the hotel, we dined its La Veranda before retiring for the evening... and we were exhausted enough to just retire for our first evening in Rome.

The next morning, Charly and I saw the *Fontana di Trevi*, the Trevi Fountain in Rome. I shared with Charly the folklore of my mother regarding the fountain. Mother said whoever throws three coins over her shoulders into the fountain, she will come back to Rome. Not ones to test fate, Charly and I threw three coins over our shoulders into the fountain—and we did this three times because we certainly wanted to return to Rome. The fountain itself is a statue of Neptune and two Tritons on each side. It was designed and built for Pope Clemente XII and completed during the latter part of the 1700s. Next it was off to the *Foro Romano*, the Roman Forum, which was the religious, political, and business center of ancient Rome.

After the Forum, we visited one of Charly's favorites, the *Scalinata di Spagna*, the Spanish Steps. Francesco de Sanctis built these twelve flights of steps in the 1700s. The elegant steps descend to the Franciscan Church of *Trinita dei Monti* built in the 16th century. Although Charly appreciated the historic significance of the Spanish Steps, she seemed more excited that they also lead to the Piazza where she could window-shop at Rome's most fashionable boutiques.

After some rather lavish and out of character shopping for Charly, we visited another ancient ruin in Rome, *Circo Massimo*, the Circus Maximus. This historical site was built to entertain emperors and sat over 300,000 spectators who applauded the competitive chariot races of Imperial Rome. Then, as quickly as it started, our second day came to an end. Charly and I were tired yet filled with excitement, making falling to sleep a challenge. We started a fire in the fireplace to set the ambiance. Charly and I kissed and cuddled, and love came easy that night. We finally drifted off to sleep as the passions of love faded with the embers in the fireplace.

For the next two days, Charly and I toured the more religious sites of Rome in preparation to our trip to Vatican City. We visited the courtyard and garden of the *Church of Santa Cecilia*. This church was constructed in 800 AD and also had a gothic tabernacle. We then visited several catacombs in Rome, those of St. Sebastian and St. Callixtus. The latter was the first Christian cemetery in Rome where the remains of 9 saints and popes are entombed.

Charlie and I then set our sights on the sites of Vatican City, the Holy See. The Holy See is the center of the Roman Catholic Church. The national name of Vatican City is *Stato della Citta del Vaticano*. The Pope who then was John Paul II rules it. The College of Cardinals elected Pope John Paul II in 1978. Vatican City State lies on Vatican Hill on the right bank of the Tiber River. As the second smallest sovereign state, the pope has complete legal, executive, and judicial powers. The chief advisory body to the pope is the College of Cardinals. A major role of the College of Cardinals is to elect a successor for life upon the death of the reigning pope.

Charly and I started our tour of Vatican City at the *Basilica di San Peitro*, St. Peter's Basilica. St. Peter's Cathedral is the spiritual center of the Vatican. The building boasts the works of many of the great Renaissance architects, including Bramante, Raphael, and Michelangelo. We viewed Michelangelo's Pieta in reverence. St. Peter's Basilica is said to be built over the very spot where St. Peter was thought buried after his martyrdom in Rome—believed by Catholics—questioned by scholars. We entered the Basilica through the *Piazza San Pietro*, St. Peter's Square—where lay people receive the pope's weekly blessing. From the outside, St. Peter's is sheltered with magnificent columns and domes designed by Michelangelo. On the inside, its ceilings and floors are decorated in great detail. The ceilings are quite high and always decorated by paintings. There are numerous statues and tombs inside as well as the main altar of St. Peters. Many of the paintings and statues are mosaics made out of small pieces of colored rock.

Also within the Basilica of St. Peter's is said to be the relic of Veronica's Veil. Like the relic of the Shroud of Turin, the Veronica Veil is said to have the image of the face of Jesus Christ. To many, the image on the Shroud of Turin was the burial cloth of Christ following His crucifixion. The image on the Veronica Veil is reported in history as Jesus' gratitude for a woman named Veronica who wiped His face while he carried the cross through Jerusalem before His crucifixion. The Veil is not publicly displayed, but said enclosed near an altar by inscription. Below the main floor of the Basilica, is the

Vatican Grottoes—the tombs of popes and saints—a place of worship and thought provoking wonder of the past—and the mortality of one's soul. We also saw the *Porta Santa*, or Holy Door, which is opened by the Pope for Holy Year celebrations.

After meditating and praying within the awe of the Basilica of St. Peters, Charly and I visited the Sistine Chapel, *Cappella Sistina*. This Chapel is famous for the awe-inspiring artwork "The Last Judgment" by Michelangelo. This mural covers about 10,000 square feet of the ceiling and wall. Pope Clement VII commissioned the fresco back in the 16th century. We spent some time in the Vatican Museum, but quickly realized that we would not be able to traverse the more than 5 miles of corridors in the museum. Evening arrived and so did our fascinating tour of Vatican City. It was time to return to our last evening at the Majestic Hotel in Rome before heading south to Naples. Love between us came effortless.

On our fifth day, Charly and I took the train south to Naples. As we entered the northwestern Naples, the Phlegraean Fields was first on our tour—a site of volcanoes, craters, and lakes. I wanted to visit Pazzuoli, but Charly did not see the need even though it was the birthplace of Sophia Loren. Women... go figure! Naples is an important artistic and cultural center in Europe. Charly and I visited the Monumental Center and Spaccanapoli, with open markets, shops, and restaurants. We also went to Mount Vesuvius, which is the only active volcano on Europe's mainland. We saw the Ruins of Pompeii, which were buried by the eruption of Mt. Vesuvius back in 79 AD.

It seems no Italian city is without fountains, and Naples is no exception as we saw La Fontana dell'Immacolatella and La Fontana di Monteoliveto. By late afternoon, we entered the square of Piazza del Plebiscito and viewed its monuments, including the Church of San Francesco di Paola and the Naples

Royal Palace. By evening, Charly and I wanted to sit down once again and relax. We decided to go to the theater in the historic Teatro San Carlo before returning to the Best Western San Germano. We danced alone and without music in our room for another hour before love filled our bed.

In the early morn of the sixth day, we headed north to Florence, which took several hours by train. The first stop in Florence was the *Duomo*, the Cathedral of Santa Maria dei Fiori. The Cathedral's dome has become to symbolize Florence as it dominates the Florentine skyline. We also saw the *Ponte Vecchio*. This is the most ancient bridge in Florence. It is made of three arches and two wide arcades on each side housing the *botteghe* or shops. Any tourist attraction with *shops* was pre-approved by Charly. There was no need for discussion, so we shopped... and shopped. Then Charly and I rested being worn out by our travels and fell asleep quickly.

The seventh day began leisurely with a late breakfast. Early in the afternoon, Charly and I visited the *Giardini Boboli*, the Boboli Gardens. It is one of Florence's most beautiful gardens dotted with flowers and fountains. Then we shopped late into the evening once again, albeit window-shopped, in the upscale shopping district of the best in Italian fashion, the *Via de' Tornabuoni* before turning in for the evening.

On day eight, Charly and I continued our trek north to Bologna. We primarily toured religious and historical sites in Bologna, including the *Catello Estense, Mausoleum of Galla Placidia, Basilica di San Petronio, Basilica del San Domenico*, and *San Giovanni Evangelista*, the Abbet of St. John. We ended our day, as with emerging regularity, with shopping at the *Piazza del Nettuno*. Charly continued to do well with our budget despite our outreach to *Piazza's*.

Charly and I continued north to the amorous city of Venice

where we would spend two days and consider our visit to Venice as the core of our honeymoon. We began with St. Mark's Square, which is in the heart of Venice. Charly thought it would be a change of pace if we shopped at the chic sidewalk boutiques surrounding the square rather than at the end of our day. She was rather transparent, but I too wanted to end our day on a romantic gondola journey on Venice's main water thoroughfare, the Grand Canal. To my surprise, Charly did not shop until she dropped, as we headed to the Rialto Bridge, Venice's landmark bridge displaying its 24-foot arch.

Not wanting to be grounded, Charly and I took in the Campanile di San Marco or bell tower. Although originally built as a lighthouse, tourist like us rode an elevator to the top of the bell tower for an exquisite view of Venice and the mountainous Alps in the distance. By early evening, Charly and I found ourselves dining and drinking at the *Bacaro Jazz*— a jazz bar. We enjoyed the music and food, a tasteful prelude to the evening ahead.

As suspected, Charly had planned a romantic evening on the waterways of Venice. Transportation on the Grand Canal could be by gondola, by vaporetto (water bus), by traghetto (gondola ferries), or by motoscafo (water taxis). Of course, Charly already planned to traverse the canal via the carefree and leisurely gondola. We went to the place of embarkation and to Charly's surprise and somewhat displeasure our gondolier was a woman. Again to Charly's surprise and somewhat displeasure, I was not experiencing similar emotions. Yet, these were primitive male feelings that faded quickly. Our gondolier greeted us warmly, "Ciao;" and she also spoke in labored English. She identified herself as Mia Mama. Hmm… No, couldn't be. We returned her greeting with upraised eyebrows, as she motioned us to sit at the rear of her gondola.

Mia began her artful stroking of the oar, as we slowly left the dock and began our excursion up the Grand Canal. Although we initially took interest in the landmarks highlighted by her—Palazzo Molin, Palladian Church of San Giorgio Maggiore, the House of Marco Polo—our interest slowly turned toward each other. Ah, amore! Such affection was obviously not foreign to Mia as her voice quieted and the still of the canal was broking only by the whispering swish of the gondolier's oar and occasional sounds of motorized crafts as they passed near us. Mia told us that the ride would last under an hour, so Charly and I considered this our foreplay for the evening. Actually, Charly thought this might be a stretch for us—meaning me—and asked me to try to control myself and be all that I could be or perhaps be even a bit more... hmm...

I ignored Charly's attack on my manliness and put my arms around her. I pulled her toward me and we embraced in a slow, never-ending kiss. The light breeze, stirred by the leisurely pace of the gondola, drifted calmly across our faces helping to compensate for the warmness stirring in each of us. Mia seemed oblivious to our stirrings and likely had us filed under *I ain't seen nothin' I haven't seen before*. Similarly, as Charly and I continued our embrace, we became oblivious to the sights and sounds around us. We were further lulled into a false sense of isolation by the gondola's supple swaying on the surface of the water. Yet, in reality, we were not alone in the confines of this small world. The longer we embraced, however, the less that seemed to matter or even be noticed.

Charly and I held each other tight as time passed without notice. Our embrace was interrupted only by the required brief gasps for air. As we continued to kiss, we gently massaged each other in our most familiar and desired places. Charly and I learned early in our relationship how to provide each other pleasure, and this unselfish focus brought mutual satisfaction. Yet, tonight was different. The grandness of the canal, the Venetian skyline, the drifting under the canvas of the stars, and perhaps the voyeurism by Mia—all enhanced the excitement that Charly and I were experiencing. We did not want our time here to end, but a glimpse of our gondolier maneuvering toward the bank of the canal betrayed our desires. Charly and I disengaged, but the separation did not take away our warm smiles and the closeness we felt toward each other. Mia gently docked her gondola and helped us step out to the bank. She told us "Ciao" and did not have to ask the customary question of whether we enjoyed the experience. We did. Charly and I headed to our hotel to continue on land what we started off land, driven by our romantic memories in Venice. We never left our room the next day and continued the pleasure of our romantic bliss that originated on the Canal the night before.

For whatever reasons, Charly and I started our eleventh day with seemingly benign smiles, as we headed westward on our two-day trek to Milan. As the train chugged toward Milan, Charly squealed with excitement, not from our romantic evening, but from a notation in our Italia guidebook—another shopping quarter. However, Charly's cry of joy turned to a shriek of death as she read that the *Quadrilatero d'Oro*, the Golden Triangle in Milan, and the *Via Monte Napoleone* were shopping districts for the very wealthy and fashion conscience—neither of which applied to us although I at times can be a fashion freak. I on the other hand was OK with not having to tour another shopping district no matter how exquisite and famous. However, before I could declare victory, Charly found several other shopping districts in Milan that perhaps, she thought, we could afford.

Our first landmark we visited in Milan was the Leonardo da Vinci National Science and Technology Museum. Besides being a great artist, da Vinci was a creative inventor whose flying and war machines are on display at the museum. Charly and I also made a point to see da Vinci's famous painting of *The Last Supper*, which is displayed at the Santa Maria della Grazie cathedral. As fast as it started, our eleventh day came to a close.

Charly and I began our twelfth day in Italy by touring several more cathedrals, including the Duomo Cathedral where noblemen and princes donated many of the stored vestments, tapestries, and sacred vases; and the Basilica of St. Ambrose. St. Ambrose was the bishop of Milan during the fourth century and is the patron saint of learning. Next, Charly headed us toward an outlet store, the Arris, which the guidebook said was for bargain hunters like us... and yes, it was quite touristy for people like us! Finally, we ended our time in Milan in the *Navigli* quarter where we enjoyed live jazz at the Grillo Parlante before dining at the King's Pub. Need I ask you who was king for the night?

After nearly two weeks in Italy, Charly and I continued our westward trek on our thirteenth day to the city of Turin. However, it was obvious to each of us that we were tiring after almost two weeks of expansive travel and torrid romance. We planned to rest in Turin and decided we wanted to *see* only one landmark—well, we would not actually be able to see it. Charly and I rested for several hours in Turin before traveling to the *Cattedrale di San Giovanni*. This is the Cathedral of St. John the Baptist and the *Shroud of Turin* rests in a chapel behind the altar in the Cathedral. This Cathedral was constructed for the sole purpose of housing the Holy Shroud. This relic is believed by many Catholics to be the cloth in which Jesus was wrapped after His crucifixion. Charly and I knew that we would only see the shroud in photographs, as it is rarely on view and not scheduled for viewing by the public until the Holy Year of 2025; but at least we could say how close we were to this holy artifact. We returned to our hotel in late afternoon and dined. Charly and I turned in early that evening for needed rest so that our bodies could draw alongside our minds and dreams.

My anticipation was building as Charly and I were beginning our fourteenth day of vacation and we were only one day away from my mother's native land of Carrara. We turned south from Turin and headed for Genoa. It seems Charly and I were becoming less spontaneous and made plans to tour a few sites in Genoa during the day and then head for the Italian Rivera in the early evening. Although there were a number of beaches to choose from in Genoa, including *Bagni Alderbaran, Bagni Marechiaro, Bagni Marinella,* and *Bagni Maddalena,* the Italian Rivera was best known and would readily hold are attention.

We started our day at the *Cattedrale di San Lorenzo Campanile.* I was aware that the chapel housed the bones of St. John the Baptist, the patron saint of Genoa. Charly and I later toured the Aquarium, a maritime museum whose displays included some original letters from Christopher Columbus. Columbus was born in Genoa. Next, Charly and I walked through the many medieval narrow alleys of Genoa, which are known as *carruggi.* Charly was able to find another shopping district and open markets Via XX Septembre. As we walked this street, we came across a bridge built around the 16th century. The bridge housed a World War II monument to all the allied soldiers that were killed in Genoa.

As the sun began to set, Charly and I grabbed a bite for dinner—a light dinner as we still planned to enjoy the evening on the Italian Rivera. The Italian Rivera, Liguria, forms the shore of the gulf of Genoa and is snuggled between the Mediterranean and Maritime Alps. As you travel southward down the thin region of the gulf, the panorama shifts from old fishing villages and small resorts to the more expensive yacht based resorts. No matter where Charly and I were on the Italian Rivera, we were enchanted by its scenic presentation. We did not do much talking that evening, but held hands, glanced often toward each other, and kissed romantically, as the experience was both exhilarating and sensual. Charly and I stopped on occasion to admire what God and man had given us, and gaped in awe as the far away rising sun drifted seemingly ever closer while setting in the gulf. Serenity mingled with thoughts about nothing in particular for Charly and I were in harmony and at rest... and in this state of accord, it did not take us long to find a relatively secluded spot to uncheck our emotions. The Mediterranean sunset and night fell—together oddly enough. Charly and I were mesmerized. In the cloak of darkness, our passions grew quietly only to explode as we fulfilled each other. The gentle, warm breeze off the gulf added to our calm and lazy rest. We lay there not noting the passing of time or anything else for that matter; yet, time was growing short as we would be on our way to Carrara the next day and part of my personal living history would be written.

Charly and I awoke on our fifteenth day in Italy with childlike excitement. Even though she was not of Italian descent, she shared my anticipation about my mother's homeland. We headed southeastward by rail toward Carrara, which is about 50 miles from Genoa and they said 30 minutes by train. We would spend the final days of our honeymoon in Carrara, which lies at the foot of the Apuane Alps. The Alps are known worldwide for the precious marbles and other building stones. Carrara is particularly famous for its white marble. Michelangelo was known to travel to the quarries for the blocks of stone that he would use to create his works of art… and we all know he was a man of good taste.

Charly and I arrived more or less on time at the Carrara-Avenza station where several of my mother's relatives met us. Mother's niece and her daughter, Maria and Isa, greeted us with warm smiles. A chorus of 'Ciaos' echoed around us. Charly knew few words in Italian, mostly learned from me; as for me, my understanding of and ability to speak Italian has progressively lessoned over the years. Fortunately, Isa spoke English very well and directed us toward the station parking lot. The four of us entered a small Fiat and Isa sped out of the rail station. Isa broke the brief silence: "Have you've been enjoying your vacation in Italia?" Charly, the less shy one among us, replied, "Very much so. It is amazing all that we've seen and where we've been—Rome, Naples, Florence, Bologna, Venice—oh, remember Venice honey? And then there was Milan, Turin, Genoa… and now Carrara." "It's amazing all the shopping that Charly has done" I chimed. Isa smiled and Charly shoved me. Maria then spoke Italian to her daughter, "Domandi Gregory come è madre e padre è." I understood 'madre e padre' was my mother and father, and guessed she was asking about them. Before Isa could translate to use, I said to her, "My parents are fine—older, but living generally well." Isa smiled and interpreted my response to her mother. Maria also smiled and said, "Buono." Isa then indicated that we would be home soon.

My mother's birth home was nestled in the side of a small mountain in Carrara. Isa turned in the long curving driveway that led to the house. The traditional orange-red roofing tile could be seen from a distance. The house was a two-story structure set in white stone and brick. The window shutters were a shade of dark green. A deck porch extended from a second story room. The home was set between two large verandas. The main front porch was screened and contained a variety of comfortable outdoor furniture used for chat, cards and other table games. The rear porch was rectangular and the wide base lent itself to an extended dinner and siesta table. Many flowerpots hung from the home. The traditional Italian grapevine draped the perimeter of the porch causing the sun's reflection to appear as moving dots on the table. There were several splendid gardens where flowers of every color and shade were planted. Several bird baths and many statues and busts decorated the yard.

We were greeted by a number of relatives of my mother, most who spoke no or little English. Isa served as our competent translator. Even though we were countries and cultures away from America, the conversation was much the same—How are you? How was your trip? What did you see? How long are you going to stay? And of course, the Italian traditional "Lei come alcuni vino?"—Would you like some wine?

Charly and I planned to spend most of our time left in Italy in Carrara, with a brief visit to Pisa about 15 miles away, before flying out from Pisa and returning to America. We intended to arrive home by Saturday, which would give Charly a couple of days to recover before returning to work on Monday. I, of course, would continue my summer school vacation. Yet we had a week in Carrara, which was sprinkled heavily with traditional Italian foods—pastas, pastries, meats, breads, vegetables... and of course, vino. Meals occurred often and were the time-honored mainstay of Italian family life. What we could not bridge in the cultural gap in language, we bridged through the international language of food.

For the next three or four days, we planned to rest and visit with my relatives and friends who came to greet us. Our visit would also include touring the famous marble quarries of Carrara, the quarries often visited by my grandfather Edgar, as

146

he pursued his livelihood as a sculptor. We would then drive to Pisa to see the legendary leaning tower.

After considerable rest and food in the morning, Isa drove Charly and I to the marble quarries of Carrara, and a cavalcade of relatives followed us. These Carrara natives were more than just familiar with the quarries. They genuinely seem to enjoy our company and perhaps felt linked to the Americas where so many of their relatives immigrated through the years. Isa told us about their Marble Museum detailing the history of quarrying the marble. The trip to the quarries was a living history in itself of Carrara's marble workmanship with its many buildings and monuments on display standing the test of time. The mountain scenery was glorious. Although it was a warm July, the mountains of Carrara look like they were snowcapped to Charly and I. Isa told us it was the marble quarries that only gave the appearance of snow. Isa shared that there were about 200 quarries in northern Tuscany and noted with a smile that we would not be visiting all of them!

Isa and our motorcade turned into a special area although she would not tell us what may this particular quarry so special. I knew that Michelangelo secured much of the marble he used to create his masterpieces in the quarries of Carrara. Isa brought the motorcade to a stop and we all ventured out into the warm summer air. We followed a well-worn path used by natives and tourists into the quarry. There were many artisans working hard at their trade as well as quarryman cutting and moving the heavy marble blocks. Isa approached one of the quarryman and asked, "Dove Michelangelo ha tagliato il blocco di marmo per il suo Pietà?" I later learned that this quarryman was asked this question many times every day, yet he still smiled broadly and pointed with pride to a spot far up a well-used quarry wall. "C'è dove taglio del Michelangelo il blocco" said the quarryman. Isa turned toward

Charly and I and pointed in the same direction as the quarryman. She told us "This is where Michelangelo cut the block of marble that he created into his Pieta." The Pieta is Michelangelo's famous statue of the seated Madonna holding her son's lifeless body in her arms. Michelangelo sculpted the statue in the late 15th century and it is displayed at St. Peter's Basilica in Vatican City. Charly and I just stared at the spot seemingly forever trying to imagine what it was like some 800 years ago; what Michelangelo was like; what drove him to create the Pieta—so many questions from a time that the world has not forgotten.

We walked around the perimeter of the quarry for about an hour before returning to our Italian motorcade. Isa pointed her little Fiat southward and headed toward Pisa. We thanked her for the visit to her native quarries that permitted us to see a part of ancient history. Pisa holds many ancient churches, town squares, and museums. We had not the time for these, but made a beeline for the Leaning Tower of Pisa. At the writing of this book, the Leaning Tower of Pisa is open to the public. At the time of our trip, Isa informed us that we would not be able to walkup the tower due to concerns for public safety. She noted it was closed to the public in 1990.

When we arrived in Pisa and at the Leaning Tower, one thing that Charly and I could bear witness with a great deal of certainty is that the Tower was indeed leaning. Information provided to us indicated that the *Torre Pendente Di Pisa* was constructed as a bell tower or *Campanile*. The Tower is about 185 feet in height and tourists use to be able to climb to the top of the Tower using its almost 300 steps. The Tower is circular in construction and consists of eight floors of limestone and lime mortar. The eighth floor holds its seven bells. The Tower is covered with exquisite marble on the outside. During its construction, the Tower leaned precariously first to the north, then to the south due to its faulty foundation on unstable soil. My only hope was that ongoing construction efforts would never fully correct the Tower's lean—it would certainly lose much of its architectural personality.

Before returning to Carrara, we stopped for mid-afternoon nibble at a nearby restaurant. We had pasta, of course, as well as salads and lots of bread. Then Isa asked everyone to go back to their cars for the short return trip to Carrara. It was dawned on Charly and I that today will be our last day in Italy. That reality is one of those approach-avoidance conflicts—the happiness of returning to America and the sadness of leaving the warm people of Carrara. This reality must have come upon us at once, as a quiet silence came upon us, covering us like a canopy. We all seemed deep in thought or perhaps deep in memories. We traveled this way for quite some time when we realized that Carrara was upon us and the trance was broken. Isa was first to speak: "It is good to have you with us. We seldom have the opportunity to share our life here in Carrara with other people. You've given us energy and a special pride that we seldom show to others." Charly and I acknowledged our gratefulness for the family and friendship shown to us since our arrival in Carrara. We arrived at the long driveway to the family home and gathered together on the back veranda.

The rest of the evening was spent in relaxation, drink, and food. Charly and I knew that by early morning, Isa would take us back to Pisa to board a flight that after a stop in Rome, would transport us back to America. And that is what happened after a peaceful and restful evening. We spent nearly three wonderful weeks in Italy. The experience will be unforgettable for Charly and me, and the memories will run deep. We knew this might be a once in a lifetime experience. We made the most of it and soaked up as much of another lifetime that we could. It drew me closer to my parents and certainly made me more understanding of their history and heritage. And Charly and I suspected that the romance and sensual excitement that we experienced would most likely lead to a bundle of joy, for we did not plan otherwise. If the stork did not pay us a visit by now, then surly one of us has a fertility problem. Bello Italia!

Chapter 13

You're So Far Away

Charly and I were both exhilarated and tired after our trip to Italy. It took some effort on both of our parts to settle into the daily routine of our lives back in America. If nothing else, Charly and I were quite right about one thing: she became pregnant quickly. Of course, I attributed this miraculous conception to my inherit maleness and virility, not the romance of Italy. After all, I come from a family of great swimmers! However, amidst my shouts of testosterone, Charly scoffed at the idea and reminded me that I only provided those little wiggly, squiggly things that her mother told her long ago were evil incarnated. She teasingly suggested that she did most of the work at conception and would indeed do most of the work during birth and thereafter. Charly had me cornered and I bowed to her superior reasoning. I loved Charly very much and could never think about life without her. I could hardly remember what life was like before her. We assimilated our strengths and challenges, giving our best to each other without becoming unnecessarily diverted or divided by our personal flaws and differences. Love does that between people. I think I read that somewhere.

By Charly's fourth month, the glow of Italy had faded some and I was back to work. We learned that our baby floating in the comfort and protection of amniotic fluid was a girl. We started trading names back and forth as couples often do. We thought of Carrie, Heather, Mary, Sarah, Roberta, Janet, Myra, Ann, Wendy, Marilyn, Jennifer, Kristie, Cindy, Robin, Paula, Diane, Toni, Karen, Janell, Rose, Ashley, Sharon, Hannah, Amanda, Donja, Tori Beth—all names of

151

people we knew, people we cared about, people we could honor and who would feel blessed to lend their name to our child. We also gave fleeting thought to less common names— Petra, Isa, Edwina, Daisey, Sheba, Sade, Matilda, Josephine and Lucy. You may not think that Lucy was an unusual name, but Charly was aware of my first encounter with the other... well, the uh, the older woman. She suggested that we add Lucy's name to our nonconforming suggestions to promote peace and harmony in our marriage. I was so convinced that this was such a great idea that I did not even question her dubious motivation!

In her sixth month, Charly began expressing the usual doubts about her looks, as her ongoing changes in body contour were not flattering to her. Sometimes my *insensitive* sensitivity was of no help and made matters worse without intending to do so. During the days that my Charly was with child, I did my best to rid my vocabulary of such words as huge, vast, gigantic, mammoth, chubby, colossal, fat, enormous, massive, plump, wide, portly, broad, and fleshy, even if the context was unrelated to my love. I refused to rent the video *Titanic*, ordered nothing Mexican with *El Grande* in it, and did not super size anything at fast food restaurants. I was careful to compliment what Charly wore or did not wear, as she appeared beautiful to me no matter what her condition or what she wore. And as I graciously did all this, I wondered how other husbands who found themselves in similar situations kept themselves from forthright lying! Pregnancy becomes Charly. It is at that moment that I experienced a pleasurable flashback to the first time I met Wendy Oaks.

Charly also began having those strange, wonderful cravings for food that generally appalled men who have not experienced pregnancy. Foods in and of themselves that are not repulsive, but the combinations are grossly mind-boggling. Charly particularly liked peanut butter and eggs. She also enjoyed sugar cookies topped with sardines. There were less dramatic cravings, like ketchup and eggs and pizza with mayonnaise. I often questioned silently what these cravings were doing to our yet unborn daughter for I knew exactly what the hell they were doing to me. St. Ignauseous, pray for us! Toward the middle of her sixth month, Charly began to hemorrhage. Fortunately, it was the weekend and I was at home with my love. The day started uneventfully enough for a Saturday. Charly was busy working inside the house. I was mowing the yard and preparing to do those other sundry chores that plague the weekend warrior: trimming; hedging; weeding; cleaning out the garage; etc. You know. Those tasks that men live for… rituals that provide continuity between Friday and Monday, as if we would not otherwise understand the connection or have anything else to do.

Although it was difficult to actually hear above the moan of the lawn mower, I knew something was not right. We all have experienced that *deja vu* feeling that something is not quite right even though there is no factual or observable evidence to suggest otherwise. As I throttled-down the lawnmower, I could hear distant screaming coming from the house. I quickly throttled-off the mower and ran toward our home. My heart rate soared intensely as I entered the house and yelled, "Charly, Charly, where are you?" Charly whimpered, "In here, I'm in… the bathroom." I rushed toward the back of the house and entered the bathroom. Charly was crying and frightened. The front of her shorts were coated bright red with blood and it was trickling down her legs as she stood shaking.

I put my arms around Charly and we hugged tightly. She said that the bleeding had begun just moments ago and the flow continued as we spoke. I helped Charly to the floor to lie comfortably while I phoned her obstetrician. Dr. Kelerstein instructed that Charly be driven to the hospital immediately and that she would meet us there.

Dr. Kelerstein was waiting at the hospital when we arrived. Charly was taken directly to one of the emergency rooms. The doctors and nurses managed to slow and then arrest her hemorrhaging. However, the bleeding was serious enough that her obstetrician hospitalized Charly. A number of tests were run in an attempt to isolate the cause for the bleeding. With all that marvelous technology, knowledge, and advancement in medicine, the doctors were unable to establish the etiology of her bleeding. They were able to rule out *placenta previa* and those other high-risk conditions that complicated pregnancy.

Charly was discharged a week to the day that she entered the hospital. I was happy to have her back home again and she appeared fine. At the advice of her obstetrician, Charly stopped working. I had wished I could have taken a temporary leave myself, but we needed the income and the insurance; Charly assured me that she was fine. I did ask Wendy if she would keep an eye out for my wife and check in on her once in awhile. Wendy always cheerfully did what you asked of her without question or expectation in return. Fred was the same way and they knew that they could count on Charly and me for anything they needed. I also called several times a day from work to assure myself that everything was all right. Such communication gave a false sense of security given the distance I traveled to school each day. It was difficult to be an hour away from home during this time, knowing that I could never be with Charly quickly enough if she ever needed me. This played heavily on my mind and perhaps guilt gnawed at my consciousness, constantly reminding me of our circumstances.

Then another *beginning of the end* roared into my life. Charly entered her seventh month of pregnancy. She had been discharged from the hospital only two weeks ago. It was a rainy Tuesday morning with plenty of black clouds and gray sunshine. It was not a harsh rain, but a steady pouring of water. The kind of rain you knew would be lasting all day with no hint of blue in the skies in any direction. It was 11:11 in the morning—a day and time I will remember always for its intrusion into our lives.

I received an alarming and tearful phone call at school from Wendy Oaks. She had called Charly several times earlier in the morning to see if she needed anything. Wendy was going to the grocery and usually picked-up a few things for Charly. Having received no answer on the phone, Wendy walked next door. There was no answer to her repeated ringing of the doorbell or yelling of her name, except the constant barking—well, more like whining and yelping by Disney. Yet, she noticed that Charly's car was in our garage. Wendy ran home hastily, almost stumbling to the ground as she retrieved the spare keys to our house. We exchanged keys with each other years ago in case we locked ourselves out or in case of an emergency.

Wendy trembled and had some difficulty squaring the key in the lock. She turned the lock and hesitantly opened the door. As Wendy called out Charly's name, she gasped as she drew her hand to her mouth in horror. Charly had apparently fallen either by accident or by fainting. She laid sprawled on the stairway, her maternity dress stained heavily with blood. She was unconscious and Wendy could not awaken her by name or by shaking her. Wendy immediately dialed 911 asking for emergency help, a call she later told me was much easier than the next call she had to make . . . her call to me.

I was conducting a group for elementary students of divorced parents where feelings of loss and abandonment are prominent. There are well-defined psychological tasks for such children and the readjustments required of them will often span over the years of their childhood and adolescence, and for many, into adulthood and throughout their lives.

As the group was processing resolution of their individual losses, Edna, our school secretary, gently knocked on the door and said, "Dr. Edwards?" She excused herself for the interruption and said that she had an emergency call for me from a Wendy Oaks. My heart beat rapidly to what felt like a lethal state. I could physically feel ever heartbeat. Edna volunteered to escort the students back to their classrooms. She did so though I do not recall acknowledging her request. I was quickly reaching a state of panic, shaking visibly, and my senses were becoming numb.

My hands were trembling as I picked up the receiver of the phone. I somehow managed to utter Wendy's name and she frantically explained the events that were unfolding for Charly. I told her that I would be right there. As the words echoed and faded away, I realized it would take about an hour to get home. An hour was plenty of time to think and envision the worse. Plenty of time to wonder if this morning was the last time my wife heard me tell her that I loved her. Plenty of time to realize that we may not have plenty of time. My body began to ache all over as my eyes swelled with tears. I was trembling more and my speech was hesitant and soon sounding nasal. Edna knew something was terribly wrong, as I hastily mumbled that she cancel my afternoon schedule. She offered her assistance, but I was gone before she completed speaking her kind offer, an offer that would receive no reply.

I hastily left the school parking area, possibly laying rubber for the first time in my life. I soon reached the interstate and sped down the highway. Road signs became a blur. I had little sense of exactly where I was at any given moment, but I knew I was heading in the right direction—eastward. We all have shared such experiences of arriving at our destinations, but not clearly certain as to the particulars of how we got there. We wondered whether we observed all the signal lights and signs. We wondered whether we hit anybody or anything. Yet, we were not intoxicated and somehow we made it anyway with the help of our instinctual map hidden from conscious activity.

I was not successful in fighting back tears and sped faster than the limit allowed. I did not really care although, shaking my head, I recalled cases where motorists who were pregnant were stopped and cited before they were permitted to proceed hastily and calmly to the hospital. "Please don't," I said to nobody in particular. My mind was a panorama of flashing events, past and present. Glimpses of the future attempted to creep forcibly in my consciousness. I did my best to stop such foreboding visions because they contained the possibility of life without Charly—a prospect indeed I thought would be worse than death. I was consumed with pain and utter loneliness. I did not seem able to drive fast enough. As my senses became increasingly dull, objects around me were traveling slower, as if I was consumed by a spatial time warp. I simply could not get enough speed. I could neither catch up to events that were unfolding in my life nor could I impact them. The road was going nowhere fast and carried me slowly with it.

Upon reaching the western edge of the city, my feelings intensified. I knew I was only about 25 minutes from home; yet, the path now was through the mid-section of the city, including maneuvering through busy downtown. Traffic in the center of our large city is commonly congested and often unpredictable. Delays are generally expected. I had no time for delays and planned to avoid them even if I had to drive like a raving maniac. I attempted to convince myself that Charly was sitting up in a hospital bed recovering from a minor procedure. "This is not happening... This is not happening" I told myself over and over again. This cannot be real. I was clearly becoming overwhelmed. My head was pounding and my stomach was tied in knots. I began to pray. I needed to be in the presence of God to provide some sense of peace and help control pensive feelings of helplessness and hopelessness.

Fortunately, I did not have to become a lunatic tank driver. It was the start of the noon hour and traffic was not yet heavy. I sped through city exchanging roads, passing cars, and making yellow-reddish signal lights. I maneuvered toward the last interstate leg that pointed me eastward again and would deposit me five minutes from my home. Five minutes to Wendy . . . She said she would wait for me. Wendy would drive me to one of several hospitals to which the ambulance carrying my wife had already arrived. My apprehension increased as I pondered the fate of my love.

I finally reached that end point and angled off the interstate. It seemed to take forever, but I did not have forever or time at all for that matter. My emotions were pretty well spent during the trip, but I knew they would again arise to heightened levels once I turned into our driveway. And they did. I began aching again at the sight of Wendy. My feelings were opened like Pandora's box. Neither anybody nor anything could soothe the pain or close that impudent box.

As I rolled in the driveway, Wendy was pacing on the porch, her body stiff and arms folded tightly over her chest. She held several tissues securely in her right hand. Wendy looked no better than I. Our mutual conditions reflected the deep friendship that had grown between our families over the years. She ran toward the car and quickly sat down as I opened the door. We embraced quickly and deeply, not saying any words, but expressing our feelings through silent tears. Wendy said that Charly was brought to Eastern General Hospital, about 10 minutes due north of our home. She also told me that her mother picked up Carrie and Craig, and that they would remain with their grandmother for as long as needed.

I wanted to ask Wendy many things about Charly—a lot of things I was afraid to ask. How is Charly? Did Charly regain consciousness? Did Charly say anything? Did the emergency medics say anything? What about our daughter? Did Charly hear me this morning when I told her I loved her? Did I tell her I loved her often enough. Was this all a terrible nightmare? The questions circled through my mind like a hurried windmill in a vigorous breeze, constantly spinning but not stopping to ask any question at all. Wendy knew I wanted to say something and perhaps she did too; but we both maintained an eerie silence. I wanted badly to pace, but the confines of the car did not permit such relief of tension.

We arrived at Eastern General at 12:22 p.m., another time frozen in my memory. We drove up the emergency ramp and did not worry about parking the car. Wendy and I ran into the entrance of the emergency room. It was crowded that day. Physicians and nurses were dressed in hospital white. They walked rapidly, seemingly chaotically, yet heading toward destinations known only to them. The sick and injured were lying on stretchers and sitting in wheel chairs. I did not see Charly as I rapidly scanned this very uninviting and unpleasant setting. Suddenly, your isolated crisis was now in the midst of many—all mixed in a single bowl—yours no more important than those of others. It was difficult not to be selfish in spite of your training to be empathetic. I wanted my Charly and nothing more. I cared about nobody else. Others be damned! I wanted my love. And in all that emotion I managed to muse to myself that I was certainly no Mother Teresa.

Wendy and I approached the nurses' emergency station. Everyone appeared busy and we were not greeted. I began pleading: "Excuse me? Excuse me?" However, only Wendy heard me. We implored together and a nurse working at a computer glanced upward toward us. Her nametag identified her as Cindy. Cindy's smile changed in an instant, as she quickly became aware that we were in considerable stress, trauma that she must experience over and over each day in her duties in the emergency room.

I identified myself as Gregory Edwards and told them that my wife, Charly Edwards, had been brought to the emergency room over an hour ago. Cindy excused herself and sat at the computer console, punching the keyboard with rapid strokes and then paused to retrieve the pertinent information. Cindy returned to us and told us that my wife's obstetrician, Dr. Kelerstein, was the physician in charge of Charly's case. We learned that Charly was in emergency surgery. I was uncertain as to what I had heard next. I became deaf and the silence confused me. Then I realized I heard that our unborn daughter was dead. I closed my eyes and shook my head. The news was numbing and everything was frozen for the moment. I was unsure as to what to say or do. I no longer saw or heard anything. Then I felt Wendy's arms around me, comforting me, and perhaps comforting herself.

Chapter 14

Gray Horizon

Wendy held me for what seemed like a long time although I really was not conscious of the passage of time. The words kept lingering in my mind—"I'm sorry, we could not save your daughter. A partial placenta laceration, which probably happened when your wife collapsed, forced a large amount of blood loss to your daughter." If you are wondering whether one can become attached to an unborn child, you need not. If you question whether the agonizing pain and numbness you feel can worsen, you need not. A deeper void was created, a crater with a seemingly bottomless pit. As much as I ached about my daughter, thoughts of Charly pushed to the forefront of my mind. I needed to know. I needed something on which to hang some hope. I paced and paced until I was no longer conscious of my steady walk.

Wendy and I continued to wait for word about Charly's condition. I could not help but assume the worst. The fact that our daughter died indicated that Charly had lost significant amounts of blood. Whatever was sustaining my wife was insufficient for our daughter. Foreboding thoughts quickly passed in and out of my mind as we waited. I began feeling more isolated and alone as time moved along. Here I was attempting to cope with personal tragedy and I realized that the world did not stop because of personal misfortune and heartbreak. Doctors, nurses, and orderlies all dressed in white continued their routines as my wife lay near death. No matter what happens today, they will all leave at the change of shifts to continue their lives. More and more I was being consumed by feelings of isolation, knowing that the world was not going to stop just so I could get off.

It was now approaching 2:00 p.m. The emergency surgery reports were intermittent and unbending—"Your wife's still in critical condition and we're doing the best we can." A subsequent report indicated that the physicians had stopped the bleeding. For the first time, I was given hope that my love would survive and we would be together. I have never been a stranger to prayer although routinely did not attend church. This was quite an irony given my seminarian background and will leave it to the reader to ponder the paradox.

I was praying without promises: "Lord, if you let Charly live, I'll . . ." Such promises were always superficial and one cannot imagine that they would sway God. I did pray and pondered simultaneously how one never forgets some things, like *The Lord's Prayer*. Amidst churning emotion, I recalled why we pray. How it brings us into God's presence and celebrates our relationship with Him. Why we pray: confessing to God what we think we did wrong; in praise and thanksgiving of God to show our appreciation for His blessings and provisions; in asking things for others; and in asking for things for ourselves. It is sometimes hard not to be selfish in prayer and I was indeed asking for something. We pray when we don't understand things that happen—why this person died, why that person suffers from disease, why nature reeks terrible injury and death.... What we do not understand seems endless. And when we do not think our prayers are being answered, we begin to doubt the power and value of prayer. Prayer gives us hope. Prayer gives us understanding. Prayer lessens isolation. Prayer gives us peace.

My momentary reflection and release from pain stopped in an instant. I was not aware that Wendy had called Fred earlier that afternoon. He arrived hustling as he always did as he walked. He put his hand around my shoulder and we grasped tightly. This act alone without words stimulated another stream of tears. Fred attempted to be encouraging despite that he always tended to keep his feet planted securely to the ground and dealt in realities rather than emotions. He is a kind man, stingy on sympathy, but not short on empathy. Like Wendy, Fred Oaks was there when you needed him.

It was 2:25 p.m. when I caught a glimpse of two tired-appearing gentleman approaching us. Like many others, they were dressed in white making the spattering of blood on their sleeves and shirt more ominous. As they came closer, I realized I was wrong about them. They were not tired-appearing. They were grim and solemn. I began to breathe rapidly and heavily as my pulse quickened. I closed my eyes and shook my head, saying repeatedly—"Please, no; please, no; no God, please . . ." The doctors stared intently at us but did not say a word. They did not have to. They bowed their heads and we knew Charly's fight was over. I knew, but did not believe that she was gone. Charly could not be gone because I was just with her this morning. I smiled at her this morning. I told her I loved her this morning... and she expressed her love to me. I kissed her this morning. I said "goodbye" this morning. I told Charly I could not wait to see her again. She was so alive and vibrant this morning. That was this morning some six hours ago... and now she is gone.

The weary physicians that approached us were Dr. Kelerstein and Dr. Burks. They apologized unnecessarily as they explained that the bleeding was too extensive. No matter how hard they worked, the marked loss of blood was insurmountable in attempting to revive Charly and stabilize her condition. They reported they brought her back more than once only to have her repeatedly slip away. Fortunately, I was centered between Wendy and Fred as I started feeling faint and my knees buckled.

Charly was gone. I heard their words, but the finality of them had not yet made their mark. I had to see her one more time. Although the doctors began to argue that we were not allowed in the surgical room, they stopped almost when they started. I needed to see the person who cared for me and gave me so much. Maybe she was not really dead; yet she was. I could not do this alone. Silently, Fred and Wendy walked on either side of me, as we headed toward the ER. Talented doctors and advanced technology could not give my love back to me. Her lifeless body was all that was left and belied the heroic efforts of many who spent the last moments of her life with her.

The ER was like the rest of the hospital, sterile white in appearance but deceiving. For in the middle of the room lay Charly. Cold technology pierced her body, as machines that could not sustain her life were nevertheless a part of her. They were no longer beeping or recording, adding to the eeriness of the room. The operating room floor was stained with blood and covered with discarded medical supplies. No movement occurred anywhere underscoring the finality of Charly's death.

As I approached the operating table, I began shaking and my gait became unstable. My legs were giving away and I would have been on the floor if not for the Oaks. I was so involved with myself and my own emotions that I failed to observe the pain and anguish that Fred and Wendy were experiencing. Charly was my wife, but we were all so very close celebrating friendship in all its binding sincerity.

As I reached Charly, I gently touched her face with my trembling hand and wept openly. My pain reverberated hauntingly in the ER. I bent over and embraced Charly, holding on and asking God to take me with her. In her death she had taken part of me with her. I never understood why good people who harmed no one died while contemptible

164

characters routinely roamed the earth in seemingly endless numbers. I did not want to understand. I was angry and hurting. I did not want to let her go.

Fred and Wendy began gently raising me from my embrace of Charly. I did not want to go as my tears turned to sobs. Of all things that mattered a short three hours ago, nothing mattered now. They kept tugging at me, kindly asking me to "let her go." I did not want to let Charly go. Damn it, I was not going to let her go. I expected her to regain consciousness and brighten the room with her warm smile and soft voice. Oh, how I wanted so badly to see and hear Charly again. Fred and Wendy continued to guide me away. As the door closed and Charly remained within, part of me remained with her. She was part of me, the best part, and she was rudely taken away.

Fred and Wendy walked me slowly out of the hospital. I never looked back or stopped. Fred said he would drive me home in my car. Wendy followed us in Fred's car. We did not talk during the trip home although Fred occasionally touched my shoulder in an attempt to provide comfort and reassurance. As we turned the final street corner, I saw our home through my glistening eyes. It was somewhat of a blur as I gazed at it through tears. Somehow my mind imagined Charly in the front yard tending her tulips and ferns. She turned around with her warm smile and then faded as we drove in the driveway. Charly was gone. Like a mirage, she was never there.

As we parked in the driveway, neither Fred nor I made a move to leave the car. Wendy parked in her driveway and came over to the car. Fred slowly made his way out of the car as Wendy opened the passenger door. Wendy made eye contact with her husband and suggested that I not enter my home at this time. Fred started walking me toward their home. Wendy knew that the bloodstained stairway with discarded hypodermic caps and other emergency trauma paraphernalia would be the first glimpse of my home without Charly. True to form, Wendy did not accompany us to their home. While I was grieving at their house, she was doing the best she could to clean up the disturbing evidence that was to torment me for days ahead.

Fred offered me a drink and some food, both of which I turned down. I lay on the Oaks' couch in the living room where Charly and I had spent much time. I grasped a pillow and lay in a semi-fetal position, softly crying and covered with an unrelenting stream of tears. Fred sat there and neither of us spoke. He knew I appreciated his presence and found him supportive for just being there, much as he has done in the past. Although I was not sure how much time passed, it did without notice until Wendy entered.

Clearly, Wendy too had been crying continuously. Her face was flushed and her eyes red with tears. Wendy's nasal voice trembled as she asked us if we needed anything. Over the phone, one might have asked if the individual had a cold; yet, in person, the nasal source was unmistakable. Wendy came over to me and rubbed my shoulder as I lay there to let me know that she was there. She then walked slowly over to Fred and they sat together holding each other. The stark reality that I was embracing a pillow instead of Charly made its presence cruelly known. This reality would often occur in the days ahead.

It was approaching 6:00 p.m. Typically, Charly and I would be sitting down to dinner. It was a time when we checked schedules, asked and answered questions, etc., as we prepared dinner and set the table. I glanced at Fred and Wendy. Although I felt alone, I knew I needed to be alone. I thanked my dear neighbors for their help and support. I knew that I would become more unglued if it were not for them.

It was difficult to say "goodbye" and leave the security of

their home, but I had to go home. I was tired and hurting. As I mumbled a "goodbye" and "thanks," Fred and Wendy arose and we embraced. They had done what nobody else could have done. Because of our friendship, their thoughtfulness helped ease my feelings of grief—a sense of sharing our unique and longstanding friendship. They said they would check on me later and to call if I needed anything or just wanted to talk. I left the warmth of their embrace and closed the door behind me, feeling isolated and lost.

As I walked the short distance from the Oaks' home to our home, the neighborhood appeared as it always did. The sky and its horizon were gray. Darkness was setting in earlier this evening because of the daylong cloudy and raining conditions. I reached for the front door and entered the doorway. In front of me lay the steps where Charly had fallen. Wendy did what she could to clean up the stains, but they were apparent nonetheless, even in the twilight of the evening. There was an eerie silence in our... in my home. The telephone answering machine blinked steadily, as it silently announced that six calls awaited my response. I did not bother at the moment. I went upstairs to bed and sobbed myself to sleep. My clothes, already wrinkled, remained on me. Disney lay at the foot of the bed, confused yet sensing that something was terribly wrong. The *beginning of this end* was over.

I arose with a shudder, screaming from a night terror whose contents I did not recall. Upon composing myself, I glanced at the clock. The glowing red digital screen indicated that it was 8:30 p.m. The bedroom was very dark. Out the door, I could see a hint of light that no doubt was the living room timer set to turn on at 7:00 p.m. each evening. I turned on the night light in the bedroom and slowly made my way downstairs.

I sat in the chair that Charly and I often shared, usually shrouded together in an Afghan that my sister had made for us one Christmas. The answering machine continued to flash its steady beacon. Now it had received ten calls, but I just sat there, motionless. The doorbell rang piercing the lonely silence. It was Fred and Wendy dropping by, keeping their earlier promise. They asked how things were going, a rhetorical question as they knew how things were going. They too were experiencing similar emotions. I fought back the tears for I had cried enough. Wendy asked if there was anything they could do; of course, there was not. What could anybody do in a similar situation? Words are always so inadequate at these times. There is nothing one can say that will alter past events. One can only share the warm memories, but even those were too painful to recall at the moment.

We began discussing some pragmatic necessities—funeral arrangements—to which Fred and Wendy volunteered to do whatever they could. Although the help was appreciated, several things had to be done despite one's grief that no one else could do. I had yet to call my parents to share the tragic events of the past 8 hours. Charly was an only child whose parents were killed in an automobile accident before I met her. Her best friend, Robin, would want to know. This would be difficult, as Robin had known Charly much longer than I and they shared a genuinely close friendship.

We talked for a while and then Wendy and Fred left. They reminded me to contact them if I needed anything or wanted something done. Then they were gone and the silence returned. Disney gazed at me as if he knew that something was wrong and probably wondered where was mommy. Yet, he could not express his thoughts. I knew he also must be hungry, as he had yet to be fed. I prepared Disney's food in his monogrammed dish. Afterwards, the difficult task of contacting family and friends as well as making funeral and burial arrangements was upon me.

People cope and recover differently with trauma and tragedy. I often find catharsis in writing and coping with the death of my wife and unborn child was no different. In grief and loneliness, I penned the following:

Some Measure of Comfort

Time moves on; passes with each day–
Just slipping, just fading away.
Asking for time of gone by years
Yields no reply and falls on deaf ears.

The future was once twinkling bright;
Now the stars fade like those on a cloudy night.
Begging for time, time the way it was
Becomes an obsession, and that's exactly what it does.

Hopes and dreams are no longer future things.
Memories and what could have been now bring–
Some measure of control of one's destiny,
Alas, a cruel joke with little hope of recovery.

Time is fleeting, unable to stop.
Memories grow, yet many are forgotten.
The divergence of what was and what's now
Wears wearily, tiring somehow.

Time moves on; passes with each day,
Unable to reconcile the yesterdays and todays.
The future is unknown and may bring hurt,
While time that was provides some measure of comfort.

Having exhausted my energy and emotions, at last I drifted off to a restless sleep.

Chapter 15

In the Still of the Night

The moment in time of the tragic deaths of Charly and Heather Elizabeth seemed like only yesterday. Yet, the passage of time indeed provided some measure of comfort for their loss. It was dawning on me that I might be single for the rest of my life and buried the same. There were too many years left if I lived out my natural life according to the insurance tables. Of course, my height and weight never matched the insurance tables and I've always wondered if they made a big mistake. If you reverse the weight and height tables, I'm definitely of average height and weight. Besides, I have tried everything to lose weight short of exercise and diet!

With summers free and time on my hands, I decided to pursue my interest in becoming a P.I.—a license private investigator; otherwise known as a private dick, gumshoe, peeper, sleuth, gumheel, shamus, or snooper... *The Rockford Files...* It was a position that would take much focus, much energy, much interviewing, much interrogation, much persistence, and possibly much risk. Somehow it was the 'risk' part that held my interest at the time.

Also, I just love 'detective talk...' "Me and the other dicks were staying at the local flophouse (cheap motel) where wags (vagrants) shot the works rolling rats and mice (dice) and dummerers (beggars) hung around until their big kick off (death). I was known as the croaker (doctor). We just finished jawing at the hash house (cheap restaurant) not being able to afford the local clip joints (high price bars) when we took a hack (taxi) to the clubhouse (police station) for none of us had our own heaps (cars). We were trying to get the dope on some goons (thugs) who busted out of the booby hatch (jail) and took it on the lam (escaped). We snoopers had our tickets (P.I. licenses), but did not carry buzzers (police badges) and were not necessarily favorites of flatfoots (police), unless they were highbinders (corrupt officials) with their high-priced mouthpieces (lawyers)—you know, the same mouthpieces that chased meat wagons (ambulances) and slipped you a mickey (drugged drink). The hoods were not just grifters (confidence men) and yaps (petty cheats) flimflamming 'C' notes (100 bucks), madison portraits (500 bucks), or even grands (1000 bucks). One was the best peterman (safe breaker) in the game. These guys were packing iron (carrying guns) and would drill (shoot) you before you could grab air (surrender with raised hands). Your molls (girlfriends) would have to pickup your stiffs (corpses). The mugs were pinching marbles (pearls) and ice (diamonds) from the local saps and rubes (fools), hoping to soak (pawn) the jewels when the heat's off. It would take more than a fin (5 bucks) this time to finger a stoolie (informer) in the bunch to keep them from beating the rap (charge)... and I would not give two bits (25 cents) for what I just said... boy, I just love 'detective talk.'

Anyway, I found that there are no formal education requirements to be a P.I., although there is a preference that they be college 'edumacated.' Well, college educated I was, and then some. I was not, however, from the typical pool of occupations where P.I.'s originated, such as former law enforcement officers, government agents, or military investigators. Although there were no formal education requirements, private dicks are required to be licensed. It took six months of evening and weekend training, and then passing oral and written exams before the National Association of Lawful Investigators (NALI) licensed me. Eventually, persistence made me something once again; in this case, I was now a certified legal investigator and ready to pursue my practice in criminal investigations—a.k.a. James Rockford, Joe Mannix, etc. It was my hope that I would eventually be hired by one of our town's more successful law firms where I would assist in finding witnesses, serving legal papers, preparing criminal defenses, conduct police and potential witness interviews, collecting and reviewing evidence, and testifying in court. The thought of such duties at this point in my life was invigorating to me.

I found that my background was appealing to many lawyers and law firms—not that I had any criminal investigative experiences, but that my communication, diagnostic, and court experience enhanced my fluid reasoning—sort of the ability to be able to think on one's feet. This type of reasoning seemed to balance, in their minds, my lack of actual criminal investigation experience, as critical and natural reasoning skills were not typically acquired or something that could necessarily be taught.

With some effort, I managed to achieve my first break with the law firm of Lest & Lestor, Inc. Attorneys Leslie Lest and Carry Lestor were very capable men and headed a prestigious law firm in town. They seldom advertised as their reputation and fair balance preceded them. Both were family men and had many organizational ties that benefited our community. Mr. Lest was a tall, thin, towering of a man. He dressed impeccably and his formal wear was a good fit for his reserved presentation. Lest was suited well (forgive the pun) for the organizational and business sense of the partnership. Mr. Lestor was more casual in his dress, a rather stocky man whose friendly face was warm and inviting.

Lest & Lestor started me out on some rather routine investigative casework. Although they had some confidence in my skills or they would not have hired me, they knew I was as green as grass on an early spring day. I welcomed easing into this branch career and getting my feet wet before the rest of my body followed suit! Much of my work involved securing documents in fraud and divorce cases for court testimony. It was routine work although I constantly attempted to find clues that would break my cases—clues that never existed. Yet, it was my way to spoof Sherlock Holmes less hat and pipe of course!

As the months passed, I was able to assimilate my counseling skills more and more into the undercover arena. My caseload grew in number and complexity, as my attorneys became increasingly confident in my investigative prowess and accuracy. I was pleased with my growth and accomplishments, and certainly was kept busy day, night, weekends, as well as on the eighth day. I was energized and focused, and this provided me internal stability and an emotional balance not realized this past year. Diversion may not be true growth, but I found it was working rather well.

Toward the end of my first year as a P.I., Lest and Lestor decided it was time to challenge me beyond routine casework. I remember clearly that late June morning when school was out of session. Mr. Lest called me into his impressively hallowed office. It had been raining for three days and it was unusually dreary for this time of year. There was flooding in our town. My residence and neighborhood were spared, as they were not near any creeks, rivers, or levies. The only impact for us was that the sewers were barfing much like the blowholes of whales or geysers found in Yellowstone Park.

Mr. Lest congratulated me on my performance to date and then sat quietly, seemingly in deep thought. I sat respectively waiting when Mr. Lest broke the silence that he initiated. "Greg, we have a case we would like you to tackle, but you can turn it down if you so choose." Mr. Lest paused for a moment and bowed his head before he continued, "We would like you to assume a murder investigation." I sat still and must have appeared paralyzed as Mr. Lest called, "Greg? Greg?" I managed to mumble a "Yes, sir" and welcomed the opportunity to be challenged and of greater service.

Mr. Lest stood and said, "There is one more thing, Greg. The alleged victims are very young infants and in some cases, aborted babies. A physician and nurse at Park Hospital is suspected of infanticide." Mr. Lest did not look away and scrutinized me thoroughly, as if my body language might belie my reply. Lest and Lestor knew of the tragedy of my personal past and my current contacts as a counselor with children—live children. I could understand how Mr. Lest might have concern that working such a case might trigger emotions that would compromise my investigator skills or at the very least, may spawn post-traumatic stress issues. I thought for a moment and knew that he need not be. Time had passed during which I gained new confidence, energy, and productive skills. I spoke assuredly, "Mr. Lest, I am honored that Mr. Lestor and you think so highly of me to involve me more intimately with your practice." My response brought a smile to Mr. Lest's face if not a sigh of relief that he had not misjudged me. Mr. Lest walked slowly to his desk, grabbed a number of file folders, and handed them to me saying, "These are the case files." I slowly took the folders from Mr. Lest and stood transfixed for perhaps too long as Mr. Lest said with a crumpled forehead, "Is there a problem?" I replied in a slow stutter, "No. No." Mr. Lest commented, "Don't take this personal." I nodded, left his office, and thought to myself that murder was about as personal as you could get... so much for objectivity. Well, I guess you can run, but you can't hide.

As I sat in my office and before I began opening the case files, my investigative training and experience taught me to organize my mind and procedures. I would need to establish method, motive, and opportunity. Forensics should provide information about the modus operandi and the causes of death. Hard investigation would provide information about the remaining aspects of motive and opportunity.

Investigation would also provide a complete background history of the victims. Unlike adult victims where you would investigate such background information as lifestyle, employment, marriages, divorces, reputation of the victim, drug/alcohol abuse, financial difficulties, and personality traits, the child investigation has a focus much like a welfare investigation.

I felt a little sick and nauseous, as I was about to open the file and read the detailed autopsy report—not so much from the medical examination and descriptions, but knowing that if this was my child, her lifeless body would be cut into pieces on the autopsy table. She was just a matter of parts even though the medical examiner was highly respectful, the parts were returned to her, and sutures knitted her back together to create a bastardized whole body. Neither child nor parent has a choice in a criminal investigation. Neither the child asked to be murdered nor the parent asked to suffer a loss.

Upon opening the first file, the autopsy report was front and center. I reviewed it carefully and somewhat tearfully line by line:

PATH MD: Steve Kelerstein
AUTOPSY NO: 1027B51
DEATH D/T: 2-25-1988 @ 12:22
AUTOPSY D/T: 2-25-2000 @ 1533
ID NO: 525252
COR/MEDREC# 1310-NCA
SEX: F

AGE: Unborn
NAME: Heather Elizabeth Edwards

SCREAMmmmmmmmmmmmmmmmmmmmmmmmmmmmmmm
mmmmmmmmmmm!!! NOooooooooooooooooooooooooooooooo
ooooooooooooooooo!!! I arose sharply and sat rigidly in bed.
My body was coated in a film of sweat than infiltrated what I
was wearing. I could hardly catch my breath, as taking in
oxygen did not seem to fill my lungs. For a moment—a
moment that seemed to last a lifetime, I was not oriented and
did not know the time or place in which I found myself. I was
aware that something was terribly wrong and that I was
frightened and scared to death. As the terror faded, I began
gradually to recognize my surroundings and to piece together
what had transpired. Panic and fear gave way to grief and loss,
as I became conscious that I was not a private eye, that several
years had not passed, that Charly and Heather Elizabeth died
tragically today, that I had just experienced a horrifying
nightmare, that... that this was my first night alone in our
dream house. I wept openly and after some considerable time
drifted back to sleep.

Chapter 16

Respects to the Young and Innocent

Black Thursday had ended. Charly and I had not prepared for what happened yesterday, as we were young and thought we would live forever or at least had the illusion that we would still be alive today. We talked that such distant matters could wait until the birth of our daughter. We were wrong. As an adult, this is the first time I had to cope with a death in the Edwards' family. I now must prepare for Charly and Heather Elizabeth's funeral service. I decided that their life and death would be celebrated together... that it would be impossible emotionally to separate their services... to separate my family.

Fr. Bob would commemorate the funeral service at the Catholic Church of my youth, St. Therese of the Infant Jesus. I had an appointment today with Joe Hamms of the local mortuary to complete all the necessary paperwork and select the caskets for Charly and Heather Elizabeth. Unbeknownst to me, the mortuary had a casket 'showroom' much like an automobile dealer's showcase. Joe escorted me into the showroom and explained the different features and makeup of each casket on display. I gave a half smile as I observed the price of each casket was marked clearly, although not itemized like an auto dealer sticker.

To help ease the trip through the showcase, I told Mr. Hamms that I desired a matching adult and infant casket. Again, he pointed out a myriad of features and accessories. As much as I tried to listen to what was said, my decisions were still emotionally based in nature. I chose matching caskets that I thought would be pleasing to Charly.

Mr. Hamms directed me back to his office where we

reviewed a myriad of options and completed an endless amount of paperwork. The list seemed to be endless, as I had not realized all the details, not to mention the costs, of all that was involved in planning a funeral and burial service. Visitation would occur Sunday afternoon and evening. The funeral and burial were planned for Monday morning. I was instructed to bring Charly's burial clothes and shoes to the mortuary later today. Mr. Hamms suggested a white baptismal garb for Heather Elizabeth. He asked me about the golden cross necklace that was part of her possessions from the hospital when Charly's lifeless body was delivered to the mortuary. I informed Mr. Hamms that she never spent a day without it and asked that he prepare it for her burial.

I returned home and observed Fred and Wendy working out in their yard. I saw that somebody thoughtfully mowed my yard and knew of Fred's kindness. As I parked the car, Fred and Wendy came walking toward me. We embraced and I thanked Fred for taking care of the lawn, which quite honestly like many other routine chores were missing from my list of things to do. Wendy asked about the funeral arrangements and I related the details to her. She said that they would support me during the hours of visitations, as Fred acknowledged with a nod of his head. As expected, the Oaks would be attending the funeral and burial services.

Wendy asked about Charly's burial dress and if I needed some help in choosing her resting garments. I knew Charly's favorite outfit, a long flowing aqua blue dress and matching shoes. She was never without her golden necklace with a small cross that Mr. Hamm already had in his possession. I told Wendy that the funeral director suggested a white baptismal dress for Heather Elizabeth. Without my asking, she said that she would shop for one today and bring it by later. I smiled thankfully at Wendy and told the Oaks 'goodbye,' as I entered my home to begin my life without Charly.

Disney was at the front door as always. I sat in the chair, motionless except for petting Disney, which I seemed to do for hours. He kept gazing at the empty chair where Charly often sat; unfortunately I could not share with him why she was not here—that she did not abandon us voluntarily. Although Disney appeared to enjoy the attention, he had that hungry look on his face. I slowly removed myself from the comfortable chair and headed for the kitchen with Disney in tow. His tail was wagging frantically, as he knew instinctually that his next meal was just around the corner.

I finished feeding Disney when the doorbell chimed. It was Wendy who had purchased a baptismal dress for Heather Elizabeth. In several more months, its symbolism would suggest celebrating her newborn existence in her baptism of everlasting life. Instead, it will be used to celebrate her eternal life in death. I smiled at Wendy and asked how much I owed her. She became tearful, shook her hands and head, and left quickly for her home.

I placed the baptismal dress in a clear, large plastic bag that contained Charly's funeral dress. I also gathered some pictures of Charly and I that were taken during those glorious weeks in Italy. They would be placed with both my wife and our child, as Heather Elizabeth owed her miraculous beginning to that romantic Roman holiday. I found Charly's favorite book, *To Kill A Mockingbird*, whose cover was tattered and worn in testimony of the number of times that she faithfully read and reread the story. I will place it with her, as I know that Charly would want to read it at least one more time. For Heather Elizabeth, I gathered some of the infant belongings purchased by Charly and those given to her at baby shower of several weeks ago. I took a long, hard look at Heather's sonogram picture taken recently that detailed clearly her beautiful features. I envisioned what she would look like at birth and created in my mind through *mental* age progression what a beautiful young woman she would have become. Charly will hold this picture of her daughter in her hands for the rest of her earthly stay.

I made a copy of the poem that I wrote for Charly about her favorites: angels and lighthouses...

The Angel and the Lighthouse

An Angel looks down from clouds above,
A lighthouse peers through foggy mist off the sea.
One is Divine, the other manmade with care and love;
Protecting us, keeping us safe and free.

An Angel's mission we honestly don't know.
The lighthouse reaches out to us in the dark of night.
Yet, both comfort us, protecting us from foes;
One rather mysteriously, the other a beaconed light.

When facing thunder from others—even daughters and friends,
Or storms brew from within;
When our heart aches and seems not to mend,
Or our past confuses us as to where we've been.

When life's trails lead us in, but not out;
Or we desire a lower berth and get an upper loft.
When we want to still the spinning and just shout:
"Stop this world I want to get off!"

Take heart—the Angel and the lighthouse are forever there;
We're vigilant for one—the other we solemnly beseech.
Both lighten the load that we bear,
We take our comfort, profess faith in each.

When the world and it's troubles become too much to bear,
When you just don't know which way to turn;
When you're alone and feel no one is there;
Trust in your Guardian Angel and beacons that burn.

Angels and lighthouses always were and will be;
They shield and guard you in every way.
They watch over you and your daughter you see,
Guiding your lives each moment of the day.

I tore the poem in thirds so that Charly, Heather Elizabeth and I would share one thing in common. I took the possessions with care to the car, as I told Mr. Hamms that he would have them today so that he could prepare my wife and child for the visitation on Sunday. There was little solace in this act, but at least it provided some closure, sharing, and hopefully some peace for Charly, Heather Elizabeth, and me.

It was now Sunday afternoon and almost time for the mourners to share their grief and pay their respects as tradition stipulated. The doorbell rang and by the time of the clock, I knew the Oaks were here for the ride to the mortuary. We would arrive an hour earlier than the visitation time to allow for my last private moments with my wife and daughter. I would see Charly for the last time; however, I would never see my daughter as she evolved from Charly's womb to the closed casket of her final resting place.

Wendy, Fred, and I embraced as we clenched with each

other before beginning the emotional trip. I walked with the Oaks to their car and we were on are way for the short drive to the mortuary. We said little in the car—nothing of substance, as if we were saving our emotional strength for the moments that lay ahead. Within fifteen minutes, the mortuary came into view and before I was really ready, we were really there.

We slowly moved out of the car and headed toward the main entrance of the mortuary. There was no wind, but some force seemed to push against us during the short walk. I had asked Mr. Hamms that Charly's casket remain closed until my arrival, hoping to blunt the reality of her death for a few more minutes.

Mr. Hamms greeted us at the door. He ushered us into the mortuary and asked that we follow him to the visitation room. I did not know whether I was ready for this; well, I knew I was not ready. However, there was no stopping these unfolding events for the course of death was as natural as the beginning of life. It was like having surgery where the anesthesiologist starts the flow of anesthesia, and all of a sudden you think of one more question... but it is too late and the arm holding your finger in query drops suddenly. You were committed to a course you could not change. As Mr. Hamms turned the last corner, he stood solemnly at the open door and held out his hand for us to enter.

I did as I was requested and entered a room decorated in somber mortuary motif. In the center and toward the front of the room, many flowers and wreaths surrounded two caskets. The adult casket holding my beloved wife Charly was familiar to me, but I had not yet seen the infant casket holding our daughter Heather Elizabeth. I was struck by the extreme difference in size and how miniature the infant casket appeared. I must have been standing without motion for a considerable length of time because Fred and Wendy gently grabbed my arms and guided me toward my wife and daughter. My tears that were held in check for such a long time began streaming down my face. I stopped my approach and the Oaks stood motionless with me. However, I knew that I could delay, but not stop what was about to happen. Wendy, Fred, and I continued our approach to my wife and daughter.

When I was within several feet of my family, the Oaks released me from their supportive grasp. I walked slowly to Charly and stood next to her. My tears flowed more openly now. Even though I could not see my wife, I felt her presence, as if she was reaching out toward me. I stood for a very long time experiencing many unconnected thoughts roaming through my mind. I seemed to have no influence or control over them as they streamed my consciousness. I stretched my arm slowly and rested my hand on the barrier that separated Charly and I. Again, I stood for a very long time unable to influence or control my streaming consciousness; yet, this simple act seemed to give me some solace. I kissed my fingers and held them to the head of Charly's casket before turning toward Heather Elizabeth. I stood with head bowed, as I thought of all the things that she would not experience and all the things that I would not experience with her—normal things like sitting up, crawling, her first words, her first steps, going to school, and all the family events and experiences of a lifetime. How much I had wished that Heather survived so that part of Charly would always be with me. But this was not to be.

At some point, I became conscious of others in the room. Wendy, Fred, and Mr. Hamms were standing respectfully at a distance. Grieving is sometimes a very selfish act, as it intensifies the experience of one's own loss and makes one forget how many people were touched by Charly's presence and love. I smiled weakly through my tears and beckoned for

184

Fred and Wendy to join me. They walked slowly toward me and then stopped to pay their respects. The Oaks' eyes were no dryer than mine and it was clear that they ached just as terribly.

Mr. Hamms gave us considerable time to mourn our loss before he approached us. He asked that we step in a side room while he prepared Charly for the visitation. The Oaks and I made fleeting eye contact and spoke nothing to each other. We were all lost in our own thoughts and emotions, as we tried to control and make sense out of what we were experiencing. Within fifteen minutes, Mr. Hamm interrupted us and waved for us to return to the visitation room by his outstretched hand.

What little solace I had mustered was now gone and a whoosh came over me draining my emotional strength. The Oaks and I entered the visitation room once again. From a distance, I could see that the top half of Charly's casket was now open. My flooding of tears blurred my vision of Charly. I hesitated momentarily, as I blinked my eyes to clear my vision; but this did not help much.

The Oaks stopped their approach as my trek to Charly reached its final steps. She appeared peaceful and at rest, although this belied the fact that her earthly existence had come to an end. Charly's favorite novel, *To Kill A Mockingbird*, was slipped into the sleeve of the casket to the side of her. Also there was her third of the poem, *The Angel and the Lighthouse*. I could not see, but I knew Heather Elizabeth had her third of the poem close to her. The sonogram of Heather Elizabeth was entwined tenderly between the fingers of Charly's folded hands. My tears rushed once again, as it dawned on me that Charly was never able to hold her baby until now. I stood at Charly's side for what seemed like an eternity thinking thoughts, reviewing memories, mentally listening to her voice and envisioning her warm smile, saying those fundamental prayers, and dearly, oh so dearly wishing to turn back time and altering reality. I held Charly's lifeless hands and gave her a kiss that would not be returned. I then stepped to the right near Heather Elizabeth and kissed the closed casket of our daughter.

I stood motionless and slowly composed myself before turning to Fred and Wendy. I simply nodded softly, needing to say nothing for them to begin their approach. Wendy and Fred strongly embraced me before they paid their respects to their neighbor and dear friend. Wendy could not control her tears and wept openly as she neared Charly. Fred moved aside his wife and supported her physically. I realized I would never again have such an opportunity with Charly. Wendy's tears stirred my own vacillating emotions once again much like the extreme feelings of joy and fear experienced on a roller coaster ride. Fred and Wendy touched softly Charly's hands and then placed their hands on Heather Elizabeth's casket. The visitation hour was drawing very near, as I felt my worse *beginning of the end* slipping away in my life. As marriage partners, the good and bad of Charly and I meshed in unity. Now, we were being ripped apart without mercy.

The Oaks and I headed for the chairs arranged by Mr. Hamms and sat in the front row awaiting the mourners. It was not long before they arrived to pay their respects to Wendy and Heather Elizabeth, and their condolences to me. The mourner entered the room, as I mentally sorted them into five types of mourners: close and dear friends; family and relatives; business colleagues; other family and friends that one does not see except on the days of weddings and funerals; and quite frankly some individuals who you do not know or possibly remember.

Emotions came very high as everybody expressed their grief over their loss of not only Charly, but also a baby that they never would get to know, never see. As I experienced in attending other funerals, there was a carnival-like atmosphere—perhaps not the best choice of words—but there were moments when friends shared memories that brought joy and happiness, if only for intruding periods of time.

The evening continued beyond the closing time for visitation, as a long line of well-wishers attended. Charly would have been honored to see so many people here... and she would be crying and laughing with the rest of us. It was after 9:00 pm when I said goodbye to the last mourner. I approached Charly one more time and held her lifeless hands as I gave her my final, everlasting kiss. I then stepped to the right near Heather Elizabeth and kissed the closed casket of my daughter. I turned slowly and shook the hand of Mr. Hamms thanking him for all his professional care in his preparations for my wife and daughter. At that, the Oaks and I left the mortuary and Fred drove us home. It was over... It was late... and the Monday morning funeral services would arrive quickly.

Chapter 17

The Last Farewell

I was tired and emotionally exhausted, as sleep came more readily than last evening. The night ended as quickly as it arrived absent of any conscious nightmares. The clock alarm glared its music yelling it was 7:00 am. I awoke not sensing initially the significance of the morning and what transpired last evening. However, reality quickly stuck its head in the door like an unwelcome marketer. The services for Charly and Heather Elizabeth would begin in two hours and then my family would be laid to rest.

Time moved slowly ignoring the significance of this morning. Wendy called at 8:00 a.m. to say that they would pick me up in about 15 minutes for the brief prayer service at the mortuary and then the motorcade to the church. We arrived at the mortuary at 8:30 where Mr. Hamms greeted us once again. Many of the mourners from last evening were already present and sitting solemnly in their chairs. Charly and Heather Elizabeth were both hidden from view by their steel barriers. I declined Mr. Hamms offer to open Charly's casket one more time. Seeing her lifeless body would neither ease the pain nor change of the course of her tragic death.

Mr. Hamms stepped up to the mortuary podium and motioned for us to rise. He spoke some words of support and then asked that we join him in the universal prayer of faith:

"Our Father, who art in heaven, Hallowed be thy Name.
Thy kingdom come.
Thy will be done, on earth as it is in heaven.
Give us this day our daily bread.

And forgive us our trespasses,
As we forgive those who trespass against us.
And lead us not into temptation,
But deliver us from evil.
Amen."

Mr. Hamms recited several psalms from the bible and then closed the prayer service by beseeching God to take Charly and Heather Elizabeth into his care. He then asked that the pallbearers remain while the others to return to our cars. Among family and friends, I selected six pallbearers for Charly and four pallbearers for Heather Elizabeth. The Oaks and I return to their car, which was parked directly behind the single hearse that would carry the caskets of Charly and Heather Elizabeth.

It was a short time before we saw the pallbearers exit the mortuary with my wife and daughter. We all sobbed quietly seemingly trying to cope with our separate grief. The pallbearers walked solemnly down the steps and stopped behind the jet-black hearse. Charly's casket was the first to be placed inside the hearse followed by our daughter who came to rest beside Charly. Mr. Hamms entered the hearse after everything was in place to his approval. The siren of the motorcycle policeman, which shrieked momentarily, interrupted our grief, and then the hearse drove slowly forward. Fred aligned himself with the hearse, and the mourners merged into the motorcade behind us in single file. We said nothing as the motorcade procession drove slowly to the church. The silence of the motorcade was broken only by the momentarily shrill of the motorcycle policeman, as he sped past to control traffic at approaching intersections.

We soon arrived at the church of St. Therese of the Infant Jesus. As we entered the drive that arched in front of the church, Fr. Bob stood at the top of the steps awaiting the living and the dead. Fred came to a stop and parked the car a short distance from the hearse. Wendy, Fred, and I stepped out of the car and stood silently as the pallbearers began gathering behind the hearse. The six pallbearers for Charly aligned themselves and slowly removed her body. They turned so that the head of the casket was perpendicular to the church steps. They walked slowly and stopped at the bottom of the first church step. The other four pallbearers for Heather Elizabeth slowly removed her body. They turned so that my daughter's casket was parallel to that of her mother's. The pallbearers walked slowly and stopped directly behind the body of Charly. It was impossible now to check my tears, as they flowed effortlessly.

Fr. Bob walked down the steps to bless Charly and Heather Elizabeth with holy water and prayed, "The grace of our Lord Jesus Christ and the love of God and the fellowship of the Holy Spirit be with you all. May the Father of mercies, the God of consolation, be with you." Those gathered responded, "And also with you." He sprinkled the coffins in turn and prayed, "In the waters of baptism, Charly and Heather Elizabeth died with Christ and rose with him to new life. May they now share with him eternal glory." Fr. Bob then returned to the top of the church steps. After remaining motionless for a moment, my wife and daughter were carried up the five steps of the church. Wendy and Fred held hands behind me, as I joined the procession to begin the funeral Mass.

Fr. Bob, Charly, Heather Elizabeth, Fred, Wendy, and I entered the church. Fred and Wendy covered the coffins of my wife and daughter with the funeral pall symbolizing the white baptismal garment received at baptism and our unity with Christ. Roman Catholic Canon Law professes that a child who died before Baptism may be given Christian burial if the parents intended to have the child baptized. Fr. Bob sprinkled the caskets with holy water as a reminder of baptism's redemptive waters. The mourners, who had been seated, arose for the start of the funeral procession. I knew who they were, and yet I did not for I was lost in my grief and focused only on my wife and child in front of me. Charly and Heather Elizabeth were placed head-to-head at the front of the altar next to the Easter candle that symbolized their unity with Christ and hope of resurrection. Crucifixes, as symbols of the Christian life, were placed on the caskets. Then, Fr. Bob began the funeral Mass and invited us to pray:

"Let us pray." He bowed in silent prayer and then continued, "O God, in whom sinners find mercy and the saints find joy, we pray to you for our sisters Charly and Heather Elizabeth Edwards, whose bodies we honor in Christian burial, that they may delivered from the bonds of death. Admit them to the joyful company of your saints and raise them on the last day to rejoice in your presence forever. We ask this through our Lord Jesus Christ, your Son, who lives and reigns with you and the Holy Spirit, one God, for ever and ever." The congregation responded, "Amen."

Fr. Bob prayed:

"God of all mercies, you make nothing in vain and love all that you have made. Comfort us in our grief, and console us by the knowledge of your unfailing love, through Jesus Christ our Lord. Amen."

"O God, who brought us to birth, and in whose arms we die, in our grief and shock, contain and comfort us; embrace us with your love, give us hope in our confusion and grace to let go into new life, through Jesus Christ. Amen."

"God of love, you have bound us together in life with Charly and Heather Edwards those we love and opened the door of heaven through the suffering and resurrection of Jesus;

look upon us in your mercy, give us courage to face our grief, and bring us all to the fullness of the risen life; through Jesus Christ our Lord. Amen." The funeral Mass continued as the rituals and bible readings flowed to the eulogy. Fr. Bob asked that everybody be seated. I watched him through my tears as he began his eulogy:

"I wish to express my heartfelt condolences to Greg and to all the relatives and friends of Charly. I have known Greg for a very long time dating back to our seminary days together. I have also gotten to know Charly in more recent years. It is difficult to say 'goodbye' to a loved one and most difficult to let go of a young wife and unborn child. Like Greg, I was looking forward to the birth and baptism of Heather Elizabeth and welcoming her to God's earthly world. Instead, we gather here to ask that God accept Charly and Heather Elizabeth into his care and provide them life everlasting."

Fr. Bob continued:

"It is sometimes not earthly possible to make sense out of the tragic events that brought us together today. Charly and Greg were young parents to be, full of enthusiasm about their daughter and providing her guidance to express her faith and realize her dreams. So, how do we explain how such young lives are gone, a young infant even before taking her first breath of life and seemingly protected in her mother's womb? What do we tell Greg who can no longer share life with his beloved and who will never realize the many family and fatherly experiences with his child? What do I tell all of you who have come here today to mourn the loss of a close friend and her child whom neither you nor her parents have ever seen?" My grief became more intense, as the image of Fr. Bob blurred with the tears.

Fr. Bob paused for a moment, as a tear tried to force its way from his eye. He then continued:

"We know that free will and the eventualities of life are allowed by God to exert their force and consequences, to follow the laws of cause and effect. Death and suffering are evils, contrary to the original will, against the will of God. But God does not ordinarily interfere in these casualties or with the laws of nature. Even to use the expression "an act of God" is theologically inaccurate. Destructive storms, upheavals of nature, and medical tragedies are not positively willed by God, but play their part according to the laws of nature."

Fr. Bob paused again before continuing:

"So, perhaps it is not that bad things happen to good people. Rather, it is that things happen... period. Roofs leak, fruit rots, pets die, houses burn, children are stillborn and orphaned, cars crash, spouses are widowed, and hearts just stop working. At some point, every human, regardless of how good he or she may be, will encounter one or another of those eventualities. These are not decisions made by God, but these things happen anyway."

Fr. Bob wiped his forehead and continued:

"These words may not be comforting to you, Greg, having lost not only your wife, Charly, but your daughter, Heather Elizabeth, upon whom you have never laid eyes. A few weeks ago I conducted the funeral of a gentleman who had died at the age of 89. The circumstances of his death were such as to suggest that he was 'ready to go.' His family seemed comforted by the fact that he had had a long, active, rewarding life. Although grieving and sad, they were accepting of his death and felt that there was a 'naturalness' about his death. That 'naturalness' was also helpful to me as the one conducting the service, as I could speak about his life, his character, and what he had accomplished through his many years here on earth."

Fr. Bob paused and continued once again:

"The death of a young mother and unborn child is neither part of a long life nor a 'natural' ending. I thought of some rather trite sayings that we often offer such as 'God only gives us what we can handle.' Although such statements may contain some truth, they do not truly explain such events or offer ample support to those who mourn their loss. How can a husband or a wife 'handle' the loss of a spouse? How can parents 'handle' the loss of their child? Heather Elizabeth has faced death before the time of her birth. We did not have the opportunity to witness the joy and privilege of knowing this gift that God presented to Greg and Charly. We will never see her cuddled in her mother's arms or playing with her father. We will never see Heather Elizabeth grow up." My tears flowed heavily now and I was conscious that I was not the only person expressing my grief.

Fr. Bob bowed his head and gathered spiritual strength to speak:

"There are no earthly comments that I can say to you, Greg, or to your family and friends gathered here today that can give reason for your loss and ease your grief. It is difficult enough to cope with one death, but how do we cope with the death of two young and innocent persons? Coping with their deaths you will do so over time using your emotional and spiritual strength, and the widespread support of your family and friends. Draw upon your faith and those of us gathered here when you find the road bumpy and difficult to travel. Draw upon those of us gathered here on those days when you are lonely and do not feel like reaching out, but you need to reach out, for we will be there. Draw upon your faith when your grief seems unbearable. Draw upon your faith on those days when anger consumes you. Draw upon your faith and those of us gathered here on those days when our friendship is not only needed, but also simply desired, for we will be there. And draw upon us when you want to share memories of Charly and Heather Elizabeth, for we will surely be there and readily share our memories with you."

Fr. Bob bowed his head allowing those gathered here, including me, to regain some composure, as there was not a dry eye in the church. He then asked us to arise as he continued the service by offering prayers of thanksgiving for my wife and daughter, for those who mourn, of penitence, and for readiness to live in the light of eternity. The liturgy continued with the preparation of the altar, the taking of the bread and wine, the Lord's prayer, offering the sign of peace to each other, the asking of forgiveness for our sins, and communion.

Fr. Bob bowed to the altar and with the servers of the mass who held the incense and holy water, descended the steps to come aside the coffins of my wife and daughter. He began the final commendation with an invitation to prayer:

"Trusting in God, we have prayed together for Charly and Heather Elizabeth, and now we come to the last farewell. There is sadness in parting, but we take comfort in the hope that one day we shall see them again and enjoy their friendship. Although this congregation will disperse in sorrow, the mercy of God will gather us together again in the joy of his kingdom. Therefore, let us console one another in the faith of Jesus Christ."

Fr. Bob then sprinkled with holy water and incensed the casings holding my wife and daughter. He prayed, "To you, O Lord, we commend the souls of Charly and Heather Elizabeth your servants. In the sight of this world they are now dead; in your sight may they live forever. Forgive whatever sins they committed through human weakness and in your goodness grant them everlasting peace. We ask this through Christ our Lord. Amen."

Fr. Bob continued, "In peace let us take our sisters to their place of rest." The pallbearers took their places with my wife and daughter, and followed Fr. Bob who led the procession out of the Church. All of us who gathered to mourn and celebrate their lives followed behind them. The procession was accompanied by the singing of the antiphon: "May the angels lead you into paradise; may the martyrs come to welcome you and take you both to the holy city, the new and eternal Jerusalem."

Outside the church, I held on tightly to Wendy and Fred and felt the supportive presence of Fr. Bob behind me. The pallbearers carried Charly to the hearse and then my daughter. The Oaks and I returned to the car to join the motorcade in its short trip to the cemetery. We attempted to wipe the tears from our eyes, but they were replaced by more tears.

As before, we said nothing as the motorcade procession drove slowly to the cemetery. The silence of the motorcade was broken only by the momentarily shrill of the motorcycle policeman, as he once again sped past to control traffic at the upcoming intersections. I knew that this *beginning* is *ending*. This *beginning of the end* was the most devastating in all my life.

The procession entered the cemetery and drove around the grounds until it reached the final place of committal. The final resting place was inescapable even to strangers, as the customary tent, chairs, and green tarp that covered the mound of dirt would soon cover my loved ones. The Oaks and I left the car and walked behind Charly and Heather Elizabeth to the gravesite. The pallbearers placed each coffin on their respective supports. Fr. Bob waited to say the final prayers as people gathered around us. He then began the rite of committal and invited us to pray:

"Our sisters, Charly and Heather Elizabeth, have gone to their rest in the peace of Christ. May the Lord now welcome them to the table of God's children in heaven. With faith and hope in eternal life, let us assist them with our prayers. Let us pray to the Lord also for ourselves. May we who mourn be remitted one day with our sisters; together may we meet Christ Jesus when he who is our life appears in glory."

Fr. Bob continued, "We read in sacred Scripture: Jesus Christ is the firstborn of the dead; to him be glory and power forever and ever. Amen. Lord Jesus Christ, by your own three days in the tomb, you hallowed the graves of all who believe in you and so made the grave a sign of hope that promises resurrection even as it claims our mortal bodies. Grant that Charly and Heather Elizabeth Edwards may sleep here in peace until you awaken them to glory, for you are the resurrection and the life. Then they will see you face to face and in your light will see light and know the splendor of God, for you live and reign forever and ever. Amen."

Fr. Bob paused before continuing: "In sure and certain hope of the resurrection to eternal life through our Lord Jesus Christ, we commend to Almighty God Charly and Heather Elizabeth, and we commit their bodies to the ground: earth to earth, ashes to ashes, dust to dust. The Lord bless them and keep them, the Lord make his face to shine upon them and be gracious to them. The Lord lift up his countenance upon them and give them piece."

Fr. Bob bowed his head in silent prayer. He then gazed at the mourners gathered today and said: "Dear friends, in reverence let us pray to God, the source of all mercies. Gracious Lord, forgive the sins of those who have died in Christ. Lord, in your mercy hear our prayer. With longing for the coming of God's kingdom, let us pray:

Our Father, who art in heaven, Hallowed be thy Name.
Thy kingdom come.
Thy will be done, on earth as it is in heaven.
Give us this day our daily bread.
And forgive us our trespasses,
As we forgive those who trespass against us.
And lead us not into temptation,
But deliver us from evil.
Amen."

Fr. Bob then began the concluding prayer: "God of holiness and power, accept our prayers on behalf of Charly and Heather Elizabeth Edwards; do not count their deeds against them, for in their hearts they desired to do your will. As their faith united them to your people on earth, so may your mercy join them to the angels in heaven. We ask this through Christ our Lord. Amen."

Fr. Bob then invited us to bow our heads and pray silently for God's blessing. Then he prayed over us: "Merciful Lord, you know the anguish of the sorrowful, you are attentive to the prayers of the humble. Hear your people who cry out to you in their need, and strengthen their hope in our lasting goodness. We ask this through Christ our Lord. Amen."

Fr. Bob turned toward Charly and Heather Elizabeth and prayed: "Eternal rest grant unto them, O Lord. And let perpetual light shine upon them. May they rest in peace. Amen. May their souls and the souls of all the faithful departed, through the mercy of God, rest in peace."

"May the peace of God, which is beyond all understanding, keep your hearts and minds in the knowledge and love of God and of his Son, our Lord Jesus Christ. Amen. May almighty God bless you, the Father, and the Son, and the Holy Spirit. Amen. May the love of God and the peace of the Lord Jesus bless and console us, and gently wipe every tear from our eyes: in the name of the Father, and of the Son, and of the Holy Spirit. Amen. Go in the piece of Christ. Thanks be to God."

As the service ended, Fr. Bob offered me his most sincere condolences, which I acknowledged silently through unbridled tears. As he greeted my family and friends, I walked to the caskets of my wife and daughter a final time. I picked a rose from each and said a silent prayer. I also spoke wordlessly to Charly one last time: "Honey, even though you will not be with me, I will keep you both in my daily thoughts and prayers. My memories of you and our life together will give me the strength to survive your absence in my life. I know you will take care of Heather Elizabeth until one day we meet again."

At that, I gave a final kiss to Charly and my daughter. I sat down as Fred and Wendy made their way for their final goodbyes. Other family and friends paid their final respects and then came by to share their condolences with me. As the final mourner gave me a hug, it was over. The Oaks supported me as we returned to their car and the quiet drive home.

Chapter 18

WWPM

It has been two years since the deaths of Charly and Heather Elizabeth. I had not forgotten my graveside promise to Charly and *spoke* to her daily. More recently, these *talks* provided me comfort and strength, a far cry from the sadness and despair of just two years ago.

The summer of 1991 was in full swing. The decade of the 90s pushed all of us, ready or not, into the electronic age. Most of us eagerly welcomed the excitement of the computer age; and yes, there were some of us who were crying for our slide rules and abacuses, as we were dragged into the wonderful world of processors. What is now known as the World Wide Web or WWW had its birthday in 1992. How people communicated would never be the same, at least not until the next technological revolution. By the late 1990s, over 100 million people were online whether or not they knew what to do in cyberspace. *You've got mail* was no longer restricted to the cry of letter carriers who promised that neither sleet, snow, rain, hail, or the dark of night would keep them from their appointed rounds. The Internet was not dependent on the weather. Our language changed and grew to accommodate the catch phrases of the electronic age.

At the start of the decade, part of the world was at war once again. Saddam Hussein and his Iraqi forces poured across the border into Kuwait and took control of Kuwait City. United Nation decrees were ignored and the Gulf War began in January 1991. Desert Storm would last less than two months, as the U.S. led coalition brought about an Iraqi ceasefire on February 28, 1991. There were more war years in the nineties than peaceful ones: 1993, Somalia in Africa; 1994, Haiti; 1996, Bosnia; and 1999, Yugoslavia. U.S. troops would find themselves deployed often alongside with U.N. troops in all these hotspots. If war violence was not enough, there was a new way for undercontrolled, isolated students to express how they feel in more than a dozen incidents of school shootings during the decade, which eventually showcased the passage of the Brady Bill in 1994. The Brady Bill required a five-day waiting period before purchasing a gun. In addition, television viewers got more than a distasteful experience of how our judicial system conducts itself in 1995 with the trial of the decade: O.J. Simpson was accused and acquitted of murdering his ex-wife and her male companion. Later that same year in April 1995, the Alfred Murrah Federal Building in Oklahoma City was bombed and obliterated in seconds by domestic terrorists. Peace in the decade was seldom given a chance.

Bill Clinton was president, but seemed to be spending just as much of his time defending himself against allegations of sexual misconduct as running the presidency. Much of offense was spurred on by the media, as polls of U.S. citizens showed that they were less concerned about the president's behavior than the status of our country. Clinton's wife and then first lady, Hillary Clinton, also found herself defending against Whitewater—although after 8 years of investigation and $73 million dollars of our tax money, prosecutors were unable to prove financial misconduct in her personal investments. I guess there was no better way to spend $73 million dollars.

Welfare-to-work programs gained initiative in the early nineties and the Aid to Families with Dependent Children (AFDC) Act was eliminated in 1996. The new block grant entitled Temporary Assistance to Needy Families (TANF) converted state funding to a fixed percentage. The high school graduation rate doubled from 41% of the population in 1960 to

82% in 1997. As a nation, we were becoming more educated—perhaps still lacking commonsense, but more educated nonetheless. Ritalin was the drug of choice dispensed to students diagnosed accurately or wrongfully as having Attention-Deficit/Hyperactivity Disorder, and to this day most people mistakenly believe that sugar matters—well, at least it does if you want to avoid obesity and cavities.

As for me, I was still employed by the public schools, and, as always, off for the summer vacation months. Summers without Charly were not good times for me. Charly and the Oaks could tell you that I was not very good at coping with down time. Wendy often sensed my emotions and remarked accurately, "I can tell you've got too much time on your hands..." This personality flaw was an idiosyncratic weakness during my single life before I married Charly and a overwhelming one since her death. I am sometimes more motivated by others than myself. I knew this well even though I was never able to combat it successfully; yet, I was not aware it was to be the catalyst for another *beginning of the end* in my life. But, once again, I am getting ahead of myself...

The Oaks moved that summer about 30 minutes east of our neighborhood. With Carrie and Craig growing, their two-bedroom home was no longer comfortable. I still spent considerable time with them. I also was becoming dependent on their friendship for my own emotional survival. Whether this occurred naturally, unknowingly, or with denial as an accomplice, relations were changing in my friendship with the Oaks. Their daughter, Carrie, would be in the first grade this coming school year and their son, Craig, would begin preschool. The Oaks' priorities, family lifestyle, and composition of friends were changing, but my own feelings and needs were not. Yet, I was naively unaware of these approaching transformations.

And why should I have been? That summer was a typical one, as summers go. With Fred at work and Wendy home with her children, that summer was much like the others except the Oaks had many *new* home improvement projects. I always asked Wendy if she needed help with them and she seemed happy to receive assistance. The Oaks' home improvements were being completed and my solitude was being compensated. We did many things that summer. We painted the shutters of their new home, shutters that Wendy insisted on taking down. The only thing I can say about the chore of taking down shutters is to please leave this to the professionals! We also painted their tool shed and garage door. I mowed their lawn when asked and was happy for the exercise and spent calories the exercise afforded me. I watched Carrie and Craig when asked, as we were like family. I would never let harm come their way and they reminded me of what might have been with Heather Elizabeth.

Like clockwork, Wendy always had a garage sale during the summer. Charly and I often contributed to her sales and sat the endless hours in the heat waiting for some rich individual to arrive. We fantasized that a wealthy person would utter "I'll give you five hundred dollars for everything you got." We often joked about this as the heat of the day intensified.

Like years before, summer was soon over and I would be back in the comfortable routine of school. Hindsight being what it is, I suspect the Oaks were also happy that my life had other pursuits to engage me. Being exposed to their family life, something that Charly and I were engaged in at the time of her death, enhanced desires for my own family once again. I knew that being with friends was meeting my social needs on the surface, but they were not altering my inner desire to be a husband and father. Those roles died abruptly with the death of Charly and my daughter. No matter how close I was to the

Oaks, this part of me remained unchanged. I was left to face the void of my world, circumstances supposedly healing since Charly's death three years ago—for as people say, time heals.

As the school year progressed, it became more difficult to maintain a single lifestyle. It was not only the sense of isolation and loneliness—both of which have lessened since Charly's death—but also I was 40 years old now. Yep. The big 4-0! How an individual copes with being 40 seems highly influenced by whether you are a "glass half full" or "glass half empty" individual. Unfortunately, my glass was seemingly more empty than full during this period in my life. Father Time was telling me to "bend over" and I was obliging.

Women often speak of being concerned with their "biological time clock." I was discovering men had one as well. My lifespan was probably half over. It was not the concern of remarrying—that can happen at any age. However, dreams about raising a family are another matter. One would like to envision attending their children's high school graduations without needing to be propped up by others or being too senile to comprehend or sense the emotions of the moment. Besides, people are rather offended by uncontrollable drooling and arbitrary farting!

I had not envisioned that my lifespan might soon come to an end. A day after my fortieth birthday I was sitting on my bed watching some unusually boring television. My bedroom is on the second floor of my home and my bed near the bedroom door. I heard a sudden pop and saw a small puff of smoke protruding from a small hole in the wall facing me. I thought the incident involved an electrical problem and concerned about a potential fire hazard, called Wes, an electrician who has worked on my home many times. Wes arrived within the hour and began examining the wall. After several minutes, he stopped and looked quizzically at me.

Then he walked out the bedroom seemingly following a linear path. Wes stopped at the wall outside the bedroom door and pointed at the hole in the bedroom wall. He then followed his arm to the back wall and asked me to come and take a look. Wes said with some surprise in his voice, "Greg, you don't have an electrical problem." He pointed to a small object planted in the back wall and said "See this? This is bullet. You've been shot at." He somewhat jokingly asked, "You greatly offend anybody lately?" After mentally reviewing my friends and caseload, I assured him I did not—at least not to the point of taking a bullet. I reflected on the angle and eventual position of the bullet. The angle suggested that it had to zip by my head before exiting the bedroom door. A taste of mortality flashed by as well. Wes advised that I contact the local sheriff's office to investigate the incident.

County Sheriff Stephen Austin arrived within 20 minutes of my call. He too examined the area and eventually dug out the bullet from the wall. Mr. Austin stared intensely at the fragment before speaking, "Looks like a 6 mm-284 from a long range hunting rifle." He paused and then asked, "Do you know anybody that might want to do you harm?" In essence, I said "No." I shared my profession with the sheriff, but did not suspect that my kind of public school caseload harbored a potential murderer, or at least I really wanted to believe that. I also could not think of any personal or business transactions that have soured to the extent of calling for my demise. Blind dating may be blind, but certainly not lethal. Without any leads or people of interest, Sheriff Austin concluded that given the size of the bullet, this was a stray shot from a long-range hunting rifle. The woods laid about 100 yards out my backdoor. He noted that this was not the first time that hunters have hunted carelessly. Sheriff Austin gave me the bullet fragment as a souvenir and requested that I contact him should a similar incident occurred. I reminded the sheriff that if a similar incident occurred, I might not be the one to contact him! We both laughed uncomfortably.

I had not dated at all since Charly's death and it was not until this year that I wanted to do so. For the past three years, I had spent much of the time with friends, particularly the Oaks. I was feeling more and more a part of their family although events constantly reminded me that I was not. No matter how enjoyable the experience, no matter how much I loved being with Fred and Wendy or playing with Carrie and Craig, when it was over, they stayed and I left. The pain of losing Charly obviously was causing more hurt than I realized or acknowledged. I was unaware that my hurt was also taking a toll on the Oaks, particularly Wendy. Unbeknownst to me, another *beginning of the end* was slowly and silently creeping into my life.

I continued to find strength in the Oaks, as attested by their family life and friendship. The more I was with them, the more I was envious and desired what they found in each other, and what I lost in Charly. I also knew that meeting and dating women would provide the only opportunity of realizing that goal. I had not taken such risks since Charly's death. In fact, I only took one conscious risk that I could remember in recent times—I changed the brand of my deodorant. Not much of a risk you say? My brand seemingly was being phased out, as the price of the deodorant got higher and the quantity harder to find—the old *supply and demand* inherent in capitalism I guess. I will resist mentioning brand names for obvious reasons of litigation. I am not a man of rich means. But changing my deodorant—boy that was a big mistake. I began smelling, literally, similar to somebody I did not care for. I met him while hiking at the local park and now I knew why I disliked him. I now knew why he smelled so bad over the past two years when the wind was headed in my direction—his deodorant was now my deodorant. I sure know how to pick them!

Take risks? Please! You already know how I feel about the dating arena. It was time, however, to push myself back into the incredulous and glamorous world of dating. Not to do so would mean eventual emotional death—a fate perhaps worse than death itself. I attempted meeting women at work, but a busy schedule and the distance traveled inhibited successful opportunities. As chance would have it, the local newspaper began a kind of matchmaking service. But, dating in the '90s? Sometimes you just wished life was a "do over."

For the matchmaking service, one simply placed an ad and description of whom you were seeking: men seeking women, women seeking men, men seeking men, women seeking women, anybody seeking anybody, and a column for "sports, hobbies and other interests" in case you were seeking nobody. Well, at least you could not blame the newspaper of playing favorites.

As I surveyed the greetings under "seeking women" to prepare my personal yet magnetic greeting, there were more abbreviations than one could shake a pen, some of them I did not immediately recognize while others genuinely scared me: BM, BPM, SBPM, DVM, SWM, SWPM, DWPM, GBF, GWF, WCPM, WF, WM and WWWM. If you did not get lost just trying to figure out what type of guy you thought you really were, other abbreviations to describe yourself and your desired mate amplified the confusion: N/D, N/S, SW/AF, and SW/HF.

The first fear, of course, was that I would make an error either inserting or interpreting the initials and find myself calling on a brawny, he-man of a construction worker! However, I'm not into construction. Even if I managed to correctly incorporate the initials to describe my potential date and who I was, what should I say?

I found a sampling of greetings under "seeking women" to be varied and doublewide in content. They included: "...too rich, too thin Irish Catholic Male... seeks . . ." "Challenge me! Danes and Bernards... seeks lady... who thinks lace and elevators are boring . . ." "king of the henhouse seeks cute chick to strut and lay eggs..." "Affectionate, nice-looking, warm, caring, but tough when have to be, seeks . . ." "Renaissance man coming of age seeking woman for portraits and other specialties..." "SE side Marlboro Man... seeks . . ." "still hitched guy looking for new hitching post for western fun..." "...financially secure, above-average inside and out... seeks... who considers herself above-average also, no kids . . ." "Guy with doublewide and now out of bankruptcy seeking empty nest woman with own nest egg..." and "One response is all I want as long as it's from the right Lady." The greeting that received my award for exhibiting the greatest unbridled magnetism was: "...unattractive, unfinancially secure, heavy drinker, lazy, smoker, gambler, no sense of humor, no kids or pets, seeks . . ." Gee, how do you compete with all that honesty?

Well, you don't. I could not compete with all that and decided to be straightforward. Honesty is the best something or other... even in the '90s. With that in mind, I submitted the following greeting (initials explained to curb your fantasy): *WWPM [widowed, white, professional, male], 41, no children, n/s [nonsmoker]. Seeking PF [professional female], around 30-40 with very young or no children, who is interested in a relationship that might mature into marriage. Enjoy meeting the challenges of raising a family together.* I found out later that this was the easy part and the ad was placed for a rather nominal fee. A telephone mailbox number that respondents could dial for a similar nominal fee followed the ad. I also could retrieve the eager respondents, if any, again for a nominal fee per caller. The dating world was just full of nominal fees.

A "greeting" for the mailbox had to be recorded as well. Again, before recording the greeting, one had to press the appropriate number: "press one if you are a male seeking a female, press two if you are a female seeking a male, press three if you are a male seeking a male, press four if you are a female seeking a female, and press five if you don't know who you are and what you are seeking." I prayed to God that I heard and pressed the correct number! How do you explain to somebody bigger and hairier than you that you genuinely punched the wrong number? Really! How would you? And would they even care?

The instructions to the dating service indicated that you should be "creative" and "imaginative" as you had "two full minutes" to record your greeting. The message also suggested that you should use as much of the two minutes as possible to say something about yourself and whom you were seeking. Of course, this probably had nothing to do with the fact that women (if I pressed the right number) who responded would be charged again a nominal fee of $1.49 per minute, and I would be levied the same fee for retrieving their messages. Well, love is love and business is business... and love is business.

Again, my greeting message was direct: *Hi, this is Greg. Thanks for calling. I'm one of those 41-year-old WWMs with no children. I'm looking to develop a relationship with a nonsmoking, professional female around the ages of 30-40 who has very young or no children. I like to do different things in the city as well as the quiet life. I listen well and can be quite supportive in a relationship. I'm interested in someone who, quite frankly, is seeking a relationship that will mature to marriage. I'm also interested in someone who enjoys family living and would like support in meeting the day-to-day challenges of raising a family. If you would like to share further, please leave your name and phone number and tell me something about yourself. I appreciate you calling and hope that you find your special someone.* Now, does that just not make you feel warm and fuzzy all over? Gives you goose bumps... or some kind of bumps, doesn't it?

The ad ran in the paper each weekend for three weeks. Before it was over, my greeting was changed three times as I searched for that "right" woman, as she had not yet responded to my ever so *sincere* greeting. I was trying to find somebody to enjoy a similar reciprocal relationship, as I had with Charly. Simple enough?

On the first run, I received 22 responses. To this day, I do not know whether the number of responses was due to the content of my greeting or, more than likely, because of great positioning in the paper that my first ad received; that is, the first greeting in the first column of the newspaper page. Right there on top. Talk about great positioning! Go AAAAAAAAAAAAAAAAAAA....

I thought to myself, "Great, 22 women who had similar interests and desires." Right? Wrong! I guess I can be really naive at times. I tried not to be picky. My main objective was to find someone who wanted to share her life with me and wanted to raise a family. Of course, that meant that she must be around childbearing years or have children from a previous marriage or relationship or something.

I returned calls to as many women as I could and desired to, I guess. Some I did not call because of their ages or the fact they had teenage children. As much as I wanted family life, I attempted to avoid having to develop a meaningful relationship, not bonding mind you, but a meaningful relationship with an adolescent in his or her turbulent years. I still shudder at the possibility of being a stepfather to an emerging step teen. Something I envisioned to be like *Godzilla Meets Monster Zero.*

Interestingly, most of the women who risked $1.49 per minute were educators. Many women identified their height, weight, and color of hair and eyes. I assumed that they saw that as important or they were trying to share directly what they perceived as important to men. Almost all the women left their first name and phone number. Some did not identify themselves at all and left brief messages that were neither telling nor enticing. One called to say that she did not meet my age parameters, but called to . . . Another woman left her phone number only. Still, another woman left no name, but her work phone number. She left the message that if I talked with her secretary, she would refund the cost of my initial call. Now, there was a fair-minded woman. One woman called to say that she did not believe that this was a proper way for women to meet men and men to meet women, but left me her phone number anyway—go figure.

Other responses were a bit more unique and colorful. One woman wanted to know my "sign" and if I believed "in the positioning of planets." She also said that she could "read my palm" to determine if there was a future to our relationship. Now, my palms were often sweaty and it concerned me that this would cloud her interpretation, united us forever when we were never meant to be. Another invited me to a craft party for our date and suggested that "if things did not work out," I would "not leave empty handed." Some women are so thoughtful. However, I could buy Tupperware at a variety of discount stores without the risk of blind dating.

A woman who boasted she was a follower of numerology explained that my box number 1010 indicated that my ad mailbox path was 2 (adding the 4 digits) and said the following of me: You are loving and a peacemaker, but are stuck on details, do not speak up in public situations, and are lonely. You have a need for harmony and order, and a life goal of finding the right relationship. Based on my calculations, you are probably a member of the diplomatic corps or a counselor—whew, too spooky and besides, I was never very good at doing anything by numbers, including dating.

One woman of foreign intrigue somehow saw the ad and in her native tongue said something—she sounded real nice, but I do not know what the hell she said and thought the better part of valor was to not risk losing my home and just leave her alone—she was probably part of some mail-order bride group. Then there was the mother of a woman who called for her daughter and well... Yet another woman claimed she was "abducted by aliens" and the experience somehow made her "more sexually responsive to men." In all honesty, I shamefully considered returning this call. Finally, one message was from a guy and he said... well, let's just say it was technically possible... Geesh!

The messages from respondents were one thing. The actual dating experiences were another. First of all, blind dating has to give you some of the most emotional high of highs and low of lows. These temperamental highs and lows are experienced in compressed time—the brief time spent waiting in the lobby of a restaurant or movie theater awaiting your date. You really do not know whom your date is based on the limited description shared over the phone. A myriad of women walk through the door and you just do not know which *PF* is yours. You experience the range of first impression dating emotions. Each time the door opens, you think to yourself, "Oh, please, yes" soon to be followed by "No, God, please, no." And the no's will get you every time. It was all so unnecessary. First impressions based on physical attributes are a very poor way for making lasting judgments; but it does happen and often impacts on the course of one's dating experience.

There also occurred one interesting pre-dating experience. One date was very concerned that I might not be the person I identified myself as and expressed some apprehension about her safety. However, she agreed to come with me to the home of the Oaks who would identify "me" as "me." Why my date would not think that the Oaks and I might be partners colluding in some dastardly crime escaped me. Yet, she apparently felt relieved that one stranger vouched for another stranger. She left the Oaks with me, apparently satisfied that Fred acknowledged I was who I said I was, and relieved that nobody was going to drop a house on her too! Ah, dating in the '90s.

A year went by and after numerous ads and dating experiences, this man was still seeking a woman. If nothing else, the experience taught me that there were more married people dating than single people. Such speculation was later supported by surveys that found 30% of individuals who surfed dating sites are indeed married. My undeniable conclusion: Marry first and worry about dating later!

Chapter 19

Wizard? Certainly You Jest-Sir!

I was being so successful at this blind dating thing that I decided to try my hand at starting a neighborhood card club in 1992. I was new in the neighborhood and thought it would be a good way to meet others; and who knows, my special someone just might be a card player. Probably not, but you never know. Well, probably not. I printed 100 notices about the proposed *Euchre Club* and delivered them to home after home in suburbia. To my surprise, this approach was more successful than blind dating, as the notices netted 11 people—5 couples and a single male—oh well. I needed to finish what I had started.

The next impossible step was to find an evening mutually agreeable to all. This process took several weeks of negotiating and one would think that an armistice to end a conflict was being parleyed. After considerable consultation, the first Thursday of every month was determined as the most convenient time for the club—and so it was.

The card club members were: Joe and Toni, Bob and Mary Lou, David, Jack and Marilyn, Jim and Clona, Rosella, and Joe M. and Barb. These 12 and me 13 started out playing Euchre. Yes, I know that '13' is such a lucky number. We were a loyal bunch and seldom missed attending the first Thursday of every month; however, vacations, illnesses, and unexpected job duties kept some of us some of the time from keeping our appointed game. Such unanticipated absences left me scurrying for substitutes to keep the continuum of four players per table, a traditional requirement for classic Euchre.

Within a year, we switched our play from Euchre to *Wizard*

(U.S. Games Systems, Inc. under license from the Wizard Cards International, Inc.), which had similar rules for following suit and collecting tricks. The play is competition among each other—no teams, and no need to find substitute players. The Wizard deck of 60 cards includes the standard 52 cards found in any deck, plus 4 Wizards and 4 Jesters. The Wizards and Jesters add a wildcard element to the game, as you can play these at any time negating the requirement to follow suit. A Wizard played by the first player always takes any trick. A Jester is a pass card and takes nothing except for the unfortunate player who throws out a Jester and others follow with a Jester—whoever threw out the first Jester must take the trick. Many a player has snootily declared, "Fight over it, boys" and ended up taking the trick herself. Certainly you jest-sir!

The card club helped forge new friendships and enhanced feeling of community in the neighborhood—at least around my corner. The top two scorers from each table moved to the next table to keep conversations original. The couples took turns bringing snacks and I provided the prizes for the top 5 scores and the 1 booby prize. I know the players were coming for the company and food because the prizes were valued at $2.00 or less—well, perhaps 'valued' is not the right word here. Besides, if you know anything about the card game, you know how sinfully addictive it can be.

We also had a charter and our own *Wizard of Independence*:

"In the course of human events, there is a time when it becomes necessary for 13 people to enhance the social bonds which have connected them with one another in an otherwise static neighborhood. We hold these truths to be self-evident: that not all card players are equal; that some achieve the Boobies more often than not; that they are endowed with certain alienable Rights, including Trump, Jester and the pursuit of Wizards. That to secure these Rights, a Card Club was instituted in the neighborhood, deriving its Just Powers from the consent of its members. That whenever members excel in their pursuit of the cards, they shall be rewarded with small tokens, not to mention the admiration of its members.

We, therefore, as representatives of the Wizard Club of the United States of America, the Republic of Indiana and the colony of the far eastside, in General Congress, Assembled, appealing to the Supreme Judge of the world for the rectitude of our intentions, do, in the Name, and by Authority of the 13 members of this colony, solemnly publish and declare, that this Wizard Club is, and of Right ought to receive Free food, drink and prizes; that the members are Absolved from the Allegiance to their employer for one evening each month of the Calendar Year, and that all connections between members and their employ, is and ought to be totally dissolved for the time specified each month; and that as Free and Independent Members, they have full Power to lead trump (albeit this is akin to levying War), conclude Tricks, contract with members 'to Work with Me,' establish High Score, and do all the other Acts and Things which Independent Members may of right do even though they would not do such said Acts and Things in their own homes.

And for the support of this Declaration, with a firm reliance on the protection of Divine Providence, we, as members of the Wizard Club, mutually pledge to each other our Lives, our Fortunes and our sacred Honor... or at least we pledge to get the Hell out of the Host's Home by 10:00 in the evening to avoid exciting domestic insurrections.

In order for members to pursue such Acts and Things in accordance with their Rights, including the Right to feel as stuffed as a Turkey; to Yell; to Laugh; to Scream; to Swear; to

Cuss; and to leave with Trinkets... the Wizard Club will meet on the eve of every first Thursday of the month. For fear of being thrown in the stockade or having thy heads separated by the ugliness of its members, we will take turns in serving refreshments to sooth the savage colonists."

There was no booze or liquor served, but we were a rowdy bunch with a competitive edge. Card night had its ritual and course. The game was addictive and player attendance stable, so that 'special someone' never had a chance. And our card gathering gathered for 10 years...

Chapter 20

Foreshadowing

Periods of sadness and depressed mood have plagued me since the death four years ago of Charly and my daughter Heather Elizabeth. You try not to blame yourself when something bad happens to people you love and care about, but neither guilt nor past events are so easily erased. Growing up Italian generated a complete database of guilt—real and virtual. Thoughts of what might have been are sparked into consciousness by random, seemingly innocent events and intruded to the forefront of your mind.

On the home front, I was making another concerted effort to date again in late summer 1992. I also continued to spend time with the Oaks. My mind and heart were more at peace with them than with any other experience or people in recent years. Guilt and self-blame took a holiday during these times.

My solitude drove me to file for membership in the Oaks' family and provided me a group identity. During the summer, helping with the garage sale, mowing the lawn, supervising Carrie and Craig, and participating in little home projects occupied my time with the Oaks as in the past. In return, the Oaks spent time with me, perhaps more time than they wanted and/or did with their other friends. I took great pleasure in taking the kids to the movies, and on occasion, sleepovers at my house. Spending time with Carrie and Craig helped ease my own unfulfilled role as a father.

The family life of the Oaks was changing and has been shifting for some time. Such family changes were both natural and expected. Craig would soon enter kindergarten and Carrie the second grade. Carrie also became increasingly involved in age-appropriate activities like the girl scouts, gymnastics, swimming, etc. Fred received a promotion and spent more time away from home than in the past. Wendy returned to work part-time in the evenings. The lives of Oaks became increasingly busier.

School was soon back in session and time with the Oaks was limited once again to mostly Saturday visits. These visits occurred routinely until February of 1993. It was a freezing, snowy month even by midwestern standards. Craig was beginning to recover from the measles. Wendy and Fred were doing everything possible to help Carrie catch the disease. They believed that as an adult, Carrie would have a more difficult time coping with the measles. So, Fred and Wendy encouraged their children to hug a lot, kiss a lot, share the thermometer a lot . . . anything "a lot" to ensure that Craig would give Carrie the red-spotted affliction. Initially, these tactics did not appear to work. Within several weeks, however, Carrie began showing the early signs of the measles. Mission accomplished!

I had talked with Wendy early in the week of February 22nd and had learned that Carrie had become more seriously ill than Craig. Her fever was higher than her brother's and she had significantly more spots. When I came home from work on Friday evening, the answering machine blinked its eye indicating that one message had been received. It was from Wendy. She said that things have been hectic that week and she had a terrible day. Wendy called to say that she would not be up for a visit this Saturday. I was never good at "reading between the lines" even though Fred and Wendy often assumed so. It was not a day I would forget for tragic events were unfolding for our country at the time—the first terrorist explosion of the World Trade Center in New York City on February 26, 1993.

My first thought about Wendy's phone call was that Carrie's illness had become severe and they went to their family doctor or hospital emergency room. I called the Oaks and there was no answer. As close as I was to the Oaks, I would at times become worried or upset when problems arose in their family. For me, there was no release or outlet for such anxieties. Such feelings I expected would arise from my own family experiences some day and I needed to develop coping strategies that would be helpful. In the meanwhile, I began my usual pacing as a way of coping with the unknown until I finally reached the Oaks. It was Wendy. Carrie was fine. I was not. The problem was not Carrie. I was the problem. Wendy said that she felt overwhelmed and I, in part, was weighing her down. I mumbled 'goodbye' and hung up the phone. I was left both confused and devastated.

Was this another *beginning of the end*? I was trying to recover from an earlier loss and resolve the associated blame I placed upon myself. I shuddered to think I would soon be experiencing another loss; that I may have unintentionally hurt the one I cared about the most. This time I had control over the unfolding events. Or did I? Had I already gone too far? Was I out of control? Was nine years of close friendship unraveling? These and other questions darted through my mind, but were brushed aside. I really did not want to know the answers to them, at least not right now.

When I talked to the Oaks, no specific answers were forthcoming from Fred or Wendy. The general sense was that I was spending too much time with them and their family. They perceived my unhappiness as unyielding even with the time spent with them and their children. Apparently it was my personal unhappiness that was taking its toll on the Oaks, especially Wendy. She was experiencing her own stress at the time, independent of and unknown to me. For me, I thought naively that they enjoyed the time we spent together.

The obvious upshot of this crossroads in our friendship was the spending of less time with the Oaks. I was smothering them and they wanted—no, they demanded their space. I was confused, saddened and hurt. Feelings of anger toward the Oaks gradually surfaced for the first time in our friendship as hurt and anger often coexist to share the same space in our lives. I was aware that this crossroads was brought about by my emotional presence. What I wanted and needed most at the time was now all but gone.

By the end of summer and return to school, the *inter*changes between the Oaks and I were largely unchanged. And it was this relational experience that sparked *inner*changes in me. In October 1993, I made a very reluctant decision and attempted to bring our friendship to a close. The pain of the decision was just as unbearable as the hurt in the relationship. And it was those cyclic feelings of hurt that became insufferable and drew my relationship with the Oaks to a close. No matter how much I desired to be identified as a member of the family, I was not. I was told I was not. I knew I was not. Yet, none of that mattered. Feelings of loss were once again upon me. Was this indeed the end of our friendship? Would I never see Craig and Carrie again? Not watch them grow up, as I would never watch Heather Elizabeth grow?

The hurt that I felt in my relationship with the Oaks was now replaced by a deeper hurt. I went through the house and packed away gifts—memories—given to me by the Oaks and their children. I was trying to tell myself that it was for "the best" and that part of my life was now over. I assumed... I believed... I feared that the Oaks neither wanted to see me nor cared about me, as they made no attempts to communicate with me.

I did not attempt to contact the Oaks for several months.

My hurt and anger gradually gave way to feelings of loss... and I missed them, all of them. It was two weeks before Christmas. I called the Oaks and Wendy answered the phone. Our conversation was brief. I said I was "a voice out of the past" and wanted to talk. Wendy agreed to see me and I drove hurriedly the ten minutes to their home.

Upon arrival, it was breakfast time. Wendy, Craig and Carrie were eating at the kitchen table. Fred had already left for work and I recalled that Fridays were one of his busiest workdays. Small chat occupied the time at the breakfast table. I could not say what I wanted, needed to say in front of Carrie and Craig. I wanted badly to pace to relieve the inner tension, but could not. I then asked Wendy if we could talk alone and she agreed.

The children were left at the breakfast table and we entered the family room. I both stared and looked away from Wendy, as I attempted to formulate in words what I was experiencing in emotions. I was breathing faster and my stomach ached. Dead silence permeated the family room except for the distant conversation and giggles from Craig and Carrie.

My emotions stirred and I began to cry. I tried to explain how I perceived recent events in our relationship, took blame for what I could, and apologized for my decisions. I told Wendy that I missed them and wanted very much to resolve whatever differences were keeping us apart.

Wendy did not interrupt me, as I expressed my thoughts with deliberation. Fear set in as I voiced my final thoughts. Wendy then spoke for the first time: "It did not have to be this way—that there was no reason for us not to see each other." Wendy related what I already knew about the transitional changes in her family. She noted that time was at a premium and they were busier now than ever before in their lives. Limitations would necessarily be placed on our friendship.

Wendy was true from her point of view and thus honest with me. Our differences were not fully expressed or resolved, but the exchange drew us toward each other. Unlike Charly and Heather Elizabeth, the Oaks and I would once again be a part of each other lives. The future of our friendship was uncertain and unclear, but the opportunity was provided by Wendy to restructure the balance of our friendship. And for that I was truly grateful.

Chapter 21

Friendship Takes A Holiday

Christmas 1993 was a happier time in my life. The Oaks and I may not have resolved our differences, but at least they were put aside for now. We were back together again. How good it felt to be seeing each other. How good it was to be shopping for Christmas presents for Carrie and Craig.

The school year finished quickly and the summer of 1994 was upon us. This particular summer was not so different than many others. I again spent time with the Oaks. As always, half the time was spent visiting and the other half involved in those perennial activities: helping with the garage sale, supervising Craig and Carrie, painting, mowing the yard, shopping, etc.

What was important and still missing for me were those interpersonal exchanges between the Oaks and I that had mysteriously ended without explanation. With a tendency toward self-blame, I was certain that I said or did something to offend Fred and Wendy. There was no other logical reason and the periodic asking "Why?" provided no clues.

As fast as the summer ended, the school year warped by with no out of the ordinary events. The summer of 1995 rushed in and with it arrived an early heat wave not customary until the dog days of August or cat days of September. This summer was more unsettling than in previous years. By the end of the school year, I had decided to leave my position of the past 10 years. My boss, Ronnie, whom I had known for 18 years, had retired. He was a good friend. Moreover, it was time to find something geographically closer to home. I was getting older and in my old age was becoming less enthusiastic about the long, tedious drive to the office. A drive I reminded myself that perhaps prevented me from making a difference in the lives of Charly and Heather Elizabeth.

Having made the difficult decision to leave my colleagues, I was embarking to search for a "New World." Well, at least my little corner of the "New World." Perhaps my priorities were not prioritized, but distance and time became the primary search parameters in this job quest. Living and working in the same county had glamorous appeal, but this had been elusive to this point in my career. I began the employment search by drawing a circle on the local map that represented a driving distance of no more than 30 minutes. To underscore the point, I cropped that which remained outside the circle. Résumés were flung at any school or agency remaining within the circle. No one was spared. No enemies were taken. No stone was left unturned. No...

This net flinging scientific approach to my job quest netted several second and third employment interviews. A decision was made and I was hired. My new office was about 20 minutes from home—a vast improvement over the driving of the last decade. *I'm off the road again...*

This new position afforded me fresh opportunities for not only new beginnings, but also for, do I dare say? ...for new relationships. I was the only male in the office and kind of liked the odds. This new position also brought something unexpected in my life during the second month of employment: walking pneumonia. Now, walking pneumonia is certainly a contradiction in terms. It was debilitating even for a strong, somewhat youngish man as myself. I learned first-handed why the fragile and the elderly often succumb to the condition. It was God-awful. You did not feel like walking. You did not feel like doing anything. The chills and sweats alternated unexpectedly like pervasive mood swings. You found yourself wetting anything you sat or lay on forcing you to change clothes 3-4 times a day. The malady turned you into a social outcast, as people in passing crossed their index fingers in an attempt to ward off the evil spirits that possessed me. Nobody wanted to be near you. You could even hear over the phone the hissing sound of disinfectant spray weakening the ozone layer with fluorocarbons, as they attempted to avoid your curse. You were a virus off the Internet! You were not user friendly. You were unclean.

While suffering with the illness, it was the only time that I can recall being limited physically to what I could do. Grass around the home grew steadily and did not take notice of events inside the home. My lawn had to be mowed. I was more at ease in giving help than asking for assistance— something in my upbringing I suppose. I called the Oaks and asked reluctantly for help. Wendy obliged and I was grateful. She arrived the next day and my lawn was uniformly leveled. Only the fragile mantels of the gaslight suffered ill effects of her lawn care. They disintegrated into a heap of pulverized dust with the noxious bump of the mower against the base of the lamplight. As I began replacing the mantels, Wendy asked surprisingly, "Did I do that?" My response was a smile and an affirming shake of the head. My smile diminished as I reflected that this was one of the few times that Wendy had visited my home over the past three years. What I did not know or even suspect was that it would be the last time anybody from the Oaks family entered my home.

Pneumonia, walking or not, maintains an unyielding grip on your lungs. My left lung was mostly affected making it impossible to sleep on my left side. I tossed and turned frequently and this limitation in sleep was quite annoying. There was no pain in sleeping; however, the lung creaked and gurgled like a sponge absorbing water when pressed against. It was like listening to bad plumbing. It was difficult to sleep with all that noise and eerie sensation.

Returning to work was froth with false starts. In the morning, you are sure you feel better. By mid-morning, you think you feel good. By lunch, you know you do not feel good. And before the days end, you feel awful and return home. My health improved gradually with the periodic prescription of antibiotics. However, after missing 15 days of work, I was terribly behind and undoubtedly was making a "great" first impression with my new boss. The initial forging of relationships with my new colleagues had been arrested. Life in the schools gets busy quickly—like turning on a light switch. One day, there are no students and the next day you have a caseload of 185 of them. I was the new guy on the block while my colleagues were well established at the school. They had been employed at this particular school for the past 8-10 years. We seldom saw each other due to our hectic schedules. Moreover, their families and established social ties consumed their lives away from the office.

By March, I was making headway in managing my caseload. I was beginning to see the light at the end of the proverbial tunnel or perhaps the light was just blinding me. In any case, as quickly as the school year started, it was over. And the summer of 1995 had arrived.

My friendship with the Oaks was essentially unchanged. The differences that arose less than two years ago remained unresolved. I kept my emotions in check when I could, but they were essentially raw and obvious to others when confusion or uncertainty reigned. Right or wrong, I believed the Oaks were simply tolerating me because of the number of years they had known me. I was expected to visit the Oaks if I wanted to see them, but they did not seem to want to take their time to visit me. The Oaks' garage sale would begin next week and signaled the official start of the summer of 1995 in our lives. Even though I volunteered to help, Wendy had not called to ask me to help prepare the sale as she had done over the previous eight years. I was losing my role in the Oaks family. My confusion was worse. My hurt was deeper. The beginning of the end was upon me once again.

I drove unannounced to the Oaks' home two days before the scheduled start of the sale. Wendy and a neighbor were busy taking down boxes out of the attic and setting up the tables in the garage. We said "hello" and not much else. I had so many questions to ask even though I wanted to hear none of the answers. I attempted to formulate my thoughts, prayed some for guidance, and repeatedly choked back my emotions. I did what I always had done before in the state of tension—I paced and then I paced some more. I was so scared and uncertain that I paced for several hours in the Oaks' garage. I would not have been surprised if Wendy asked me to leave, but for some reason she did not.

We were again at the crossroads of two years ago and I did not want to be there. Wendy was unsuspecting of this approaching intersection in our lives and continued unpacking and arranging. I reflected about the Oaks. I tried to understand why events unfolded as they did. I tried to accept why events occurred as they did, why things important to me in our friendship no longer seemed important to them. And I left.

That evening I was in a bottomless pit and was unable to grab onto anything of substance, anything that would pull me out. My emotions were similar to my first night without Charly with one glaring, terrible exception: Wendy and Fred embraced me and supported me that evening. They were not here tonight.

I convinced myself that I had done something wrong. With no information from the Oaks, there was no other explanation.

I could not understand why Fred and Wendy tolerated me as long as they did. I was hurting and wanted the pain to stop. Generally, when you are emotionally distraught, it is not a good time to make decisions. Like many people do, however, I did. Pain pushed me to make choices that were diabolically opposite of what I really wanted. I wanted my friendship with the Oaks to continue, to be restructured, but I did a poor job of coping with the confusion and hurt.

In the bewilderment, I chose to jump ship. A poor decision at best, but there it was. I returned to the Oaks the next morning. Wendy, Carrie and Craig were eating breakfast in the kitchen. I was hoping to find some answers or reasons as to why. Something to change the course of events that were unfolding. Something in the nine years of our friendship that would make things OK once again. But none occurred and the hopelessness was unyielding.

I tried not to say what I was thinking and choked back my emotions. I had brought Wendy a meat/fruit tray for snacking during the garage sale. I purchased the tray that morning. As in years past, I brought some items from home to be donated for the garage sale. Wendy said that I should price them and collect the money like everybody else, something she has said to me every year. I recall telling her that I was not like everybody else and added reluctantly that I would not be back. Wendy spoke that it did not have to be this way. Oh, how much I wanted to believe that, to accept that. I wanted time to turn back to nine years ago when Charly and I first met Wendy, as she cultivated her flowers that early spring day. I wanted to embrace Wendy, Craig and Carrie and ask them not to let me go. I did not want to end our friendship. Oh, God how I did not want that!

Wendy did not try to argue differently or offer other options beyond her assertion of not having to be this way. An eerie silence permeated the kitchen. I was scared and did not know what to do. I only knew that I wanted the hurt to stop. I mumbled a faint "goodbye" and asked Carrie and Craig for a final hug. I told Wendy that I would miss watching them grow up and being a part of their lives, as I had been for the past nine years. The kids and I hugged. Emotions were no longer kept in check and I hastily retreated to the car. As I backed out of the Oaks' driveway, tears streaming down my face blurred my vision. The last I saw of Carrie and Craig was shrouded in a haze. They were at their front door waving goodbye. And so it ended.

The next week was a long week. I experienced some good days, some bad days—mostly bad days. A week had past with no contact from the Oaks. Then the spare keys to my house arrived in the mail. They were wrapped in blank lined notebook paper. Although there was no letter or note, the message was unmistakably and painfully clear. The Oaks had kept my spare keys for nine years, the same keys that Wendy used to gain access to our home on the day that Charly and Heather Elizabeth died. For me, the keys were a symbol of our trust in one another. Upon losing that trust, a special friendship died.

Chapter 22

Loss and Found

We were taught in our youth that when God closes a door, He always opens a window. I am uncertain as to what God does when there are no windows. The days passed—some good days, some not so good. Some were very bad. Some days were spent visiting friends or helping them in their home projects much like with the Oaks before except less frequently. Other days were spent in utter solitude. The loss of nine years of friendship weighed heavily on my mind and crippled my coping responses.

Friendships are like any other relationship—marital, partnership or otherwise. It takes words and actions from both parties to sustain or drive apart a relationship—or to forgive. I fought not to do what occurred in 1993 when the Oaks and I separated briefly. And I did not. I did not pack away the photos, cards, pictures, gifts and drawings given to me by the Oaks. The fern plant that Wendy gave Charly and I stood on the television set, as it has for the past ten years. The family and individual photos in each room of the house marked the growth of Craig and Carrie over the past nine years. The drawings and little gifts made by the Oaks' children were particularly special to me. Like the hand-made boxes that Carrie and Craig learned to make last month. Craig gave me twin teddy bears and two pennies. Carrie traced and then knitted with red and brown yarn a Christmas reindeer. They also made animals out of clothespins and paper butterflies and airplanes. Countless drawings and thank you notes adorned the refrigerator on all sides. All cherished remembrances of what was.

It is important that one survive tragedies that storm into one's life. Indeed to do better than mere survival if one can. The alternatives to endurance are sometimes unthinkable and unspeakable. It was important to overcome this void in my life, and as always, deliverance was by friendship.

I called friends, even those that I had not seen in quite awhile, and tried to forge new friendships in an effort to schedule every waking moment of my everyday life. The difficulty was that I had few *single* friends. At my age, most of my friends were either on their first, second or third marriages with their respective children, stepchildren, and engaging responsibilities in tow. So, it was again time to forge new friendships with finding that special someone in the balance.

I knew of a young family that moved into the community about two years ago. Jon and Marie had three children: Joseph; Jacob; and Melissa—all under the age of five. Our relationship to this point can best be summarized as brief pleasantries as our paths crossed on sidewalks—literally. One Sunday morning, however, was going to be different. I mustered sufficient courage, armed with the belief that "no" can no longer hurt, and asked Marie if she would talk to her husband about having the family over for a cookout. I shared honestly that I was trying to get better acquainted with new families in the neighborhood and not to feel obligated.

Poor thing. Not only did my request for friendship force a break in Marie's brisk pace, the look of shock and horror that suddenly morphed her face took even me by surprise. You might have thought I asked her to enter into an affair. However, Marie recovered from my forwardness and her broken stride. She indicated that she would talk with her husband. I expected nothing from the interchange and received predictably no response. However, Jon managed to utter a brief "hello" the next time our walking paths crossed. For the past year, I had thought off and on about attending a singles group, which I knew was sponsored by a local Methodist church. My other untried and untrue methods of dating had been less than satisfactory over the past several years. It was time for a change and new approach. It was time to risk again. The last risk I took was changing my brand of deodorant for heaven's sake. It was a very poor choice you might recall! At this point in my life, there were no other acceptable options. My subsistence depended on recapturing what I had with Charly and would have had with Heather Elizabeth. It was something special yet natural. There was no other means of survival. It was clear to me that the roles of husband and father were necessary for sustained happiness. I wanted to be a member of a family where I did not have to leave, where my wife uttered terms of endearment once again, and where my children called me 'daddy' long before I became their 'old man.'

As often is the case, this particular singles group was an outreach ministry of a local church. It was a popular group with a very large following of single adults. The organization attempted to provide a caring atmosphere where singles could gather to grow personally and in fellowship. It was where new members were likely experiencing personal pain or loss of a relationship. I was no exception to the rule.

The thought of being in a gymnasium-sized room filled with about 300 people was exhilarating, but not in the productive, useful sense. I did not want to do this. I really did not want to do this, but I believed I needed to do this or something similar. My apprehension grew as the day of the first meeting arrived. It was a Wednesday. As most new people who attend a similar event, you leave yourself sufficient time to travel in order to compensate for the inevitable traffic delays. As always, you leave yourself too much time and you arrive early.

The leaders and organizers of the singles group know immediately that you are a new member. After all, you arrived early—too early! "Welcomes" greeted the new person as the leaders noted that new members always arrived early. For those members who may not have identified you as "new," you were given a special green nametag with your first name written in bold letters. Perhaps the color green was not chosen by happenstance—green for rookie or green to match your pale face?

You were ushered into a large auditorium. One by one, other singles arrived and the once rather expansive auditorium quickly shrunk in size. Yes, it was indeed exhilarating to be standing among some 300 strangers. As time ticked slowly ahead, you attempted to make the kind of superficial small talk typical in such situations: occupation; weather; current events; length of group attendance; present marital status and history thereof; etc.

After numerous introductions and large amounts of small talk, announcements blared over the auditorium's audio system. We were welcomed and a wide variety of programs were identified for the evening from which members could choose. For new members to the singles group, a "get acquainted" session was identified. This evening, anxious new members numbered about 30 and gathered in a pleasantly decorated room located in the church center. We sat in the inevitable circle of folding chairs facing and inadvertently sizing up each other.

A handsome and older Scottish gentleman identified himself as O'Hara. He spoke his introductory remarks in his native brogue, which was mesmerizing and pleasing to the ear. O'Hara summarized the goals and activities of the singles group. In his oration, he noted that we were likely here because we had suffered some loss or break in a relationship or friendship. Tears began to swell as I briefly thought of Charly and the Oaks.

The group leader continued his remarks sprinkled with humor and what seemed like sincere concern for our plights. O'Hara noted that the women in the group traditionally sought each other out, initially attaching themselves to each other and generally avoiding men. They slowly "dangle their toes in the water" when they feel ready to involve themselves in a male/female relationship. O'Hara addressed the men in his familiar sense of humor, beseeching them to "try and show more sensitivity than usual" and "resist your hormonal urges." He continued that we should "show some restraint" and "try not to hit on these women on their first night." The group instructor's message and humor were well received although undoubtedly for some men fell on deaf ears.

This particular singles group boasted of a wide variety of educational, recreational and athletic activities. Its schedule for the month justified their self-appraisal. A survey of the monthly schedule included the following activities and events: motivation and self-help discourses; worship and liturgical services; recreational activities such as volleyball, hiking, tennis, canoeing, baseball, and basketball; ballroom and country line dancing; card games such as euchre and bridge; music fests for all tastes—jazz, blues, popular, rock; and drop-in dinners and restaurant outings. Truly a smorgasbord of events for the choosing as friendships and perhaps something deeper are fostered through increasingly meaningful and enjoyable social contacts.

I was starved for socialization and driven by the same. I was both running toward the need for friendship and running away from loss. I participated in as many activities as time and courage would allow. I did well most days. I stumbled and mumbled through the singles social arena. It was not long before I looked forward to seeing particular individuals and truly enjoyed their company each Wednesday night.

I hiked with a group every Saturday morning at one of the local state parks. Communing with nature was good for the body and quieting for the soul. The unwritten rules for hiking in a singles group became increasingly clear with each hike. Women tended to communicate and pair with their female counterparts. The goal of most men was to break this pairing and insert themselves into the coupling. Most women enjoyed hiking with other women. Most men were not into male bonding. It became more interesting to observe the choreographed dance by men in their attempts to find that "special" someone, whether to fall in love or run the bases, than it was to actively participate in the maneuvers. There was considerable social and personal stress if your only weekly goal was to try and find that "someone" in your life. Moreover, you tended to ignore what nature's best had to offer you. It was months later before I developed the mind-set of *Que sera, sera*—whatever will be, will be. It was then and only then that I could seriously enjoy the hike and the accompanying creatures and sounds of nature.

Chapter 23

Laughing Your Way Through Singledom

Ironically, participating in the single's group kept me single through the 1990s. As an active member of the singles group, I had the opportunity to signup for support groups and courses designed to promote our knowledge and emotional and/or social growth. I tended to steer away from support groups as a rule. The intelligence of any group, after all, is usually the lowest IQ of a member of the group divided by the number of people in the group.

Fortunately, there were a wide variety of courses offered. Some of the classes included:

- Creative Suffering

- Overcoming Peace of Mind and Join the Rest of Us

- Guilt Without Sex;

- Sex Without Guilt

- The Primal Shrug

- Whine Your Way to Alienation

- Tax Shelters for the Very Indigent

- Looters Guide to America's Greatest Cities

- Needlepoint for Junkies

- Bonsai Your Pet

- How to Convert Your Vacuum to a Fully Automatic Rifle

- Cultivating Viruses in Your Refrigerator

- The Joys of Hypochondria

- Biofeedback and How to Stop It

- Tap Dance Your Way to Social Ridicule

- Optimize Your Body Functions

- Incarceration and the Social Benefits

- How to Date and Eat at the Same Time

- Dressing Right, Dressing Left—How It Can Change You

All these alluring courses made the decision a very difficult one, indeed, but not surprisingly I chose a class in standup comedy. Humor and being humorous were comical to me. I began developing a sense of the lighter side of being single. Singledom is amusing, humorous, laughable, sidesplitting, and hilarious. I already know I have been single too long. You, the reader, knows I have been single too long! There are some well known signs, and perhaps some lesser signs, that warn us that perhaps we have been single too long—for example, you know you have been single too long when...

- Your dates start attacking your personality flaws and you counter that without them, you would have no personality at all

- You start getting rejected by dates when you ask for their phone numbers and they tell you their area code is not in this country

- On dates, you fall and can't get up or you decide you'd have a better date if you don't get up

- When somebody tells you on a date that they want to "share bodily warmth," you turn up the furnace

- A visually challenged person rejects you on a blind date

- You find yourself drinking milk out of the milk carton, eating ice cream out of the box, sipping pop out the bottle, and you don't care

- You notice green stuff in your refrigerator and not only do you not mind, but it seems decorative to you especially around the holidays

- You finally decide that it will be easier to construct a new bathroom rather than try to clean it

- You start timing how long you can stand on one foot for the entertainment value it provides you

- Your dates keep getting younger and people begin to believe that you are chronologically challenged

- You hug your TV set to get that "warm all over" feeling

- You begin channel surfing your TV set and you spend less than 5 seconds per channel because your attention wanders, you don't remember what channel you've already seen, etc.

- You begin hugging your pillow at night and not only do you not mind, but it gives you pleasure to do so

- You find you can reuse your Christmas tree with the help of just a little green spray paint

- You feel you have to deceive the food service industry employee by ordering two meals so that they don't think you're alone

- The local fast food chain offers you stock in their company in appreciation of your support

- Research people in the mall start to interest you and they identify accurately your marital status as you walk by

- You no longer know who the people are in the pictures in your wallet because they came with the wallet when you bought it

- Weddings, hospital visits and funerals begin to take on the same meaning in your life

- You begin attending more funerals than weddings

- You run your dishwasher only once every leap year

- You can no longer tell the difference between dust mites, dust, and tumbling tumbleweeds

- You begin routinely violating the color separation policy in doing your laundry and pink underwear becomes appealing to you

- You have more batteries than underwear in your dresser

- The Bureau of Motor Vehicles automatically checks your participation in the organ donor program

- Hearing "party of one" at a restaurant begins to sound like great fun

- When you carry on a dinner conversation, nobody seems to be talking to you and you don't seem to mind

- Breaking wind in mixed company no longer bothers you and besides, you can no longer help it

- You remove your name from your state's *no call* list

- You really begin enjoying talking to marketing people over the phone and you won't let them hang up

- You stop cutting out grocery coupons for the food you need and began clipping them because they save you the most money

- It no longer offends you to pay more for single serving packages

- You just purchased your fifth microwave and this time you bought an adapter for your car

- They erase your name and phone number off the restroom wall of the local singles' bar

- They erect plaques at various national landmarks in honor of your record number of visits to them

- You begin storing other peoples' stuff at your house and have established catalog numbers to identify the stuff

- The personals department of the local newspaper knows your name by voice when you place a personal ad with them

- People who answer your personal ads are the same people who have replied to them for the past five consecutive years

- You become attracted to anything that moves, that has more than one leg, and that turns his, her, or its head when you cough

- When people ask you your opinion about sex education, you tell them honestly you don't remember what that is

- Those condoms you have been saving have decomposed, hardened and make good erasers

- All your friends have been married and divorced at least three times—all your other friends are dead

- You get more and more mail from various cemeteries trying to interest you in their eternal slumber guaranteeing that they will find somebody to bury you next to

- Your parish priest refuses to hear your confession anymore because you don't have anything to say that he hasn't heard before

- Your guardian angel abandons you because you don't get much action

- You stop checking the 'divorce' box on forms and begin checking the box marked 'single' once again

- You become interested in dating people you meet at family reunions

- You are too old to be a gigolo

- You finally make it to the altar to get married, but your spouse cancels the wedding because you can't remember to say 'I do'—so your spouse to be doesn't

- Your family and friends begin to question your sexual orientation

All seriousness aside, a headliner at a local comedy club in town, Mr. Woody Gepetto, taught this particular comedy course for singles. The syllabus of the course included understanding the parts of comedy, how to write comedy, and how to present standup comedy. A total of 11 students were enrolled. There were simple exercises to help you get in touch with your lighter side. For example, the course began simple enough as we were given a list of words and asked to take our best shot at being funny. I may have been shooting blanks, but I will let you decide…

Bit – Used by women in their love potions, as in a bit of this and a bit of that;
Online – A man or woman who is in ready mode and available for use;
Seat – something that we often sit on but never tires of us;
Bat – not seen as out of hell until your mother-in-law comes after you with a   Louisville slugger;
Yard Sale – like a garage sale without the oil stains;
Plate – something that democrats and republicans over charge for, and you don't even get to keep it;
Can – half a French dance;
Seek Time – The length of time required for a man an woman to find each other;
Log – a grandson excused himself from the table and told his grandfather he was going to 'logon' to which his grandfather replied, "Good, put two logs on the fire;"
Bank – a place that cheerfully lends money to people who don't need it

We found that one can even express classical humor in poetry:

Man and Woman in the 21st Century

Differences between us always were and will be,
Yet sameness is exhorted more now than ever.

Man and woman will soon enter the 21st century,
Different as can be, yet certainly no better.

Edward Galluzzi

What one has, the other wants
Although each also has what neither embraces.
Into the 21st century, sameness they will flaunt;
Even differences will have familiar faces.

So how will man and woman be chronicled?
More different or perhaps not?
The question is actually quite rhetorical,

For we began different more than not!

Of course, sometimes you just feel like singing and you want to remember your silliest things (a parody sung to the tune of "My Favorite Things" from *The Sound of Music*):

My Silliest Things

Acne on faces and hair out of noses
Bigger love handles and warts on your toes's
Black plastic garbage bags tied up with strings
These are a few of my silliest things.

Mud covered doggies and ant dotted cookies
Jason and Freddy and all things real gooky
Wild animals that bite you and bees that sting
These are a few of my silliest things.

Psychs with WISC kits and blocks crammed up their noses
Dandruff that stays on your head in osmoses
The smelly white river floods in the spring
These are a few of my silliest things.

245

When the dog bites
When the bee stings
When I'm feeling sad
I simply remember my silliest things
And then I don't feel... so bad.

Well, perhaps you feel worse now than a few moments ago. To continue, the comedy course also involved a number of simulations and role-playing among the students. This included the creative writing of your own joke and it went something like this...

-Start of Joke- Oh, I hate restaurants—I mean I really hate going to restaurants... I mean for counselors and psychologists, they should call them 'Interruptaurants.' You're sitting quietly at your table with this Fox, and not after taking two bites you hear the manager call out: "Is there a psychologist in the house? Is there a psychologist in the house? We have a jumper at table 9! A jumper table 9!"

And you think to yourself, "I can't be the only one here tonight—please say it ain't so." And you begin thinking about all the things you could have been or people wanted you to be... my Italian mother, bless her soul, wanted me to be a Don—'cause she hated the name Ed... my dad didn't give a damn what I was as long as I left the house by the age of consent—which in the traditional Italian family is age 9... my grandmother wanted me to be a psychic... my grandfather wanted me to be a psychotic... my sister, the nun, wanted me to be a priest... my pastor, the priest, wanted me to be a nun, hmm... my dates apparently wanted me to be a magician 'cause they usually disappeared—on and on, the list is endless... but no, I became a psychologist—

So, I put down my fork, and looked at Fox with my

drooping, blue Italian eyes—you know, I give her my best rugged, romantic Steve McQueen look that everything was going to be alright—that I was in control of the situation... and just as if Fox actually spoke to me, what I didn't hear was "Yah, right!" But this doesn't sway me—as I leave, I turn around to give her my best apologetic line, and she was already talking on her cell phone! I can tell I've overly impressed Fox.

Undauntedly, I blazed my trail to table 9. And typically, it wouldn't be difficult to find table 9 'cause there have been so many of these jumpers lately that the manager conveniently numbered each table. Of course, not being the college graduate and also being slightly dyslexic, the tables weren't numbered in order and you couldn't tell if a 6 was a 9... so I randomly waded through the sea of people and crabs looking for table 9. I got to table 6, and there was this man standing on top of the table with a fork in one hand and a potato in another... I figured this must be him as it was unlikely to have two jumpers in the same restaurant in the same night—especially without a full moon!

As I approached the table, the gentleman seemed like a man I could negotiate with—he seemed as normal as I was... But when I took one more step, he yelled out, "Stay away from me or I'll jump." And for effect, he threw the potato down to the floor where it mashed nicely. He yelled again, "Stay away!"

Then the man reached down briefly and grabbed another potato. So here he was again in the familiar stance, fork in his left hand and potato in his right hand. In my most matter-of-fact, Bob Newhart monotone deadpan voice, I said, "You seem upset." I was doing that psychologist thing of checking for validation of this guy's feelings. Immediately, the fork passed by my left ear, I think dumping a piece of corn in my ear as it flew by, and then I heard the fat lady at the next table sing as the fork stabbed her in the lower left quadrant of her *gluteus maximus*!

Then the man reached down briefly and grabbed another fork. Having validated that the man was indeed upset, I tried to reason with him. I said, "Look, there's no sense in jumping here—you're only 3 feet off the floor and at best you'll just break something and make people nauseous. Now is that what you want? An anorexic party perhaps? Feeling quite clever that I had drawn upon the appropriate analogy and references, I reached toward the man. He screamed at the top of his lungs, "Stay away from me or I'll jump" and hopped several times on the table smashing the ketchup bottle and oozing what appeared like blood onto the table and floor.

Undaunted, I took several French fries from his plate and coated them in the oozing ketchup. As I was munching the small fry, I looked up at the big one and asked, "Why do you want to jump?" The man glanced slowly at the potato and said, "Spud told me to." And I thought, Oh, my God! He's already identified with the potato! Now I knew I really had my work cut out for me. What was to be a simple negotiation and a quick return to Fox would soon be bogged down in a quagmire of psychological gumbo.

I had to think quickly and clearly... what would Freud do at this very moment... I shook my head trying to clear it—that was too easy and not very helpful... Freud was only interested in sex and he'd still be eating his meal with my Fox! Drawing on my own professional experiences, I offered to pay for his meal if he would just sit down and quietly finish eating. This guy just started having a big catharsis, wallowing in his tears as if he, the fork, and Spud have been best buds for years!

I reached up slowly offering the man my hand to help him down off the peak of disaster. He gave me the fork, which I placed gingerly on the table. He then handed me the potato as

he climbed down off the table and took his seat as if nothing unusual had occurred this evening. I was about to give him back the potato when Spud turned to me and said, "If you keep him from eating me, I'll testify for you at his commitment hearing!" Although the offer was a temping one, I quickly dumped Spud back on the table. I made my way back to Fox only to find out she was right—I shoulda been a magician!
-End of Joke-

Toward the end of the class, Mr.Gepetto provided the students the opportunity to write their own material and present their act on stage—strictly on a voluntary basis of course. I was one of two students who took the risk, as there was a shortage of tar and feathers in our town. Perchance laughter is indeed the best medicine. I have long known that part of challenging yourself was making a fool of yourself. So I wrote the material and practiced it over and over. I read it, taped it, and dreamt it. I even imagined the parts where people would laugh.

I thought I was prepared, but come 'opening night' my anxiety level rocketed to heretofore-unforeseen heights. I half-stood, as if taking flight was an inspiration whose time was about to come. I was shaking and positive I was going to leave, but for some reason I did not. I thought I had a natural penchant for comedy, but I literally could not remember a single joke that I had written, not even one… not one! It was unquestionably an act of desperation rather than proclivity that in the darkened auditorium I began writing by candle light simple acronyms and any other pneumonic codes to recall what my anxiety-ridden brain could not muster. I took this cryptic note with me as Mr. Gepetto introduced me. There was a respectful warm round of applause from the audience even though they ain't heard nothin' yet.

I walked on center stage, grabbed the microphone hoping (a) that I did not drop it, (b) that I did not drop it where it would noticeably hurt, and (c) that I spoke into the end that could be heard. I spoke confidently taking comfort that I indeed was using the right end of the microphone. I knew that because I heard my voice permeate and resonate throughout the room. Some mild laughter echoed from the audience, which was all the encouragement I needed. Louder laughter followed, and even though I glanced occasionally at my cryptic notes, I remembered my lines. The only other presenter made a tape of my routine for prosperity or perhaps paucity. And here from the corner of nowhere in particular is the transcript of the comedy routine:

MC: "We had an intensive and interesting class for six weeks. And tonight, we have a couple of people who didn't have to do this, but this will be their first time on stage. So we ask that you not leave and applaud even though you may not feel the urge. And first, I would like you to welcome Gregory Edwards..." There was modest applause, as the audience was obviously holding their judgment in reserve.

"Good evening. You know, if this were a real comedy club you would all be laughing your heads off right now because you'd be half-wasted... Like you, I'm single. And I think I've been single for much too long. I know this because I use to dream about women. Then I began dreaming about women eating food. I didn't think that was too bad, as I got the best of both worlds. But now, I just dream about food!"

"For those of you who haven't guessed, I'm Italian. We Italian men tend to be excessive in what we do. When we're dating, we send lots of flowers; we hug and kiss a lot; we pinch a lot... we pinch a lot... we really do pinch a lot. And we're pretty excessive when we end a relationship too because you're likely to wake up with a horse's head in your bed . . . or even worse, my cousin Guido!"

"We don't even treat our dead with respect. Italians bury their dead with their butts sticking up out of the ground. That way when you visit the grave, you have some place to park your bikes!"

"As an Italian growing-up in America, we pretty much lived by the same rules and sayings that guided other families—we just said them a little bit differently. When the American parents tried to teach their children to always be prepared, they said, 'Don't get caught with your pants down.' My parents taught me the same thing except they said, 'No canna live in Venice with no gondola!' And when American parents told their children to 'always wear clean underwear in case of an accident and you have to go to the hospital,' my parents taught us the same thing except they said, 'No canna live in Venice with no gondola!' And when American parents told their children to 'always look before they leap,' my parents said... EVERYBODY... 'No canna live in Venice with no gondola!'"

"Like most Italians, I grew up in a Catholic family. We have many beliefs and one of them is that our guardian angel is always with us. In fact, in elementary school, the good nuns always reminded us to sit far to the left and leave room for our guardian angel that always sat on our right side. You knew this was true each time you looked in any classroom. What you saw was that the more spatially challenged Catholic students were tumbling to the floor, as they misjudged how much space was sufficient for the average guardian angel and found themselves seated on the floor at the left side of their desks!"

"Although we were Catholic, my father often tuned into one of the TV evangelists of the time. He ended each service the same way, by asking viewers—like us—to touch the TV screen as he prayed for us. Now, my father always insisted that we do this. There was our entire family, all of us, every Sunday morning at 9:27 a.m. touching the TV screen with out hands. We not only got free radiation treatments, but there was our entire family running the risk of being incinerated in an instant by a well-timed electrical storm."

"I love my parents, but talk about neurosis on parade! Stress around them is quite relative. Over the years, I've developed this three-night visiting rule. I can't visit for more than three consecutive nights. If I do, I run out of patience; I run out of energy; and I run out of Imodium—I just run out all over the place!"

"I have fond memories of my brother too. Once he agreed to teach me how to drive a clutch. This was unusually characteristic of my brother and I'm not sure what possessed him to not only allow me near his '69 Ford convertible, but he actually let me inside in the driver's seat! I don't think you get the picture. My butt was actually touching the seat! Well, to continue, my brother went into great detail on how to use the clutch and I did what he told me—I thought. The gears screeched and screamed—for mercy I guess. The car traveled about two feet, in reverse if memory recalls, and my brother calmly turned toward me and yelled, GET OUT!"

"You know, I started off in the Catholic seminary—thought I wanted to be a priest for a number of years... and here I find myself in a single's group anyway. Had I only known I was going to live a celibate life, I think I would have stayed in the priesthood!"

"Seminarians or not, we were typical teenagers. I remember once we were attending a Good Friday service at the local convent. For those of you who do not know what a convent is, it is NOT a criminal blowing off steam... you pagans!

Within this cloister of nuns, the good sisters took the vow of silence. Imagine any woman taking the vow of silence!" The nuns did not interact with the outside world. They were not on line; there was no Internet. The convent used this rotating wooden tube as a conveyance for material. A simple pull of the rope rang a bell signaling that the material was ready. My friend and I argued whether or not he could fit inside the tube. After much serious debate between the two of us, he decided to take the direct approach and jumped right into the cylindrical transporter. As my friend crouched in the tube to prove he could fit, I impulsively pulled the rope. I don't know; it just seemed like a good idea at the time."

"The bell rang and the cylinder began rotating. My friend, who was about to pick up some bad habits, disappeared into the swallowing jowls of the convent. And he was gone in an instant. I imagined, like in a bad science fiction episode where the transporters went amuck, he would return as a melted molten mess of massive mucous membranes! I began firing off 'Our Father's and 'Hail Mary's like it was my last anointing and Satan was right on my tail. Then, in desperation, the only thing I could think of saying was, 'Beam him back, Scotty!'"

"After several long minutes, the tube rotated back slowly. My friend gradually appeared, his atoms arranged seemingly in all the right places, and nothing looked obviously wrong. I asked him, "What happened? What did you see?" Even though he was in a trance-like state, he managed to mutter, "No canna live in Venice with no Gondola! Thank you all for coming tonight. Thank you very much."

The audience applauded. The lights were turned off. The camera stopped. The stage curtain closed... exit, stage right...

Chapter 24

Internet Dating – The Final Frontier?

The continuum of time crept forward to welcome in a new century and along with the passage of time, my singledom also persisted unabated in the year 2000. Born in one century, living in another. Woo-hoo! My quest to find that special someone—well, that OK someone now, forged ahead as well in the arena of the wonderful world of dating. Spanning the globe searching for the constant variety of women... the thrill of dating... the agony of breakups... the human drama of dating competition... this is ABC's *Wide World of Sports*... oops, sorry—got caught up in the moment.

As my singleness continued, the world was ushering in the third millennium of the 21st century, more or less. It was leap year and we celebrated the millennium along with the rest of the world, although the Gregorian calendar would not usher in the third millennium until the year 2001. Why you might ask? The first century began with the year '1,' as there was no year zero '0.' Makes sense to me. Why would you want a year zero? You already knew that nothing happened in the year zero!

With all the hoopla and fears of Y2K, it passes without the hyped malfunctions and computer failures. However, Microsoft is ruled to have violated U.S. antitrust laws by keeping, in the court's language, "an oppressive thumb" on its competitors. The largest corporate merger at that time occurred when American Online announced its purchase of Time Warner for $162 billion dollars. Retail giant Montgomery Ward announced it was going out of business after 128 years of service. Super Bowl 34 kicked off in Atlanta at the Georgia Dome. The state of Vermont kicked traditional marriage in the butt by legalizing civil unions for same-sex couples. The New Jersey Devils defeated the Dallas Stars to win the Stanley Cup. France defeated Italy to win the European Football final. The 2000 summer Olympics opened in Sydney, Australia.

There were a number of births in 2000 swelling the U.S. population to more than 280 million people. To balance out the birthrate, famous people who died in the year 2000 included the following: Julius Epstein (screen writer for Casablanca); Victor Borge (piano comic); Werner Klemperer (best know for his role of Colonel Klink on Hogan's Heroes); Gail Fisher (best known for her role on the detective series Mannix); Steve Allen (the original host of the Tonight Show); Ben Wicks (political cartoonist); Loretta Young (actress); Sir Alex Guinness (actor); Walter Matthau (actor); Maurice Richard (hockey superstar known as the 'Rocker'); Douglas Fairbanks, Jr. (actor); Larry Linville (actor played Major Burns on M*A*S*H); Alex Comfort (author, Joy of Sex); Durwood Kirby (of Candid Camera fame); Doug Henning (magician); Hedy Lamarr (movie star), and Charles Schultz (creator of comic strip Peanuts). France's supersonic passenger jet, the Concorde, crashed on takeoff in Paris killing all those aboard.

The year 2000 was a presidential election year: George W. Bush versus Vice President Al Gore. No clear winner was declared and after one month of the November election, the Supreme Court ruled against a mandatory recount of ballots in some Florida counties. Amidst controversy, Bush was declared the victor having won a slim majority in the Electoral College, but not a majority of the popular vote. Vladimir Putin was elected president of Russia. William Clinton was the first seated U.S. president to visit Vietnam and his wife, Hilary Rodham Clinton, was elected to the United States Senate.

Mount Etna erupted.

Iraq rejected the U.N. Security Council proposal for weapons inspections, but that probably would not lead to anything significant.

In my corner of the world, my friends and colleagues demonstrated unique sympathy by reminding me of my singledom at our employee Christmas party in December 2000. They presented me a miniature doll, a miniature limousine, and a gift card to a local department store. The accompanying note read… "You say you're looking for a good woman. Well this doll is the perfect woman. She cooks, she cleans, she already owns her own house separate from yours, and she has her own sports car. She'll dress up in an evening gown then put on an apron. She'll put on a small bikini with high heels and change her hair color also. She does all this and looks good too. So take her for a ride in a your new limo. You can even take her to the store for a new washer & dryer or buy yourself a good flick. Merry Christmas." I guess it would have been too much to ask for them to just dig up a blind date!

The radio and newspaper personals had their shot at me—literally. Yet I was still single. After their second, third, fourth or fifth marriages, women were either tired of men, switch their sexual orientation, switched their sex, or switched on their toys. Like the decline of smoking and cigarette advertising, women no longer had that "I'd rather fight than switch" attitude. Switching apparently was pretty good.

In January of 2000, I gave the recent birth of Internet dating a chance to amend my unbendable life. The important thing about Internet dating is to follow the basic rules to protect you and those like you. The rules were not rocket science, more of common sense—something that many single persons lack by the way. If you cannot use your head, use your intuition. That's why the rules were developed—for the good of the single.

Of course, as a homosapien male, being pursued by a stocking female was not going to occur. There are indeed weird women in the world and they are increasing, but percentage-wise they are still fewer weird women than weird men; quite a bit fewer actually. In fact, trying to get a female to be persistent was the usual problem. All the Internet dating services recommended that you upload a flattering photo of yourself, and by doing so individuals are said to be 90% plus more likely to review your profile. Using the unscientific method, I did find this to be true by creating the same profile with and without a photo. Indeed, 94% of respondents reviewed my profile with a photo compared to 32% when no photo was included. However, of the 94% who checked out my profile with a photo, 93.5% did not attempt to communicate with me. Of the 32% who checked out my profile without a photo, 31% did communicate with me. Of the 31%, 5% of the respondents were male. When asked for a photo to be sent to them by email, 26% of the 31% ended their contacts. The 5% of the males continued their contacts. So, no matter how I approached this Internet dating thing, I concluded that only 1% of the women cared to have anything to do with me, and my odds would improve to 5% if I changed my orientation.

Well, I stuck with the 1% or whatever fraction of 1% I could attract. Internet dating taught me a number of things. I learned that there are many beautiful women, inside and out, that live beyond my little corner of the world. I learned about photo carbon dating that emerged as a science, as some individuals uploaded photos that were, shall we say, not exactly current and perhaps 5-10-15 years old... not a fair and balanced way to preserve beauty and youth. I learned that many women were interested in companionship rather than marriage as a long-term solution to living single, and they cared very much about other people's circumstances. I learned that I was not the weirdest person in the universe, and in some cases, I did not even come close. Internet dating: the final frontier? Geesh, I certainly hope not!

Other Books by the Author
Published and to be Published by CCB Publishing

Mirror, Mirror at 1600 D.C.
ISBN 978-0-9810246-1-5

The role of the Presidency is complicated more than enough for Elizabeth Ashton without the added political burden of being the first woman elected to this high office in America. She is delighting her supporters and converting readily her critics when she is kidnapped while attending a fundraiser. The unfolding plot is a matter of survival—not only personal survival, but also hanging in the balance is the endurance of the Presidency and democracy in America. The missing President must be recovered—dead or alive.

Twelve Upon A Time...

A kindergarten-elementary aged children's book...each monthly story is unique and illustrated by the original drawings of children whose interpretation of the words can only be seen through their eyes. The stories are written to assist the imagination of children and to strengthen the parent and child bond through the sharing of heartwarming, silly, absurd and believably impossible tales.

Side Stepping the Rules: Broken or Not

There are many books about the dating relationships of men and women written by women, but men write few. Well, take heart, for now is the parody book that presents the sensitive man's guide for escaping the clutches of the woman who thinks she's Mrs. Right. And it must work because it seems like the author has been single forever.

www.ingramcontent.com/pod-product-compliance
Lightning Source LLC
Chambersburg PA
CBHW031118030726
47496CB00002BA/588